By the same author:

Belfast Girls

Danger Danger

Angel in Flight:
the first Angel Murphy thriller

Angel in Belfast:
the 2nd Angel Murphy thriller

Cover photo & design: Raymond McCullough

Angel
in Paradise

Gerry McCullough

Published by

Precious Oil
PUBLICATIONS
www.preciousoil.com/publications

ISBN 13: 978-0 9955404 2 2

ISBN 10:   0 9955404 2 X

10a Listooder Road, Crossgar, Downpatrick, Northern Ireland BT30 9JE

Angel

in Paradise

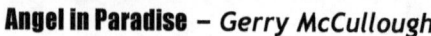

Thanks to my husband, Raymond, for cover design, editing, proof-reading and general encouragement.

Chapter One

A high wind blew over the northern end of the Greek Island of Corfu. Sophie Papadopoulos sat up in bed and found that she was shivering.

This was very unusual. Corfu, a warm, sunny island, is seldom cold except in the depths of winter, and the climate is normally pleasant and enjoyable. They called it the island paradise because it was so full of flowers and sunshine. But after all, Sophie realised, this was still wintertime – or perhaps more like early Spring – and one had to expect a measure of cold and windy weather.

She should have turned on the central heating. She would have to drag herself out of bed and turn on the switch in the cupboard on the landing outside her bedroom. Her luxurious villa was equipped with everything she could possibly need, including central heating as well as air conditioning, but she hadn't expected that it would be so cold tonight.

Sophie was the widow of a Greek millionaire who had made his money in computers, had a series of heart attacks, probably from overwork, in his early fifties, and then died. She had plenty of household help, but none of them slept overnight in the villa. Sophie preferred the privacy. Now she wondered if it might be a good idea to have one of the girls sleep over on a regular basis, so that she would be there to help in times like this. To save Sophie from having to go and turn on the system herself.

What a pain!

Sophie was seventy-eight and getting out of bed in the middle of the night was not just metaphorically, but also physically, a pain. Her rheumatism had been growing much worse recently.

It was when she had finally managed to stand upright by the side of her bed, and was beginning to drag on her warm dressing gown, that it occurred to her that the chill in the air seemed to be coming from a draught blowing up the stairs just outside her bedroom door. Surely she hadn't been silly enough to leave one of the windows open downstairs? Or had it been the noise of someone breaking a window which had woken her?

It had just crossed her mind that it would be as well to press the alarm bell and bring the local police roaring to her aid, when she heard a faint sound somewhere in the house. She moved quickly but cautiously across her bedroom floor to the switch positioned on the wall beside her dressing table. Perhaps she should have the alarm moved closer to the bed for future occasions like this, she thought.

By this time her hand was reaching out to touch the switch. Unfortunately, it was already too late. Heavy feet thundered up the staircase. The bedroom door burst open. A big, thick-set man in black was suddenly in the room. He was wearing a hooded mask which completely covered his head, except for the narrow slits through which she could see his sharply gleaming eyes. They reminded Sophie of the eyes of a wolf she had seen many years ago, yellow, narrow, frightening. The man seized her from behind before she could move.

'I wouldn't do that, Grandma,' he said in menacing tones. His voice was thick and not quite hoarse. Although he spoke in Greek there was a trace of some sort of accent. Sophie couldn't identify it. American, possibly? 'Come and sit down over here.'

He pushed her across to the nearest chair and thrust her down into it. Sophie noticed through her terror that another man had followed him more quietly into the room.

'Now then, Grandma. No need to worry. All we want you to do is give us the combination of the safe. Where you keep your jewels, see? You tell us that and nobody will get hurt.'

The second man came up behind Sophie and twisted her right arm behind her back, pushing her forward in the chair as he did so. It hurt. But that wasn't what worried Sophie most. What worried her most was the cigarette lighter which the first man had clicked on. The wavering flame came closer and closer to her face.

It was then that Sophie started screaming.

Chapter Two

Angeline Murphy sank back luxuriously into the comfortable first class seat of the aeroplane and sighed in contentment. She closed the book she had been reading and gazed happily out of the window on her left side. Below her stretched the blue, blue Mediterranean Sea, a perfect match for the summer sky above it. The sea was studded with the green of numerous tiny islands, jewels scattered wholesale by a generous hand. The Isles of Greece.

The Isles of Greece, the Isles of Greece,
Where burning Sappho loved and sung.

Angel repeated the words of Byron's poem to herself with pleasure. She could see even now that she had made a good choice for her holiday destination.

This was the first holiday she had had since that business over a year ago in Crete, where she had met Josh Smith, the young American policeman attached to Interpol, and between them they had cleared up an unpleasant conspiracy and disposed of a corrupt businessman. Angel hoped this holiday would be very different.

She knew she was lucky to be flying first class, lucky to be heading for the villa belonging to Josh's friends the McPhersons, lucky not to be taking a package holiday with a hurried change of planes in London, to stay in an apartment in the middle of a number of other holiday makers.

Not that she would have despised such an arrangement. A couple of months ago, after the dreadful business with the rock band Raving and its lead singer, she had planned a holiday in Greece on exactly that basis, and had been delighted to be able to do it. But then Josh had stepped in, telling her that the McPhersons had invited him to stay at their villa and would be only too delighted if he wanted to bring his 'girlfriend' with him.

Angel wasn't too sure if her relationship with Josh, advancing cautiously from friendship, justified this description just yet – or if it ever would. But it was tempting to see what it would be like to live in the lap of luxury for a short time. And the saving on accommodation meant that she could fly first class – also a first time experience.

A pity she'd had to change plans in London. There was no direct flight from Belfast to Corfu right now. Still, she'd had a very pleasant overnight stay in a good hotel, so no problem.

Angel could see through the window that one particular island was drawing nearer. She sat up straighter to see the details, and heard the captain's voice coming through the intercom.

'Hullo again, passengers. I hope you've enjoyed your flight with Greek Airways. We are now approaching Corfu and should be touching down at Corfu airport in approximately twenty minutes. The temperature is 35% Celsius and the forecast is for dry sunny weather – no surprise there! Please fasten your safety belt if you haven't already done so. Your hostess will come round to make sure that you have everything you need. Enjoy your stay in Corfu!'

Angel checked her seatbelt and noticed with some surprise that someone had slid unobtrusively into the empty seat beside her. A tall, well built man, lean rather than thin, with an attractive, muscular body, silver hair above a face which looked too young for hair like that, a tanned skin, and very blue eyes. Not that she was bothering to look at him, Angel hastily told herself – it was just that she had noticed him briefly earlier in the flight, when he had been sitting across the aisle from her, a seat forward. But why had he changed seats at this particular moment?

'I hope you don't mind,' the man said. His voice was pleasant, deep and with a very faint accent which Angel thought was French. 'At this stage in any flight, as the plane works up to the time when it will land, I think most of us find that it helps to have someone to talk to for the five or ten minutes – to take one's mind off what may happen. I have no near neighbour and I saw that you were in the same position. Perhaps we could help to distract each other from the dangers of landing by some light and easy conversation?'

'Why not?' Angel agreed. She herself had no fear of flying, even at the more dangerous stages of take-off or landing, but possibly this man had. Although she had to admit that he didn't seem the type in any way. However, it would cost her nothing to chat pleasantly to him for a few moments, if that was what he needed.

'You are going to Corfu on holiday?'

'Yes. I'm told it's a lovely place. I'm meeting a friend at the airport when we touch down.'

'I am going on business. I've been called in to help with a problem. The people who told you that Corfu is a lovely place are right. The climate is unbeatable, the people, like all Greeks, are friendly, the water is warm. This is a good time of year to go there – early June. Later, in July and August, it is possibly too hot for people – like yourself ? – from a more temperate climate. You enjoy swimming?'

'I love swimming. Sure, I spend a lot of my free time at home at the local swimming baths.'

'Ah – at home! I guess from your very attractive accent, mademoiselle, that you come from Ireland.'

'That's right. Belfast. And you? You're French?'

'I am Greek by birth, my dear, but I've spent a lot of time in France. My English is tainted with the French intonation, I think. I learnt both English and French at the same time, while working in France, which must be my excuse. I am Gregor, by the way. And you? Or should I continue to call you mademoiselle?'

'I'm Angeline, but I'm usually called Angel.'

'Angel to my friends, devil to my enemies', Josh Smith had said. Which one would this man turn out to be? Or would he remain only a passing acquaintance? There was something very attractive about him. Something in his eye.

'So are you staying near Corfu town, Angel?'

'No.' Angel noticed that Gregor's left hand was hovering not far above her knee. Time for an unobtrusive warning off, perhaps?

'No?' The hand descended slowly and Angel felt it gently resting on her thigh.

'No, as I told you, I'm being picked up by my friend – my boyfriend, I should really say – and we're driving to the north end of the island. We're staying at a villa not far from Rhoda.' As she spoke, Angel slid her legs discreetly across the seat, away from Gregor's hand.

'Boyfriend? Ah, what a pity!' The hand withdrew so inconspicuously that it might never have been there. 'Whenever I meet a beautiful young girl, she is always already spoken for!'

Chapter 2

'Sure, I guess that's life, Gregor.' Angel gave the Greek a sweet smile. 'But I wouldn't think a man like you had any problem meeting hundreds of beautiful girls.'

'A man like me? You find me attractive, then?' the soft voice purred.

'Ah, now, stop fishing for compliments, boyo!'

Gregor laughed. There was a sudden bump and Angel realised, with some relief, that they had touched down. Not that she minded being chatted up. It was always nice to pull. But she didn't really want to encourage this attractive stranger just as she was about to meet up again with Josh Smith. She hoped Josh would be in good time, waiting for her, so that Gregor would understand clearly that his cue was simply to disappear.

Then the air hostess was coming round and indicating the exit door for first class passengers, and Gregor was gallantly helping her to get her hand luggage down from the rack. There was no rush or scramble to get out, no crush of passengers pushing to get to the exit – so different from other flights Angel had taken. And a moment later she felt the hot June sun on her face as she stepped out of the doorway and began to descend the steps onto the tarmac of the airport grounds. It was, she reflected, a bit like walking into an oven.

The airport bus rolled up and Angel got in.

A small, rat faced man with sandy hair was sitting in one of the few seats, but he got up as soon as he saw her and took off his white baseball cap with a flourish. 'Do have my seat, honey!' he invited.

Angel laughed. 'I didn't know there were still gentlemen with good manners around these days. Thank you, I'd be delighted.'

She sat down, and the man hovered over her in a friendly way.

'On holiday, I take it?'

'Yes, and you?'

'Oh, I live here. I love the place, and I have a good business importing things from the UK, which I can get for half the price the guys here would have to pay otherwise. Jason Horowitz.' He produced a card and offered it to her.

'Angel Murphy,' Angel said in return, accepting the card. 'I don't have a card, I'm afraid, but I work for the BBC as an announcer.'

'Of course!' Jason said in delight. He continued to hang over her rather too closely for Angel's comfort. 'I knew I'd seen your face before!'

'Really?'

Since she was mainly on BBC Northern Ireland, Angel could be forgiven for feeling surprised. This seemed like a chat up line.

'So, are you from Ireland, Jason? Sure, I can't say you sound like it!'

'Nah, you're right there, pet. Cockney born and bred, that's me. But I spend a good bit of time in Ireland, north and south – business commitments, see? That's why I recognised your face – not a face anyone would forget, babe!'

'And what do you import, Jason?'

Jason grinned. 'D'you know, you're not going to believe this, Angel. I mainly import olive oil.'

'What, to Corfu? Hard to believe!'

'Isn't it? But in fact, I can buy things like that in the UK for a fraction of the price they can produce them here – even though this is where that sort of stuff is grown!' Jason grinned at her triumphantly. 'It has to go over to the UK to be processed, see? They process some here, but it ends up expensive. So I can buy the final product in bulk back home and then transport it here by trailer on board ship, and I can make a fortune by charging less than the producers here can do!'

It sounded like just the sort of twisted, ridiculous thing that might well be true these days, Angel realised.

'So, Angel, maybe you and me can get together for a drink sometime while you're here?' Jason asked, beaming at her invitingly. 'Lots of hot spots in Corfu Town or further south, especially if you're not short of cash – and I can tell you, I'm not!'

'Sure, I don't know, Jason,' Angel murmured, trying to avoid committing herself without being too rude. 'I'll be up at the north end of the island – and I don't know what plans my boyfriend has in mind for us, or how free I'll be.'

Jason's face fell at the mention of a boyfriend. Angel smiled to herself. That was the second time today Josh, boyfriend or not, had been useful to her in choking off unwanted attention.

Surely they must be nearly at the airport terminal building by now? She could do without any more of Jason's attention, harmless as he might seem.

Yes, that must be it, the low building drawing near now. Angel heaved a sigh of relief.

'Well, thanks again for the seat, Jason,' she said briskly. 'Nice to meet you. Maybe we'll run into each other while I'm here.' Then she stood up and picked up her hand luggage.

'Nice to meet you, too, Angel.' Jason smiled, a surprisingly sweet, attractive smile. 'Don't just write me off, pet. I really do like you, and I'd like to meet up again. Hey, here's my phone number, if you feel like calling.' He thrust a piece of paper with a number scribbled on it into her hand.

Angel couldn't help smiling back.

'Okay, Jason. You never know!'

A short time later, she was delivered safely at the airport terminal buildings, dodged away from Jason's disconsolate face, and, glad by now to get out of the hot sun, went inside, where she then moved through passport control with the greatest of ease, collecting a card with emergency numbers listed on it as she went. The carousel with her luggage was straight ahead. And there, too, was a familiar figure.

'Josh!'

Angel ran straight into his arms, amazed to find out how very pleased she really was to see the young American again.

Chapter Three

'Angel, honey!'

Josh's arms went round her in return. He gave her a warm hug, kissed her lightly, then released her.

'Good flight?'

'Lovely.'

'Then let's get your baggage and get out of here. The car's waiting outside.'

A voice with a slight accent spoke over Angel's shoulder.

'Inspector Smith?'

Angel spun round, to find Gregor standing just behind her, smiling at Josh as if he was an old friend.

Josh didn't seem to think he was. 'Yeah?' was all he said.

'Ah, you don't know who I am! And you wish I would go away and leave you with this beautiful girlfriend of yours! Angel and I chatted on the plane, so we are – friends, may I say?' He gave Angel a charming smile. 'You and I have also met before, Inspector. In the Paris office.'

Memory obviously returned to Josh. 'You're Captain Doukas.'

'At your service, Inspector.'

'Nice to run into you again, Captain. On holiday?'

'No, as I told Angel, I've been called in to help with this business of the jewel robberies – you've heard about it?'

'I've heard about it, yeah, but maybe I should explain, Captain, that I'm here strictly on holiday – no business whatsoever allowed in! Which reminds me, great as it is to see you again, Angel and I need to be running on. We have a long drive ahead of us. Be seeing you, Captain. Angel, honey, come and point out your cases to me and we'll get them out to the car.'

And to Angel's surprise Josh put his arm round her shoulders, turned her round and hurried her away from Gregor almost rudely. It wasn't like Josh, who was always so friendly, to cut someone off in mid conversation. Surely he wasn't jealous of the handsome Greek? Or did he just dislike him for some reason unknown as yet to Angel?

She waited until the cases were safely bestowed in the boot of Josh's cream coloured Audi, and she was sitting beside him in the front. It felt strange to be sitting as a passenger on the right hand side, which she still automatically thought of as the driver's side, as it would be at home. The car, a comfortable up to date model, was air-conditioned, and for a few minutes Angel simply enjoyed the refreshing coolness and the smooth motion as Josh pulled out from the airport complex onto the main road for Corfu Town. Then she decided it was time to find out more.

'So, Josh – who's this Doukas guy? Is he one of your Interpol people?'

'Not exactly, Angel.' Josh fixed his attention carefully on the road ahead. 'He's more of a freelance. We call him in occasionally, if we really need someone on the spot.'

'You sound as if you don't like him.'

'I don't!' Josh spoke violently. Angel jumped. She never heard Josh speak so sharply before.

'Wow! What did he do?'

Josh looked round at her for a moment and grinned. 'Sorry, Angel. Didn't mean to blow up. I don't know how to explain. I may be quite wrong about the guy. It's just that – well, a few times – lots of times – I thought he grabbed the credit for other people's work. A mate of mine did a brilliant job tracking down a drug dealer, and Doukas stepped in at the last moment, got the bosses to think that he'd done all the work, and made Pete look stupid. That's just one example.

And I also think he made a lot of dollars by helping to get someone off the hook who should have been sent down for a long stretch. And not just once. But, hey, honey, I've no evidence. I shouldn't be shooting off my mouth about him like this. Maybe he's a nice guy all the time, and as honest as they come – I just wouldn't know.'

Angel sat quietly for a moment. She was thinking about her own impressions of the Gregor she had met on the plane, and Josh's idea of the Captain Doukas they'd spoken to in the airport terminal. Did they match up or not?

Presently she asked, 'And what's this stuff about jewel robberies?'

'Corfu's had a spate of them recently. Since late winter. The first was an old lady, widow of a computer millionaire, who had her home broken into and her jewels stolen back in early March. Since then, there've been at least a dozen more.'

'I didn't know there were so many rich people on this wee island,' Angel observed.

'Oh, yeah. Lots of millionaires – even multi-millionaires – here. Time they caught these villains and put a stop to the business. Thing is, they threaten the people whose houses they break into with all sorts of violence. They're mostly elderly folks. They don't hold out for long against the threats of being burned or beaten up.'

Angel shivered. 'I suppose not. Horrible!'

'Yeah. I keep thinking, suppose it was my Mom – or my Gran. Not that either of them has anything worth stealing. But you get me.'

'I do indeed. It's a nasty business.' She looked around her at the beauty of the scenery flying past. 'I hope they catch them soon. It's hard to believe something like that can be going on in this lovely place.'

'It happens everywhere, honey. But you don't have to think about it, Angel. We're on holiday – me as well as you. All we have to do is relax and enjoy ourselves.'

'Right.'

She was silent for a few minutes as the car whizzed round a number of hairpin bends on the very edge of the cliffs which dropped down to the blue of the sea on their right. Bougainvillea blossomed on both sides of the road, purple and dazzling in the sunlight. Olive trees grew in silvery grey rows away to the left.

'Okay, Josh. Tell me more about these friends of yours – the McPhersons. Have you known them for long? Will I like them? And will they like me?'

Chapter Four

'They'll love you, honey – who wouldn't?' Josh shot her a sideways grin. 'With your gentle sweet, wouldn't-hurt-a fly nature and your shy retiring ways –'

'Josh Smith! I'll kill you!'

'Then there's how you look. Who doesn't love tall blondes?'

'Don't call me a blonde! Just because I have fair hair, it doesn't mean I go into the forest looking for a Christmas tree and give up because none of them are decorated. Etc.'

'A tall blonde walked past my window,' Josh quoted. 'I knew she was tall because I live on on the fourth floor.'

Angel laughed. 'I shouldn't encourage you.'

'She rolled her eyes at me. I rolled them back.'

'Groan!'

'I kissed her lips. She screamed. I took the cigarette out of my mouth.'

'Enough, enough!'

'Enough? I could go on for hours!'

'Back to the McPhersons,' Angel said firmly. 'Tell me about them – I don't want to meet them cold.'

'You'll like them, I think. As the name suggests, they're Scottish American. I've known them since I worked with their son Bobby. Bobby was a great guy – a real pal. He was killed in a shoot out with some Russian Mafia villains about five years ago. He and I were working together.' Josh paused as if he was finding it difficult to go on. 'We had them pinned down in an old warehouse where they stored their stuff – just about everything hot you could think of. They'd been making a fortune with it. There were a lot of bullets flying and, well –' He paused again. 'I got off without a scratch, but Bobby – well, they got him just before the local police rolled up late. It fell to me to tell his Mom and Pop. I guess since then they've sort of adopted me as a kinda Bobby substitute or something.'

Angel was silent. There seemed to be little she could say without being trite. 'I'm sorry,' she tried at last.

Josh took his right hand off the wheel and reached over to give her left hand a squeeze. 'I know you are, honey. But, hey, it's five years ago. No need to mention it to them by now.'

'So, they aren't young?'

'Not young, but not that old either. Hamish is maybe ten years older than Marge is. She's a darling – soft and warm and cuddly. He's more your typical stern-faced, intellectual Scot, but one of the kindest men I know underneath it. He made his money in publishing, and now he's bought this villa so he and Marge can have a safe, relaxing place, away from the rat race, to enjoy life now Hamish has semi-retired. He was actually supposed to be fully retired, but he can't keep away from work. He still reads manuscripts for the company, and tries to make sure they keep up the kind of standards he imposed on them when he set it up.'

'They sound – interesting.'

'That means you don't like the sound of them. But I bet you'll think differently when you actually meet them.'

Reluctant to comment, Angel asked, 'And will there be other guests at the villa, or just you and me?'

'I'd guess just you and me, but we'll see when we get there. But we won't be expected to hang around with either the McPhersons or any guests they may have, unless we want to. Marge and Hamish know we haven't seen enough of each other for a while and we'll want to spend a lot of time together. They didn't invite us in order to butt into our lives.'

'That sounds good.'

Angel was silent for a while, thinking about the holiday she had embarked on, and hoping it would live up to her too glowing expectations. Most things didn't, of course. But she had a good feeling about this one.

'This is the turn off coming up now,' Josh said presently. 'A couple of miles along that, then another turn off, and we'll be nearly there.'

They had been following the road which ran close to the blue sea, glittering and dazzling on their right far below. Now Josh swung the car off the main road to the left and began to drive, taking it more slowly, up something which seemed to Angel more like a track, leading uphill between the silvery olive trees and the many coloured wild flowers. Angel, looking out eagerly, recognised tall blue or yellow irises, orchids in almost every colour from red to cream, large white daisies, buttercups in masses – a mixture of flowers she was used to seeing growing wild back home with others she had only seen for sale at high prices in nurseries.

The next turn off was, to Angel's surprise, tarmac surfaced. She guessed that the McPherson's must have arranged and paid for this themselves. And there, suddenly coming into sight round a bend, was the Villa Callidora.

The name, Josh had told Angel, meant beautiful gift. Set up against the lovely hills and trees of Corfu, and surrounded by yet more wild flowers – Angel recognised the bright blue of borage, white orchids, yellow acanthus, red poppies and purple grape hyacinths, as well as many others she couldn't identify – the Villa Callidora certainly lived up to its name.

'Marge picked the name,' Josh explained, 'because, in a way, it was Hamish's gift to her. They certainly couldn't have bought it without his earnings from publishing. Marge has never earned much, I guess. I think she and Hamish met when she was a typist in his firm and he was still something quite junior. And as soon as they could afford it, she left to keep house and look after Bobby. They used to holiday in Corfu, and dream of the time when they could all move out here. But Bobby was grown and gone by then. And not long after, he was gone for good. But they're very happy here, in spite of that.'

'It's a place where anyone could be happy,' Angel said warmly. She had fallen in love with the villa at first sight.

'Okay, honey,' Josh said, pulling the Audi to a halt in front of the two steps which led up to the doorway. A veranda with a low white fence ran along the front of the house, and geraniums hung in pots at each side of the entrance door, while a vine spread its gracious shade over the roof of the veranda. 'Let's get your baggage out of the car and come on in and meet the folks.'

And Angel, pushing open the car door and hopping out, went forward eagerly to meet Josh's friends. She had decided already that she was bound to like anyone who chose to live in this beautiful place.

Chapter Five

The plump, sweet faced woman who came rushing out of the door to meet them had a mass of blonde hair which clearly owed something to a skilful hairdresser, a soft pink and white complexion, and blue eyes which were just as clearly the gift of nature alone. She wore a beaming smile, a low cut T shirt and cream coloured shorts.

'Josh! I heard the car and I just knew it must be you! Hullo, my darling boy!' She hugged Josh enthusiastically before turning to Angel. 'And this is your girlfriend that you've told us so much about. My, isn't she beautiful!'

'Now, Marge, stop making her blush! Yes, this is Angel.'

'Hi, Marge.' Angel found it hard to maintain her usual cool in the face of so much excited warmth.

'Angel – what a perfect name for you. Although Callidora would suit you too, wouldn't it, Josh? She's a beautiful gift for you, sweetie, isn't she?'

'Angel isn't anyone's gift, Marge,' Josh cut in hastily. What would she say next? 'Angel is very much her own woman, not any man's property!'

'Oh, honey, I didn't mean that she was – just that she's beautiful!'

'Come on, let's get in out of the sun, Marge, and maybe give your beautiful guest a cool drink? And show her where her room is? Where's Hamish, by the way?' As he spoke, Josh picked up the suitcases, which he had deposited on the ground by the veranda in order to return Marge's welcoming hug, and strode firmly up the steps to the front door, ushering Angel and Marge before him.

Inside the villa the air conditioning was on at full blast. Angel, already aware of the extreme heat outside, was only too glad to sit down where Marge directed her and to sip a long cool drink of freshly squeezed oranges straight from the fridge. Josh disappeared with the suitcases to deposit them in Angel's room, and Marge plumped herself down in a seat near Angel and went on talking.

'Hamish is over at Morrie Henderson's right now – they're looking at a new manuscript the publishing house sent them. He should be back soon – he knows you're coming. But, sweetie, you've no idea what he's like when he gets his nose in a book! I've gotta apologise for him, Angel! He'll want to see you, that's for sure – Josh's girlfriend! We're both so glad to meet you! I'm sure you'll love it here, sweetie. It's a marvellous island. The people are so nice. Only one problem right now – the jewel thieves. You've heard about them, of course?'

'Josh mentioned them.'

'Horrible villains! My poor friend – well, she's not poor, she's actually very rich, but she's poor because of what happened to her, if you understand me – poor Sophie Papadopolous, she had all her jewels stolen, well, all the ones that weren't in a safe deposit, but that wasn't the worst of it! They terrified her so much that she's had to move into a nursing home for a while. I hope she'll be able to get back home soon, whenever she gets over the threats and the violence –'

Angel interrupted. It seemed to be the only way to get a chance to speak, with Marge. 'Did you say Sophie Papadopolous, Marge?'

'Yes, that's right.'

'I think I must know her. Was she Sophie Dunlop before she married?'

'Why, yes, honey, that's right!'

'And she came from Belfast?'

'Wow, now you say so, Angel, I do believe you're right!'

'She was a good friend of my parents. Could you tell me a bit more about what happened to her?'

'Well, sweetie, she was sleeping when these awful men in masks broke in and threatened her and stole her jewellery – poor Sophie! The police came, of course, but they were too late to catch the men. She had to move out to a nursing home, like I said.

I'm planning to call with her later today, I get in to see her as often as I can, we used to have a drink together every week or so before this happened, so I try to keep up as if things were just the same – but she's not quite her old self, yet. Improving, I think. She keeps talking about going home and then changing her mind. It was several months ago this all happened – her burglary was one of the first – there've been a lot more since then –'

Once again Angel found that if she wanted to speak it would be necessary to interrupt Marge.

'Would it be okay if I came with you, Marge? I'd like to meet up with Sophie again.'

'Why, it certainly would, sweetie! I know Sophie would be very happy to meet someone from home – she still calls Belfast 'home' when she talks about it!'

'What time did you plan to leave?'

'Oh, in a couple of hours, I think. So you'll have time for a swim, or whatever you like – maybe a nap after all that travelling.'

A clatter of footsteps coming down the polished wooden stairs announced the return of Josh.

'Want to go see your room, honey?'

'Good idea, Josh.' Angel stood up. 'Thanks for the drink, Marge. I'll be ready to go in a couple of hours, then.'

'Go?' asked Josh mildly as he led Angel out of the huge kitchen and showed her upstairs.

'I asked Marge if I could come with her to visit Sophie Papadopolous,' Angel explained. 'I used to know her, when I was no age. She was a friend of my parents, before she married and moved out here. And she often came back to visit them, which was when I met her. I was very young at that time, mind you, but I remember her well.'

Josh remembered that Angel's father had been a well-known journalist, and that both her parents had been killed in an air crash some years ago.

'Sophie was quite a personality on the local scene years ago,' Angel went on. 'My father interviewed her more than once. She was a singer, in case you haven't heard of her. Sophie Dunlop. Sang Irish folk mainly. Had a real hit with her own version of Danny Boy at one point.'

'Yeah, the name rings a bell.'

'She toured the States after her big hit – so you might have heard of her then. I think it was in America she met her husband – Josef Papadopoulos, a computer whizz kid, already on his way to making a million. They fell from a great height, love at first sight for both of them. And when he felt he'd done enough hard work for a lifetime, Joe wanted to move back here to where he was born.

Sophie gave up her career and moved with him. She always seemed very happy about it, when I saw her. It was sad that he died so soon after the move. Sophie said he couldn't stop working, had to have his finger in the pie, thought up new ideas and stuff, even though the doctor warned him to take it easy.'

'Happens a lot.'

'She's a really nice person. It makes me angry to hear about what happened to her.'

'What happened?'

'The robbery, Josh. I thought you knew about it?'

'Oh, right. That Sophie Papadopoulos! I didn't catch on for a minute. Hey, honey, it's not my case, I don't have all the details at the front of my mind.'

'Sorry.' Angel laughed. 'It's just that the whole thing makes me so angry. Let's forget about it for now. What would you like to do before I have to go? How about a swim?'

'Okay – but first we need something to eat, right, honey? Don't know about you, but I'm starving! Marge will expect us to grab for ourselves, for things like a snack lunch – but dinner will be a big meal, of course.'

He took Angel into the kitchen and rummaged in the fridge and cupboards for bread, feta cheese and salad, while Marge looked on, smiling. Then, after a sufficient break, they changed, and enjoyed a leisurely swim. All too soon, it was time for Angel to get dressed and go with Marge to the nursing home.

Chapter Six

'I couldn't tell them quick enough,' said Sophie.

She was sitting up in bed in a comfortable sunny room which to Angel's eye had everything anyone could want. Venetian blinds in a soothing, neutral colour shielded the fiercest rays of the sun from the room, which was in any case air-conditioned. Sophie's bed was large and soft, with blue, flower patterned sheets. A matching duvet was pushed aside during the heat of the day. A high spec television screen hung from the wall opposite, where Sophie could watch it when she wanted to.

The windows, although it was hard to tell because of the Venetian blinds, seemed to lead out onto a balcony with a small table and a lounger. Inside the room, there were several comfortable chairs in soft pastel colours, bookcases along another wall, and on the bedside table an eReader shared space with the TV remote control and a jug of red tulips. These, and the pictures on the walls, provided the only splashes of bright colour. A restful, happy room, Angel thought.

'I was so terrified that he was going to burn me that I almost forgot to press the alarm button on the chain I always wear round my neck,' Sophie said. 'They didn't notice it – it's hidden by my nightie. I just shrank back as far as I could into the chair and blurted out the combination of the safe and waited to see what they'd do. Thank the Lord the man turned off his lighter as soon as I told him the numbers.

'I didn't really forget the alarm, mind you. I'd pressed it even while he was threatening me. But I knew the police couldn't get there in time to stop them. They arrived, puffing and blowing as if they'd run all the way, just after I heard the robbers' car drive off in the other direction. I still have very sharp ears, you know,' she added complacently. 'You need to have sharp hearing if you're a singer, to check that you're not going out of tune.'

'You seem to have got over it well, Sophie,' Angel said.

'Sometimes. It's good to see you and Marge, Angel. It gives me a lift – takes me back to the good old days. You were only a little thing when I last saw you, but bright as a button. You're the image of your mammy now, do people ever tell you?'

'Agh, I don't see too many people who knew my parents, Sophie.'

'Sure, I probably seem cheerful to you right now,' Sophie continued, 'but a lot of the time I'm the complete opposite. I still find it hard to get to sleep – I'm afraid of the nightmares. And as for going back home, I can't face it. Maybe I never will. And yet I love the place – it's where Joe and I were so happy before he was taken from me.' She shivered in spite of the warmth of the day and drew her fleecy blue bed jacket more closely round her.

'There, there, sweetie, try not to think about it!' Marge comforted her.

'If I just knew those men had been caught – I think that would make a real difference.'

Angel looked at her old friend thoughtfully. 'Maybe I could help with that, Sophie?'

'You, pet?'

'Don't look so surprised! I've done a bit in that line over the last year or so – stopped several villains in their tracks.'

'But – are you in the police, then? I though Marge said you were working in TV?'

'Oh, no, Marge is right – I'm not in the police. I just happened to get caught up in some stuff.'

'But what could you do, Angel?' With the bluntness of an old friend who still thought of her as a child, Sophie was sceptical.

'Who knows? But give me a few more details, for starters, Sophie. What exactly did these guys take?'

'Oh, all my jewels, that Joe would insist on keeping on buying for me. A brooch with diamonds, shaped like a flower, that he bought on our honeymoon in Paris, and another one with an enormous opal, so pretty. Two matching bracelets supposed to have belonged to Marie Antoinette, whether that's true or not. I know Joe paid a lot extra for them because of that. Several rings that I hardly ever wore because I only have a limited amount of fingers!

They didn't take my engagement ring or my wedding ring, because I haven't taken them off for years, and now I couldn't get them off if I tried – my fingers have swollen up. One of them hauled and pulled at the rings – hurt my hand quite badly – but he couldn't shift them, thank the good Lord. I think it would have broken my heart if they'd managed to get them. But the worst of the lot was my sapphire necklace. Joe bought it for me on our last wedding anniversary just before he died. Here – I'll show you the photo he took of me wearing it.' Sophie leaned over to take an album from her drawer, flicked over the pages, and held it out to Angel.

The photo showed a much younger Sophie, twenty years younger probably, glowing with life and happiness – Sophie as Angel remembered her. For a moment she focussed on the face in the picture, while her own memories of her parents and their friends chased each other through her head. Then, sternly turning her attention to the picture of the necklace shining round Sophie's throat, she examined it in detail.

The diamond flower brooch was also in the shot, pinned to Sophie's breast, but it was the necklace which stood out. Six large matching sapphires were set in a graceful chain of little gold links with a design of leaves surrounding each bright stone. A seventh stone, larger than the others, hung as a droplet from the centre, with its own set of golden leaves around it. The necklace was delicate and beautiful, not too heavily designed for the wearer. It was both individual and striking. Angel committed it to memory before sighing and handing the album back to Sophie.

'Thanks, darlin'. Now, maybe it's time we talked of something else, so's not to leave you too depressed. I was just remembering the time Daddy and Mum took me to meet up with you at the Stag's Head – I was far too young to be in a pub, but the owners didn't seem to mind – and when people saw you were there they insisted on you singing Danny Boy – do you remember that night?'

'That was the night your daddy came up to the front by special request from the whole pub and recited Yeats' poem, *Down by the Sally Gardens*,' Sophie said, brightening up. 'Nearly stole my audience from me, the dirty dog!'

'Och, no, Sophie – they went mad for you when you sang the song straight after he'd finished. Not a dry eye in the house!'

'Happy memories,' said Sophie with tears in her own eyes. 'Happy memories.'

It was time to leave. Sophie needed to rest, and Marge wanted to get back in good time to supervise the evening meal. They said goodbye to Sophie and headed back to the car. Neither of them noticed that the eyes of one of the nurse carers were fixed on them from behind the half closed door which they passed, on their way to the front entrance of the care home. And neither of them heard the voice of the nurse speaking hurriedly and quietly, in Greek, on the phone, a few minutes after they had passed.

'Yes, it's me. You were right. She's just been here, visiting Papadopolous. I heard some of it. They were talking about the robbery and looking at photos of the jewels. Turns out it was a good idea for me to get a job here after Papadopoulos moved in. The girl's going to interfere, I think – I didn't hear it all.'

'Okay. Thanks,' said the voice at the other end. 'Don't worry – I'll deal with this. I'll borrow a moped and pick you up in an hour or so, okay?'

Chapter Seven

When Angel and Marge got back, Marge disappeared straightaway into the kitchen, refusing Angel's offer of help. 'Maria will have left everything ready, honey. I just have to turn off the oven when the timer goes, and serve it out.'

'Maria?'

'She's our cook, honey, she's great, you'll love her food, but she goes home in the evening once she's left a meal sorted. You go on and see what's happening with that man of yours!'

Josh was lying by the pool, half asleep, just as she had left him.

'Hi, honey. Want to join me?'

'Yip.'

Angel went upstairs, slipped into her bikini, and came down to lie on a lounger beside him, all within a few minutes.

'Ah! This is the life,' she said.

'Race you two lengths!'

Josh sprang up and dived into the deep end of the pool almost before Angel had settled herself and got her breath. Seconds later, she was thrusting through the water only a foot behind him. He wasn't going to beat her by cheating. Getting up speed, she caught him up, then surged past. But Josh still had some reserves of strength to call on. They reached the far end of the pool neck and neck, and finished the second length with not a millimetre between them.

Angel, laughing breathlessly, splashed water over Josh's head, then, as he gasped and spluttered, she turned at top speed and raced back down the pool. But before she had gone very far a strong pair of arms seized her and ducked her beneath the water. Angel had enough presence of mind to grab out in her turn and drag Josh down with her.

It was as they were grappling with each other underneath the water that a shot echoed across the pool.

As they came to the surface, more shots sounded. Instinctively both Angel and Josh dived sharply. The bullets ricocheted across the pool's surface. They both knew that bullets could penetrate the water if they were aimed downwards, but as long as the enemy kept firing along the surface they were safe enough. And surely someone would notice what was going on, and send for the police?

There was a limit to how long either of them could stay under the water. Angel allowed herself to go up, her head poking above the surface briefly, just long enough to take in a deep mouthful of air and to have a quick look around. To her horror, she saw that Marge had heard the shots and was racing out through the patio doors which led to the pool. She wanted to cry out a warning, to shout, 'Go back, Marge! Go back!' but before she could get enough breath to call another bullet cracked through the air, and she saw Marge stumble and fall.

Without a second's thought Angel made for the edge and scrambled out of the pool. Running across the space between her and Marge, she fell to her knees and felt Marge's pulse. Marge was still breathing. Strong as Angel was, there was no way she could lift Marge. Instead, she grasped her under the arms and towed her back through the patio doors into the house, out of the direct line of fire.

The first thing was to see where the bullet had hit, and what needed to be done. It took Angel only a moment to see that blood was flowing from Marge's right thigh. It wasn't spurting – that was good news. The bullet hadn't hit an artery, then. Still, best to be sure. Angel looked round for something she could use. A smallish table in the dining room was draped with a linen cloth. Napkins were piled beside it, where Marge had clearly been setting up for dinner. Expensive, but Marge's leg was more valuable. Angel seized two of the napkins, folded one of them into a thick pad, and pressed it against the wound. Then, holding the pad down hard with one hand, she rolled the other napkin on the diagonal to get as much length as possible and tied it as tightly as she could round Marge's leg, to hold the pad in position.

Next – phone for the police. Where were the servants? She knew Marge had a handyman who should be on the premises, as well as a cook and a cleaner who would both have gone home by now.

It was then that Angel, looking out at the pool and wondering where Josh was, noticed a red streak colouring the bright blue of the water. For a moment she felt as if her heart had stopped.

Then she gathered herself together. Vaguely she noticed that the there was no more sound of firing. And somewhere in her mind she knew that she had done everything that could be done for Marge except sending for the doctor. But nothing else mattered just now apart from Josh.

Had he been shot? Yes, of course, where else would the blood be coming from? But how serious was it?

Angel was already moving as she thought these things. She had seen the red streak, identified it in her own mind as blood, and a second later was diving back into the pool.

The blood was making the water murky and hard to see through, very different from the clear blue lucidity which had allowed her to see so much detail during her earlier rough and tumble fun with Josh. Pushing frantically around in the depths, Angel at last felt something solid brush up against her. Seizing this object with both arms, she thrust hard with her legs and reached the surface. Yes, thank goodness, it was Josh. He was unconscious.

There was no time to spare to see what damage had been done to him. Angel pushed out for the shallow end of the pool, where there were wide low steps at the edge. It would be easier to get Josh out of the pool there. She knew she couldn't lift him out at the deep end without help.

Even so it was difficult enough. Angel was glad she had kept up her weight lifting over the last six months. It took her valuable minutes to heave Josh, deeply unconscious, onto the tiles beside the pool. Then she knelt down beside him, took a quick look to check the details, and saw that he had been shot in the left arm. There was also a graze along his scalp which was the main thing, she realised, that was making him unconscious. No time to waste. The blood from his arm was coming sluggishly. It would have to wait. Angel took a deep breath and began to give Josh mouth to mouth resuscitation.

She had been working away at him for what seemed hours, but might only have been five minutes, when she heard a heavy step behind her. Maybe it was one of the gunmen. Angel didn't care. She couldn't stop to find out.

Then a voice sounded in her ear. 'Good. Keep going. I've phoned the police and our own doctor. I must go back to Marge now.'

Out of the corner of her eye Angel saw a tall, stern faced man, his red hair streaked with grey, incongruously dressed in Bermuda shorts and T shirt. Even at that moment, she couldn't help thinking that a man of his type should be wearing a suit, shirt and tie. As he turned on his heel and headed back into the house, things clicked in Angel's busy brain. This must be Marge's husband, Hamish McPherson, the publisher.

Chapter Eight

It seemed an eternity before Josh coughed, turned his head sideways, and spurted up a lungful of water. Angel felt tears trickling down her cheeks.

'Hi, Angel. Were you kissing me? Hey, don't stop, honey!'

'I was giving you mouth to mouth resuscitation, boyo,' Angel said, recovering her cool. 'So, let's have a look at that arm of yours, now.'

But the arm seemed not to have suffered too much. The bullet hadn't done much more than graze it just above the elbow.

'I hear there's a doctor on his way,' Angel said, concealing her thankfulness as far as possible. 'He'll be looking at Marge first – but I think things aren't too serious there either. Too bad – you won't be able to skulk in bed for weeks, after all, darlin'. I know it's your favourite thing.'

'But, listen, what happened? Who was shooting at us and why?'

'Sure, let me get my crystal ball, and maybe I'll be able to tell you. You're the cop, you should know, right?'

Josh grinned weakly. 'When I get my head together maybe I'll be able to work it out.'

Then they heard the sounds of people arriving.

The doctor had brought his assistant with him, and while he dealt with Marge's leg, the para-medic came out to do what he could for Josh. It was while this was going on that

Angel, moving back a few paces to give the medic room, saw something white at the side of the pool. She picked it up.

It was a sheet of paper wrapped round a large stone and cello-taped to keep it in position. Angel unwrapped it carefully, making sure not to tear the paper. A message was written on it on the inside, in English.

'GO HOME, IRISH. KEEP YOUR NOSE OUT OF OUR AFFAIRS, YOU AND YOUR BOYFRIEND.'

The words were written in capitals in a straggly hand. It might have been done by someone deliberately using their left hand to disguise the writing further. It seemed that this was at least part of the answer to at least one of Josh's questions. Angel had only been looking into one matter since her arrival a few hours ago – the theft of Sophie Papadopulous's jewellery.

Thoughtfully, Angel dropped the stone and folded up the paper as small as possible, so that she could hold it mostly concealed in her hand. Being without a pocket in her present costume, it was the best she could do. Reminded by this, she looked round for the towelling robe she had brought down with her. There would be a pocket in that. Yes, there it was, hanging over the lounger she had spent all of five seconds on earlier. Angel moved over, picked up the robe and slipped it on, and put the folded paper into her pocket. Time enough to worry Josh about it later on when he'd had a chance to recover.

It was at this moment that Hamish came out to see how Josh was doing, bringing with him Dr. Kefalas.

Dr Kefalas was a small, chubby man with a beaming smile, red cheeks, thick grey hair and a bushy grey moustache, carrying a black bag which obviously held his medical equipment.

'So, this is my second patient?' he said. 'Okay, Paul, you've done a good job, now move over and let me have a look.' His English, somewhat to Angel's surprise, was both fluent and idiomatic. He bent down over Josh and took a syringe out of his medical bag. Before Angel had realised what he was doing, he had swiftly injected it into Josh's arm. Josh sighed and closed his eyes.

Angel was furious. Who was this man, and what did he think he was doing? She'd just worked hard to bring Josh back to consciousness. Now this doctor had knocked him out again.

She started forward, but was stopped by Hamish's hand grasping her arm hard, restraining her.

'Och, it's okay, lassy,' Hamish said quietly into her ear. 'Dr Kefalas knows what he's doing. He's the best doctor on the island – that's why I have him for Marge and me. He won't do anything that isn't for Josh's best.'

'I believe you, Hamish,' Angel said reluctantly.

'Now, since you refuse to let me take my patients to hospital, Mr McPherson, and insist on keeping them both here to be looked after,' said Dr Kefalas, half humorously and half seriously, 'and since you promise me that they will have every possible care, I want you to have this young man carried up to his room and put to bed now. It will be good for him to sleep for the next few hours. Just as your wife is already doing. Do not attempt to wake either of my patients, I insist. Let them sleep until they wake up naturally. The nurse you phoned for should be here shortly. I will wait here until she arrives, and I will give her my instructions myself.'

'I can't thank you enough, Doctor,' said Hamish earnestly. 'You must be hungry. I've dragged you out when you would have been about to eat. The least I can do is invite you to join us for your evening meal. I believe it is ready in the kitchen. I'll go and check.'

Doctor Kefalas expressed his pleasure at the suggestion. Angel was only half listening by now. The para-medic and the McPherson's handyman were, between them, carrying Josh upstairs to his room. Angel went with them, her anxiety overwhelming her. It was only when she saw Josh comfortably settled in his bed that she felt able to go back downstairs and take some action.

The first thing she needed to do was to look into the direction the bullets and the message wrapped round the stone had come from. She knew the firing had come from behind the trellised wall of bougainvillea over on the right hand side of the pool. Grimly, she made her way there.

Chapter Nine

The lovely purple flowers hung abundantly over a trellis about five feet high, set several feet away from the pool, which masked the area behind it. There was no gate handy. Angel peered over the top but saw little of interest. A closer look was necessary. Walking along the edge of the trellis, she came to a gap and made her way around it.

This was still Marge and Hamish's garden, and therefore it was laid out in grass and flowers carefully watered daily by Hamish's sprinkler system. This was a great advantage, Angel realised, since the dry, hard ground of the paths around the cultivated area would certainly have left no marks. But to come close enough to the trellis to be able to fire over it into the pool, the marksman had needed to walk across the grass and even stand on the soil of the flowerbed from which the bougainvillea plants sprang.

Angel approached cautiously. She didn't want her own footprints to obliterate anything. In fact, she acknowledged ruefully to herself, that the police, when they came on the scene, were probably going to be very annoyed with her for 'contaminating a crime scene.'

Oh, well, I don't care, thought Angel. She was determined to get these villains who'd not only robbed and terrorised dear Sophie Dunlop (as Angel still thought of her) but had now shot and wounded her sweet hostess Marge and, worst of all, her friend, or whatever she should call him, Josh Smith.

There were plenty of vague marks on the grass and clearer ones on the flowerbed.

Two people. One with larger feet in shoes with ribbed soles. Probably trainers. And one, a much smaller foot, possibly a woman – the marks, although the heels were certainly not stiletto (and who wore stilettos in the daytime any more?) were smaller than those of a man's shoe would be.

No dropped clues. No torn off buttons or ripped cloth, like the clues in old detective stories. No dropped cigarette ends or matches. Angel froze for a moment in the middle of her ironic mental comments. What was that sticking to a branch of the bougainvillea?

Peering closer, she saw that it was a tiny remnant of cloth from someone's clothing.

She shouldn't take it, of course. But perhaps she could detach a thread or two, and leave the rest for the cops?

She picked cautiously at the tiny scrap and soon managed to release a small part of the cloth, leaving the rest for anyone who might notice it.

Taking it in the palm of one hand, she examined it carefully. It reminded her of nothing so much as a part of a uniform. Dark blue, like the uniforms of the carers at Sophie's nursing home.

Angel gasped in horror as she connected up the facts. Someone had known she'd been taking an interest in Sophie's burglary. It was the only thing that note could have referred to. She hadn't been involved in anything else – hadn't been here long enough for that. And that someone had passed on the information. The result had been the shooting at the pool. And now a scrap of material reminiscent of the uniform worn by the carers at Sophie's home had turned up in the position the shots had come from.

She didn't think one of the carers had fired the shots. But one of them had probably passed on the information that Angel had visited Sophie, might even have heard them discussing the robbery, and passed that on too. And now it seemed one of them had been here, with the marksman.

Was Sophie in danger, then?

Probably not, Angel decided thankfully. If Sophie had anything useful to pass on to Angel, then she had already done so.

No, it was Angel herself who had been the target for the shots. And in that case, she, escaping scot-free, had been the cause of both Marge and Josh suffering extreme danger and being badly wounded. Angel shivered in spite of the heat. She drew her warm towelling robe more closely around her.

There was no way she was going to let this go. She would catch these guys if it were the last thing she did.

The cartridge cases from the gun that had been used should be somewhere nearby. Angel scouted carefully around and presently came on one. It was a .45, as far as she could tell. There should be two others, but she decided to leave them for the police to find. In fact, she had better replace this one where she'd found it.

The next step was to see if there were any marks left to show where these people had come from. Angel, oblivious of the fact that she was wearing only a bikini and short towelling robe, headed along the paths beside the beds of flowers and reached the nearest gate. Here there was another flowerbed, full of well watered flowers and bushes.

As Angel brushed against the shrubs in passing she released the scent of rosemary, myrtle, and bay from the beautifully tended bushes. Roses, geraniums and a host of other colourful and sweet smelling flowers grew side by side. This flowerbed might be a possible source of footprints or something. But the soil seemed untouched.

Angel opened the gate, the side entrance to the villa, and stepped outside into even more scorching heat, unsheltered by walls and plants. What were those marks she could see on the road nearby?

Alongside the high wall round the McPherson's property were the marks of some sort of machine, which must have been parked by the wall for some time to have left so much sign of its presence. Drops of oil, which must have fallen from it as it stood there. Tyre marks in the dust.

Not a car, Angel decided. The tyres were those of a two-wheeled vehicle, a motorbike at a fairly confident guess. The marks were too broad for a push bike. And the oil suggested a motorbike, too.

She walked along the road, looking for signs of where the bike had gone.

For some distance, the marks were clear enough. But then they petered out. Presently Angel came to the main road, and found, naturally enough, that the marks she had been following disappeared in the dust of many cars. It seemed that the bike had gone south, in the direction of Corfu town.

This was also the direction of Sophie's nursing home, and was some very slight confirmation of the possibility that one of its riders had been returning there. But it was clearly going to be impossible for Angel herself to follow it up any further.

Chapter 9

Time to get back to the Villa Callidora. The Corfu police might have arrived by now. They could probably put out a request for anyone who had seen a motorbike emerging from the side road at the relevant time to get in touch.

Chapter Ten

Angel was also increasingly anxious to see how Josh was doing. She was still angry with the doctor for knocking him out, but reluctantly acknowledged that it would be good for him to rest. But surely concussion patients weren't supposed to sleep for a while, until they after they had recovered?

As she approached the pool she saw a number of people on the far side, just inside the patio doors. Hamish, the doctor, and two other men. Presumably Hamish and the doctor had finished their meal. Angel couldn't have eaten. She had no appetite whatever. Coming nearer, she recognised one of the other two men. Captain Doukas – Gregor.

This was not good news. Josh didn't trust this man. While attempting to keep an open mind, Angel wished someone else had been sent to investigate. She decided that she would be very careful what she told him.

As she approached nearer to the group of people, they all looked round.

'The lovely Angel!' said Captain Doukas. ' I'm so pleased to see you again so soon.'

'It could be on a happier occasion, Gregor,' Angel said. She walked coolly past him and leaned casually against Marge's dining table. 'How is Marge, Hamish?' she asked. 'And Josh?'

'Both sleeping peacefully,' Hamish reported. 'The doctor is happy with them both.'

'Angel, I must, I'm afraid, ask you a few questions about exactly what happened,' Doukas said. 'I hope it won't upset you too much to go over the horrible events again.'

'No, it won't upset me, Gregor,' she said coolly. 'But first of all, I should tell you that the shots came from beyond that trellis.' She moved back past him, walked to the patio doors, and indicated the trellis with one hand. 'I don't want to give you instructions, but I think you'll find some useful clues there if you look now before they get wiped out somehow. There are footprints, and signs of a motorbike in the lane just outside the grounds.'

'Ah ha! I have heard of your detective skills, my dear Angel, and now I see them in operation!' laughed Doukas pleasantly.

How has he heard anything about me, when we apparently met as strangers only a few hours ago? wondered Angel. But there was no answer forthcoming.

Instead Doukas snapped, 'Lekkas, go and check this out – carefully!' and his subordinate, a thin, youngish man with dark hair and moustache in the usual Greek style, saluted and hurried off, muttering, 'Yes, Captain,' as he did so.

Doukas changed his approach at once, and became suave again. 'May we go into another room and talk, Angel?'

'What's wrong with here?' Angel replied, leading the way to the loungers beside the pool and lying down on one. The sun was lower in the sky by now, and she was comfortably in the shade, warm but not hot. Hamish and the doctor retreated into the villa out of earshot, and Doukas, looking rather embarrassed but reluctant to suggest anything else, followed Angel and sat upright on a neighbouring lounger.

'Since you don't suggest giving me time to change, Gregor,' Angel said sweetly, 'sure, I guess my costume's more suited to a sun lounger than anything else.'

Doukas realised his mistake. 'I'm so sorry, Angel, I should have asked if you'd like to change before we talk!'

Angel, having succeeded in wrong footing the captain, laughed. 'No problem, Gregor. Ask your questions.'

'To begin with, my dear, I'd like you to tell me in your own words just what happened.'

This suited Angel. She had already decided not to tell Doukas too much. She wasn't sure if she really should distrust this man. She wouldn't do it purely because of what Josh had said about him. Angel was used to making her own decisions about people. She wouldn't allow someone else's opinion, even Josh's, to influence her too much. And she'd quite liked Gregor when she'd met him on the plane.

Nevertheless, she had no intention of telling him more than the bare minimum of what she knew, so it would be easier to tell him her story, rather than to answer possibly difficult questions.

'Josh and I were swimming in the pool when we heard bullets – coming from behind the trellis, as far as I can judge,' she began. 'We both dived down and when I came up for air I saw Marge – Mrs McPherson – come running out. Then she fell as a bullet hit her. I got out of the pool as quickly as I could and did what I could for her.

Then I saw blood in the water and realised Josh had been hit. I got him out and gave him mouth to mouth resuscitation. Then Hamish came, and he called the doctor. By the time the doctor came, Josh was conscious again. That's all really.' No mention of the message wrapped round the stone. She would keep that to herself. As for the things she'd seen behind the trellis, Lekkas was there, and was perfectly capable, she was sure, of noticing the same stuff for himself.

'You've been very brave, Angel,' Doukas said admiringly. 'Not only beautiful but brave also. Inspector Smith is a lucky man. I think I should tell you that after we parted at the airport, I looked you up on the police database. Partly for personal reasons and partly business – I wanted to know who this beautiful young woman was who knew Inspector Smith so well. You must forgive me for this. But I found out nothing but good about you, as I'm sure you would expect.'

Angel was amazed to realise that she had a record on the police database. So that was why Gregor was able to refer to her detective skills. Still, as she'd told Marge, she'd been involved in catching more than one major criminal, so why not? It was annoying that Gregor Doukas had been able to look her up, but she decided to shrug it off.

'I assume you'll be able to collect up the bullets and identify the type of gun used,' Angel said crisply. 'But I don't want to tell you how to do your police work – you're the expert there.'

'Indeed,' smiled Doukas. 'I may want to talk to you some more, Angel, but meanwhile I want to go and check on what Lekkas is doing. And you will wish to change. The evenings get chilly quickly here. And lovely though you look in your bikini, I would regretfully advise you to put on something warmer soon.' His look swept up and down Angel's body, scantily covered with the towelling wrap. She shivered, not from cold. His eyes as they roamed over her gave her a strong feeling that she was wearing nothing at all.

She stood up and drew the wrap more closely around her.

'Indeed, Gregor, that sounds like good advice,' she said coolly, and walked past him into the villa and on up to her room without another glance.

Chapter Eleven

Josh was still sleeping from the sedation when Angel called in to see him on her way to bed. She left him to it, and wondered if she herself would be able to sleep after the events of the last few hours. However, jet lag was catching up on her and in fact she slept deeply and woke in the morning feeling refreshed.

This time, Josh was awake, too, when she looked round his door.

'Come in, sweetie, and tell me what's been happening,' he greeted her with his warm smile. The sun beaming in through the window lit up his face bright with pleasure. 'Last thing I remember is you kissing me and then explaining it away as mouth to mouth resuscitation.'

'The doctor thought you needed to rest. He sedated you. Not in line with what I've always thought you should do for someone who's concussed, but too late to interfere by the time I realised what he was doing. But it doesn't seem to have done any damage, I see.'

'Doesn't seem to have,' Josh agreed. 'If I start raving in another ten minutes, we can rethink that opinion.'

'Shut up!' Angel came into the room and perched on the end of the bed, and Josh pulled her near enough for a serious kiss. Presently she sat up and smoothed back her hair.

'So,' Josh said, 'tell me more about what happened. There were shots, yes?'

'Shots from behind that trellis thing. Marge came running out and she got hit in the leg – oh, she's going to be okay, they tell me,' Angel added hastily, seeing Josh's look of horror. 'And you were grazed in the arm and the head. Neither injury serious, the doctor said.'

Josh squinted round to look at his bandaged arm. 'Seems all right.' He reached his hands up to examine his head, and felt the long plaster stretching from front to back.

'Wow, don't tell me the doc shaved my hair!'

'Only a narrow bit where the graze is,' Angel assured him. 'Don't worry, he didn't spoil your beauty.'

'That's a relief. I'd have had to cancel my entry for Mr Universe next week. Angel,' Josh went on hastily, seeing Angel open her mouth to comment, 'do the cops know who did it? Or why?'

'Maybe. If so, they haven't told me. And aren't likely to. Who do you think's leading the investigation, Josh?'

'Well, who?'

'Sure, only your old friend Gregor Doukas, that's who.'

'That's a pain.' Josh thought for a minute. 'Still, he'll probably want to talk to me today, and I'll see what I can get out of him.'

'I can probably tell you more than he can,' Angel said. 'I had a look around myself while we were waiting for the cops to show up. And I didn't tell Doukas everything I found, I can tell you.'

'Angel! You shouldn't keep things back from the cops.'

'Josh, you were the one you put it into my head not to trust the boyo. Mind you, though I'm not sure I agree with you, I don't plan to tell him too much.'

'So, are you going to tell me what you found?'

'Not just tell you – show you.'

Angel fished in the pocket of her shorts and brought out the paper which had been wrapped round the stone. Josh took the paper from her outstretched hand and unfolded it.

'Go home, Irish. Keep your nose out of our affairs, you and your boyfriend,' he read out. Then he looked at Angel.

'The only thing I've taken any interest in is Sophie's robbery,' Angel said. 'And I haven't done much there, apart from visit her at the nursing home and offer to look into it for her.'

'But, hey, who would know you'd done that, sweetie?'

Angel fished in the other pocket of her shorts. 'Maybe someone who works in the nursing home and happened to overhear us?' She held out her hand with the scrap of cloth she'd picked from the trellis spread out on her palm for Josh to see. 'This was caught on the trellis near where the shots came from. Oh, don't worry, I left some of it for the police to find – if they bother to search properly. I thought it might come from a nurse's uniform, what d'ye think?'

'Could be,' Josh agreed cautiously. 'But would someone be running around shooting people still wearing her nurse's uniform? Seems a bit crazy to me.'

'Okay, see what you mean. But maybe she just hadn't time to change if the other one was picking her up. And another thing I found was the marks on the road just outside the Villa grounds of tyre marks and oil. Not car wheels, more like a motorbike.'

'Or one of those mopeds everyone rides on Corfu?' Josh suggested. 'And you didn't mention this to Captain Doukas?'

'I told him the shots came from the direction of the trellis. Nothing to stop him looking there and finding exactly what I found!' Angel retorted.

'H'mm.'

'So, are you getting up any time soon, you lazy hellion?'

'Probably. You're not very kind to an invalid. I thought you'd at least have brought me my breakfast in bed?'

'Hey, I still haven't had my own! Don't forget Marge is an invalid, too! I don't know what's likely to be happening downstairs, but just to pamper you I'll bring you up some of wherever I find going for myself – provided you get up after that! I want us to look into this business today.'

'Devil!' Josh retorted. 'Why anyone ever called you Angel, I don't know. You're a slave driver!'

'Seriously, darlin', I don't really expect you to get up until the doctor's seen you – and then only if he thinks you can. I'll do some investigating myself if you aren't fit.' A frown crossed her face. 'I feel really guilty about this, Josh. Someone was out after me, and it was you and Marge that ended up hurt. I'm going to catch the guys that did it, you can be sure!'

Josh grinned. 'Well, you'll clearly need me to help you, then, sweetie. So looks like I'll have to get up after all – provided you get me that breakfast, first!'

Chapter Twelve

Angel ran lightly down the stairs and found her way to the kitchen. No surprise to find Hamish there, but who were all these other people?

She had expected to see Hamish, naturally. The comfortable, plump, middle aged woman standing by the stove superintending the cooking of omelettes and the perking of coffee, while whisking a tray full of croissants out of the oven with one hand, must be Maria, the cook who had gone home last night after preparing the evening meal, as Marge had told her.

The man sitting at the kitchen table with a plate of food in front of him was the gardener/handyman who had helped to carry Josh upstairs last night. The other woman, youngish, cool, crisp, efficient looking, could be anyone. She, like the man, was seated at the table, a plate with two croissants and honey in front of her, sipping coffee.

The kitchen table was set with knives and forks, napkins and glasses, and the large jug of orange juice, probably freshly squeezed, suddenly looked very attractive to Angel.

'Angel! I meant to get someone to bring you up some coffee! Still, now you're here, sit down and start with orange juice.' Hamish bustled about, pulling out a chair for her, pouring juice into a tall, sparkling glass.

'This is our wonderful Maria, as I except you've guessed, Angel – the cook to beat all cooks! And this is Stephanos, who keeps our garden looking so great. And this lovely lady

– ' he beamed at the efficient looking girl – 'is our life saving nurse, Dido Marinas. We're so lucky to have Dido – she's been looking after Marge so wonderfully. And Josh, too, of course.'

'I slept in Marge's room last night,' Dido put in, speaking English in a cool voice with little or no accent. 'That way I was able to check on her regularly. And of course I looked in on Josh as often as I checked Marge.'

'So, I do hope Marge is recovering?'

'Yes, thank God!' Hamish said. 'Nurse Dido tells me she should heal up soon, and if she gets plenty of rest she'll be up and about in a week or so. Isn't that great?'

'Sure, I'm really glad to hear that, Hamish,' Angel said. She wondered if she really liked Nurse Dido. But it was maybe too soon to make a judgement. She hadn't realised that you could still get a live in nurse. Maybe it was different in Greece. Or maybe it was just different if you had the money to pay for it. How the other half (or probably, the other 1%) lived!

'I told Josh I'd bring him up some breakfast, if that's okay, Hamish?' she said. 'Juice, coffee and a couple of croissants would be fine. Maybe I could borrow a tray and sort some stuff out for him?'

'Well, of course you can, Angel! That is –' he looked doubtfully at the nurse. 'If Nurse Dido thinks that will be okay? Don't want to set him back.'

Angel was annoyed, but tried not to show it and said nothing.

'Oh, I should think a light breakfast wouldn't do him any harm,' Nurse Dido said coolly. 'I'll be coming up to take his temperature, and so on, in a few moments when I finish my own breakfast. If you wouldn't mind leaving it until I've checked him?'

A perfectly reasonable request, Angel knew. So why did she feel as if this woman was interfering between her and Josh? Stupid, right?

'No problem, nurse,' she said lightly. 'I'll sort something out for Josh whenever you're ready.'

Nurse Dido smiled with no warmth and continued to eat her croissant, spreading on more honey.

Angel finished her juice and wandered out into the garden. It was a fresh, beautiful morning. The intense heat of the sun later in the day hadn't yet taken over. As she strolled along, breathing in the fresh scent of the roses, she heard someone approaching behind her. It was Stephanos, the gardener.

'Hi, Stephanos! I'm just admiring your beautiful garden.'

'I'm glad you like it, Miss.' Stephanos spoke fluent English with very little accent.

'Agh, sure, call me Angel, please – everyone does.'

'Angel, then.' The gardener bowed his head slightly and smiled.

'I didn't know you could grow roses in this part of the world?'

'Oh, yes, it's not easy, but it can be done.'

For a few more minutes they chatted easily about the various flowers which, it seemed, were the pride of Stephanos's life, then Angel asked tentatively, 'Do you mind if I ask you a few questions? That dreadful business yesterday evening – I wondered if you'd noticed anything helpful? Anyone hanging round the outskirts of the garden just before that, or some sort of car or motorbike parked nearby?'

'Not a car – no. And not exactly a motorbike. There was one of those motor scooters – mopeds, isn't it? – that the tourists hire, parked just at the road behind the fence, back there.' He pointed beyond the swimming pool. 'I thought of telling the owner to move it, but it wasn't really on our land. Besides, there was no sign of the rider.'

'Motor scooters?'

'Yes, if you haven't seen them about yet, you will as soon as you go out on the roads. Visitors hire them to get around, and spend half their time falling off them.' He laughed.

This sounded worth exploring further. 'Tell me, Stephanos, where do you think this motor scooter came from?'

Stephanos shrugged. 'As to that, it could be any direction, if you mean where was it ridden from. But if you mean where was it hired, there are several places I know of. The nearest to here, and the best, is my brother Alexandros. I don't just say that because he is my brother, you understand.'

'And how would I find Alexandros?'

'He has a place just up the main road a few miles. Alex's Car and Bike Hire. You'll find it easily if you'd like to.'

'Thanks, Stephanos – you're a star!' Angel gave him a flashing smile. 'Hey, time's flying on. Maybe I'll be allowed to bring my friend some breakfast now, if Nurse Dido has finished.'

Stephanos smiled sympathetically, and waving goodbye Angel headed back to the villa.

The kitchen was empty by the time she reached it. Hoping that the nurse was not still in with Josh, and deciding that if necessary she could wait outside the bedroom door, Angel put things unto a tray, poured out some hot coffee to add to it, and carried it upstairs. At Josh's room she tapped and called out, and was pleased to be greeted by a welcoming, 'Come on in, honey!'

'Hey, breakfast at last! Looks good – and so do you, sweetie!'

'Glad to hear it. The nurse made me wait until she'd finished. I hope she's been and gone?'

'Just missed her. Gone back to Marge, she said.'

'And are you okay, does she think?'

'Fine. Never was much wrong with me, apart from this arm. It'll take a few weeks to mend, but nothing to spoil our holiday. Just as long as Marge is okay, too. That would sure spoil it for all of us.'

'And are you all right in the head, now?'

'Hey, girl, I recognise that as an Irish insult! My head never had much wrong with it – a bit of concussion and a graze. Don't I look dashing in the bandage? Captain Jack Sparrow in person?'

'I wouldn't quite say that.' Angel grinned and dodged the hand Josh reached out to tickle her. 'So, what did she say? Are you supposed to stay in bed today?'

'There was some loose talk of it. But I reckon I can lie about down by the pool, watching you swim, just as well.'

'Sure, that would be lovely, Josh, but I'd thought of following up a few things presently. I really want to find these guys who terrorise elderly women and shoot anyone who gets in their way.' She frowned. 'I'm feeling really angry about this whole business, Josh. And determined to put a stop to it.'

'Okay, Angel, I get you. I feel much the same. By tomorrow, when I'm allowed to walk about, I'll be right with you.' He smiled. 'I won't tell you to take care of yourself, because I already know that if anyone can do that, you're the girl who can.'

'Sure, thank you for those few kind words, sir,' Angel said lightly. She was relieved that Josh, as indeed she had expected, wasn't going to fuss.

'So, what do you have in mind to do?'

'I'd better tell you first of all what I've found so far. Then you'll understand why I aim to begin by visiting Alex's Bike and Car Hire just down the road.'

Chapter Thirteen

The sun was already hot when Angel left Josh comfortably settled by the pool with something to read and a cool drink on the low table by his side, and set off to walk the couple of miles along the main road to her objective. She was soon glad she'd picked up a shady sunhat as she left, and began to wish she'd worn shorts instead of the light blue skirt she'd picked out, pretty though it was.

Alex's Bike Hire was an ancient, rather dilapidated wooden structure, with its green paint faded and peeling a little from constant exposure to strong sunlight. As Angel approached it, she saw a young man, dark haired, tanned and half asleep, lounging on a bench in front of the veranda which ran along the front length of the building.

'Hi!' she said. The young man blinked open a pair of sleepy brown eyes and smiled at her with a flash of gleaming white teeth beneath the usual black Greek moustache, as he swung his legs down and pulled himself into an upright position.

'Hi, gorgeous!'

He had a face like one of the wise monkeys – the one, Angel decided, that spoke no evil, not the ones who saw or did no evil. It was a triangular shape, and full of wrinkles, although she retained her original impression that he certainly wasn't old.

'Can I help you?' he asked, beaming.

'I hope so. Call me Angel. My name's Angel Murphy.'

'Angel. Hi.'

'So, are you Alex? Your brother Stephanos sent me here.'

'Stephanos? He often sends people here – he knows I give them good service.' Alex flashed his white beaming smile again. 'Yes, I'm Alex.'

'Hi, Alex,' Angel said. 'I'm hoping you can help me. I think someone I know rented a motor scooter – that is, a moped – from you recently?'

'A stack of people have rented mopeds from me recently, Angel. What's your friend's name?'

His English seemed easy to follow, with a wide-ranging vocabulary and a strong American accent. Much better than her own lame Greek, at any rate, Angel thought, aware that she had no room to be critical.

Strolling over to the young man, she settled herself comfortably on the bench beside him.

'I'll tell you what it is, Alex,' she began confidingly. 'I'm staying at the Villa Callidora down the road a bit, where Stephanos works. Now, I don't know if you've heard about this, but last night there was a shooting there.'

'Yeah, sure, I heard all about it!' Alex exclaimed. 'A terrible affair. Not a thing to happen in Corfu!'

'I know, Alex. It seems really out of place in this peaceful, beautiful island. After the two injured people had been treated by the doctor, I came outside to look in the direction the bullets had come from, and I found marks just outside the Villa grounds of what seemed to me to be a moped. Stephanos thought you might be able to help me find out who had hired it.'

'Wow! That's not so easy, Angel!' Alex smiled his confiding, happy monkey grin. 'You don't know this guy's name, you don't know what he looked like –'

'Alex, I don't even know it was a man. Women hire these too, don't they?'

'Ah – yes – but not so many, in fact. Only two in the last day. You think it was a woman?'

'Well, I'll tell you. There was a hint that a nurse might have been involved, right? A female nurse, I mean. But maybe she was just a passenger, not the one who hired your moped.'

'Hey, you'll have to let me think. And look up the list of customers in my record book. How about sitting there for a few minutes and drinking something cold, beautiful Angel, while I do that?'

Angel laughed. 'Sounds good, Alex! Tell me something, you sound really American. Have you lived there?'

'Sure I have! Born in New York. Lived twenty years in the Big Apple – then I reckoned I'd come over just to see my native spot – the place my mom and pop emigrated from. Stephanos was already here. He told me about it and made it sound good. So I came, for a vacation, like. But I fell flat – loved the place as soon as I saw it. I've been here for ten years now and no plans for leaving.'

'I can understand that, Alex. I wouldn't mind moving here myself.'

Alex sprang to his feet, suddenly energetic. 'But how about that drink, babe? Rest and enjoy the sun, while I fetch you something. I know, you must try this island's speciality, Koum Quat! A fresh liqueur made from the little Japanese oranges imported here long ago, and used to make a liqueur like none else in the world!'

And to Angel's laughing protests that it was far too early yet for liqueurs, he paid no attention, disappearing into the depths of the ramshackle building with another monkey grin and a wave of his hand. Angel gave up trying to prevent him and settled back to enjoy the sun and the view out over the blue, blue sea, her wide brimmed hat tilted forward over her face.

The purple bougainvillea poured over the wall beside her, the fresh green leaves and tendrils of vines grew across the veranda roof, providing some shade. Tall orange trees with their bright fruits hanging in profusion from every branch lined the sides of the road. Angel sighed in a content which would have been absolute except for the worry at the back of her mind about Josh and Marge. Still, the doctor had said nothing serious was wrong, hadn't he?

Presently Alex emerged again from the building with a tall glass in one hand and a rather battered book in the other. 'I have added ice and water, Angel, which I hope won't spoil the flavour,' he announced, handing the glass to her.

'Thanks, Alex,' murmured Angel gratefully, feeling the coldness of the glass and holding it for a moment against her hot forehead before taking a cautious sip. To her relief it was delicious and with the added ice and water possibly not too alcoholic.

'Now,' said Alex, turning suddenly into a brisk businessman as he sat down beside her and spread open his order book on his knee, 'I can tell you the details of all my clients for the last few days – it's not wise to hire out a valuable moped to someone when you have no means of contacting them, you know? So I have names, addresses, credit card details for those who pay that way, as most do. As I thought, there were only two women yesterday, and – you are interested also in the day before? – ah, yes, I thought so. Then, two more women the day before, but none on the preceding day. Most of my customers are men, as I said. See, these are the women.'

Angel looked with interest at the names and addresses indicated by Alex's thin and slightly dirty brown finger. There seemed nothing distinctive about them, but she fished her little notebook out of her shoulder bag and made a note of each, nevertheless. They would be worth following up.

No real reason to think that the person in the woman's sized trainers who had left a tuft of what might be a nurse's uniform behind was the one who had hired the moped, of course. It could just as easily have been hired by her companion, the shooter, who might be a man. Angel's eye strayed down the list, looking at men who had hired mopeds in the last few days. Her eyes almost passed unrecognisingly over one particular name, then jumped back in disbelief.

Surely not! Could she really be seeing the name there of Jason Horowitz?

Chapter Fourteen

Jason Horowitz! Surely there couldn't be two people on this small island at the same time with that unusual name!

Angel didn't believe it. This must be the guy she'd met at the airport. And if so, it couldn't be a coincidence that he had turned up here again.

But what was he up to, hiring a moped just near where she was staying? He'd given her to understand that he would be at the southern end of the island or else around Corfu town.

'Alex,' she asked, 'do you remember this guy?' She pointed to the name.

Alex frowned. Then his brow cleared. 'I sure do, Angel. That's the sucker who dropped his wallet and let a lot of stuff fall out of it all around him! You know we don't get much wind here, but there just happened to be a bit of a breeze that day. I was running all directions trying to pick up his papers for him, and he just stood there giggling his head off! Looked like he was wasted – high as a kite!'

'And so did you get everything he dropped and give it back to him?'

'Well, I thought I had. But turned out there was one more thing – a photo that got lodged behind the veranda railing. I didn't see it until after he'd gone off on the moped. I'll give it back to him when he brings the machine back. Couple of days from now.'

Angel hardly dared to breathe. 'Could you let me see it?'

'Sure, why not?' Alex dived into his office and came back a minute later with the photo in his hand. He held it, looking dubious. 'Must be important to him, I guess. Not many people make print outs these days. Just keep the digital version. Maybe he's really crazy about this chick and wanted to carry it next to his heart. Hey, listen to me getting sloshy! Still, I better be careful with this.'

'I just want to look at it, not to keep it, Alex.'

'Okay, Angel.' Alex shrugged and handed over the snap reluctantly. Angel took it eagerly and gazed at the picture.

A youngish, dark haired woman who looked very vaguely familiar looked back at her, a triumphant expression on her face. She was attractive in an individual way, her face fine drawn, her complexion soft and pale. Her mouth was wide, her lips full. She was dressed for the evening, as if bound for a formal dance or the first night at a very up market theatre. But what struck Angel so that she found herself almost ignoring the face and dress was the necklace gleaming brightly round the woman's neck, clear to be seen.

Six large matching sapphires were set in a graceful chain of little gold links with a design of leaves surrounding each bright stone. A seventh stone, larger than the others, hung as a droplet from the centre, with its own set of golden leaves around it. The necklace was delicate and beautiful, not too heavily designed for the wearer. It was both individual and striking and Angel had seen a photo of it round the neck of a very different woman only the day before when she visited Sophie at the nursing home. It was the necklace Joe Papadopolous had bought Sophie for their last wedding anniversary before he died.

What was this woman doing with Sophie's necklace round her throat? The obvious answer was that she was involved with the thieves in some way. So, it was important to memorise this woman's face. Angel stared hard at the photo, trying to make sure she wouldn't forget it. The more she looked, the more she was sure she'd seen this woman before, but where that might have been was still something she couldn't be sure of.

She became aware of Alex moving uneasily from foot to foot beside her. Angel laughed and handed the photo back.

'I wouldn't be in too much of a hurry to give it back to him, Alex,' she said. 'This may be evidence of grand larceny, okay? So if I were you I'd hold on to it and say nothing to this Jason Horowitz.'

'Seriously, Angel? Wow!' Alex stepped back and stared at her, his mouth hanging open. 'Okay, you've got it! I'll keep it and say nothing, right?'

Angel grinned. 'You do that, Alex! Now, how about renting me one of these mopeds of yours? It sounds just the thing for getting around this island.'

'You wouldn't rather have a car?' Alex asked dubiously.

'No way! My friend has a car. If I wanted a car I could borrow his – but I'd rather not risk taking it. I'll feel freer with a moped I'm renting myself. So, what's the charge?'

A few minutes later, a debit card having been brought into use and a few brief words of instruction from Alex having shown Angel the whereabouts of the starter and brake, she perched herself up happily on the shiny green moped, waved goodbye to Alex, and headed off back to the Villa Callidora. The sun beat down on her shoulder blades, a sense of freedom washed through her, and she sang happily as she explored the intricacies of the moped's moving parts. She'd never ridden one of these before, but, hey, she could drive a car and had even flown a light aircraft, so what could be so difficult?

Liam Clancy's song came to her mind.

'*I'm a freeborn man of the travelling' people,*' sang Angel.

'*Got no fixed abode, with nomads I am numbered.*

Country lanes and bye ways were always my ways.

I never fancied being lumbered.'

This was the life!

Provided Josh and Marge were recovering well, that was.

Chapter Fifteen

Once back at the Villa Callidora, Angel parked the bike just inside the garage and hurried inside to check on Josh. He was back upstairs in his room and he was sleeping, but as she came in, moving quietly so as not to wake him, he stirred, opened one eye, and smiled sleepily.

'Hi, Angel. How's things?'

'Moving ahead, I think. But, hey, I thought you were going to lie about at the pool instead of being stuck up here? Are you okay? Do you still feel bad?'

'Sure, I'm fine, honey. But the doctor called and advised me to go back to bed and rest as much as possible today. I dropped off not long after he'd gone. But maybe I'll get up now.'

'Indeed you will not, Josh Smith!' Angel said severely. 'You'll do as the doctor tells you.'

'Bossy pants.' Josh struggled into a sitting position in his bed and stretched out his good arm to draw Angel to him. 'C'mere, honey. Now, tell me about this 'moving ahead' stuff, okay?'

'Well,' Angel said, snuggling down beside him, 'I went up to the local moped and car hire place as you know. Run by Alex, the brother of Stephanos, the gardener here. A really nice guy, and very helpful. I found out from him that one of the people who hired a moped in the last few days was Jason Horowitz , the guy I met at the airport –'

'Guy you met at the airport? News to me!' interrupted Josh.

'Oh, no, I suppose I didn't mention him. It wasn't important. But this guy Jason Horowitz tried to chat me up and I remembered him because of the name. He must have chased straight up here by taxi or something and hired a moped the same afternoon. I noticed his name on Alex's list because it's so unusual.'

'So, how many guys chatted you up on the plane or at the airport, exactly?' Josh murmured wryly. 'This Horowitz and Doukas – how many others?'

'Oh, you don't want to hear the whole list! Nobody important!' Angel said flippantly. 'I don't keep count.' Then she shrieked as Josh began to tickle her with his sound arm and hand. 'Ow! Ow! Stop it, you villain! It was your car I got into, wasn't it?'

'Fair enough. So, is that it? This guy's name was on the list?'

'No, apart from the fact that he gave me to understand he was heading for the other end of the island, there's something else. He dropped his wallet and when he and Alex gathered up the stuff that fell out of it, there was this photo that got left behind. Alex showed it to me.'

'So?'

'So, it was a photo of some woman wearing one of the necklaces Sophie had stolen! She showed me a snap of her with it round her neck yesterday when we visited her at the nursing home – I couldn't be mistaken. It was definitely the same necklace! So this woman must be involved with the thieves, even if she just knew one of them well enough to buy it from them. It's a definite lead, if we could track her down.'

'If.'

'Yes, but, Josh, I'm quite certain I've seen her somewhere – if I could just remember where.'

Josh sat up straighter. 'That sounds like something good, Angel. If you could remember where you saw her, we might really be on to something. It was here in Corfu, you think?'

'Yes, I'm pretty sure it was.'

'Well, you haven't been here long, and so you haven't seen too many people. If you could think back over the ones you've seen. Where all have you been? In the airport, for starters. It wasn't someone there, one of the staff?'

'I don't think so.' Angel sounded doubtful as she tried to call to mind the various women she'd seen at the airport – travellers and staff both. None of them rang a bell.

'Well, we got here, and apart from staff – you would know it if was one of them, wouldn't you? Yes, of course – then, the next place you went to was the nursing home – '

'Wait!' A bell rang suddenly in Angel's head. 'The nursing home! Of course! Josh, I'm sure it was one of the carers at the nursing home! I didn't think of her at first because in the photo the woman was dressed up in evening wear and expertly made up, and when I saw her in the nursing home she was in uniform and with no make up – it makes a difference. But, yes, I'm sure now that that was who it was!'

They stared at each other. Things had suddenly moved on considerably.

'Okay,' said Angel briskly. 'That settles it. This afternoon, as soon as I've seen that you have some lunch, I'll take my new moped and go straight to the nursing home and look into this!'

Chapter Sixteen

'Now, wait a minute, Angel. Don't jump off the deep end without thinking about it first.'

'I'm not doing that, Josh. All I'm doing is calling at the nursing home to see Sophie again, and having a look around while I'm there. How is that the deep end?'

'Okay. But just be careful.'

'We don't even know what sort of connection this woman has with the thieves, after all,' argued Angel.

'No, but we know it's quite likely she's the one who was here with the guy who shot me and Marge, right?'

'Oh. Sure, I think you're right there, Josh.' Angel was silent for a moment. 'Maybe we could think out just what her involvement is likely to be?'

'Let's just say, for a start, there was a woman involved in the shooting who left a tuft of what might have been a nurse's uniform behind her, right? And you recognise a woman from the nursing home, almost certainly the same one, as the woman in the photo wearing Sophie's stolen necklace?'

'Right.'

Josh was silent for a moment, thinking, and Angel waited to hear what he would say.

'So,' he said eventually, 'what I wonder is, why was she wearing the necklace? I don't think she would have gone out in public with it on – far too dangerous. So, let me just guess here, maybe she just wanted to try it on, to see what she looked like in it?'

'That sounds like a possibility, Josh!' Angel responded eagerly. 'I know if I could get my hands on a necklace like that, I'd be dying to try it on, just to see how I looked.'

'Okay, and so someone – presumably this guy Jason Horowitz – took her photo wearing it. And kept it, not just on his camera, but as a print out.'

'A strange thing to do.'

'Yeah. So why did he do that?'

Angel waited patiently.

'What I wondered was, did he take the pic, and then make a print out, so he would have a hold over this woman? For whatever reason. Money, sex, help with what he's up to, whatever. He could threaten her with exposure – if she didn't do whatever it was he wanted.'

'Josh, you've got something there. That must have been it.'

'Well, I wouldn't say it must have been, Angel. But it gives us an idea to work on. You might be able to persuade her to tell you the names of the thieves in return for the photo. If you can get it from your friend Alex, that is. You'll just need to smile at him sweetly, I guess.'

'Might not be as easy as that, Josh. He was very determined to hold on to it. He had some romantic idea that Jason Horowitz printed it out to keep next to his heart because he was crazy about this woman.'

'And I suppose that's an alternative reason for the print out, honey. If a bit less likely!'

A knock at the door interrupted them.

'Yes? Come on in,' invited Josh, and the door was pushed gingerly open by Maria.

'Here's your lunch, Josh,' she said shyly, bringing in a tray loaded with a salad, a plate holding stuffed vine leaves, sliced fried eggplant, and olives, and a carafe of red wine, together with plates, cutlery and a glass. A white napkin was folded to one side.

Josh's eyes brightened at the sight.

'And yours is ready downstairs, Angel,' she added. The hint was unmistakable, and Angel rose to go.

'I'll leave you to it, then, Josh,' she said. 'And when I've had my own, and checked on Marge if they'll let me see her, I'll head off. Don't worry, I'll be careful!'

Josh gave her a worried look, but she had gone before he could say more. He could only trust to her good sense. After all, he'd seen her come safely through several different situations, some of them much more dangerous than this, and he knew very well that she wouldn't thank him for interfering.

So, philosophically, he left her to make her own decisions, and turned with interest to the loaded tray before him. Greek food was always a delight, especially when cooked and provided by Hamish and Marge's excellent cook Maria. Josh struck his fork into an olive, poured out a glass or wine, and began to enjoy his lunch.

Joining Hamish and the nurse round a table set out on the patio behind the kitchen, Angel expressed pleasure at the sight of the food on offer, then asked, 'And so, how is Marge today, Hamish? Improving, I do hope.'

'I think she is,' Hamish replied, spreading a napkin across his knees as he settled himself at the table. 'But Nurse Dido here could give you a better picture than I can.'

Angel turned her head to look inquiringly at Nurse Dido. Dido looked coolly back at her and continued to eat her sliced and fried aubergines.

'So,' Angel was forced to inquire, 'how is Marge doing, then?'

Dido condescended to answer. 'As Hamish said, she's certainly improving. It will be a few days yet before we can say anything more definite.' She speared another aubergine slice with her fork, and picked an olive from the dish in front of her.

Angel, as had happened the last time she'd spoken to this woman, felt put down, even humiliated. What was wrong with Dido that she couldn't respond pleasantly to someone who was trying to be friendly to her?

'Well, that sounds hopeful,' was all Angel could find to say.

Hamish intervened, perhaps sensing the antagonism between the two women.

'This has really ruined your holiday, Angel. I hope you'll find something nice to do this afternoon? Please don't feel you have to hang around here – Marge is fine, being well looked after, and so is Josh, of course.'

'Actually, I thought I might go down to see Sophie Papodopolous again, Hamish. You know Marge took me with her to visit Sophie yesterday? I used to know her, back in Belfast, when I was a wee thing the size of sixpence, when she used to come over sometimes. I'd like to see more of her.'

'What a great idea, Angel! No, I didn't know any of this. But it works out well. You can borrow our car, of course.'

'No, no, Hamish, no need for that. I've hired myself a moped to get around on – I'll enjoy finding my way round by myself. I'm sure Josh has told you how independent I am!'

Hamish laughed. 'He did say something like that, now I think of it! Great. Have a good afternoon. Now, if you'll excuse me, I think I'll look in on Marge and see if there's anything she wants.' He pushed his chair back from the table and stood up. 'Please don't stop eating on my account.'

'Give Marge my love, won't you?'

Angel smiled at Hamish, whom she already felt fond of, as he left the room, hurrying to see his much loved wife. She felt desperately sorry for him, and guilty besides, since the attack which had disabled Marge had been aimed at her. But it made her all the more determined to find out who was responsible.

Chapter Seventeen

Angel finished her meal, stood up and said goodbye politely to the nurse, and went upstairs to her room to freshen up. While there she had a quick shower and changed into bright yellow shorts and top, which would make it easier to ride the moped. Her skirt had been just a bit cumbersome earlier on.

Humming cheerfully to herself, she went out to the garage to pick up the machine. Hopping up onto the saddle, she reminded herself how to start it, and was soon buzzing happily along the road outside the Villa Callidora and out onto the main coast road.

The blue, blue sea sparkled merrily beneath the wall beside her, the bougainvillea shone purple in the bright sunlight, and Angel rejoiced in her freedom, as she had done earlier when first trying out the moped. This was a great way to travel. She felt so much nearer to the country around her than in a car. The silvery leaved olives trees crowded the hillside on her right and the sun like golden wine lighted the further away hills.

'*I'm a freeborn man of the travellin' people,*' Angel sang softly to herself again, and couldn't contain her smiles.

The miles disappeared beneath her wheels and before she knew it she was within sight of the turn off for the nursing home. She parked in the forecourt and went in.

'Hi,' she greeted the receptionist, a good looking Greek girl with long black hair, an olive skin, and huge, dark eyes.

'I was here yesterday with Marge McPherson, visiting Sophie Papodopulous. I wondered if it was possible for me to call in with Sophie again?'

The receptionist cast a dubious eye over Angel's shorts and her long dusty legs, sprayed from the open road. Perhaps she didn't look quite like the person who'd arrived with Marge yesterday by Rolls, much more formally dressed for the visit. Angel was amused, but took care to show nothing.

'Well, I will see,' the receptionist said. Her English was fluent but stilted. 'It will depend if Mrs Papodopolous wants to see you. What name will I give her?'

'Angeline Murphy.'

The receptionist picked up the phone on her desk and rang Sophie's room. Apparently she got an enthusiastic reaction. Angel couldn't hear the words, but she could hear a high pitched squeaky response, and when the receptionist put the receiver down, her icy attitude had changed to a smiling approval. Apparently Sophie's attitude had allowed Angel to pass the test.

'Mrs Papadopolous will be happy to see you,' the receptionist said. 'Room 202, along this corridor to the left.'

'Thank you,' Angel said demurely and headed off in the direction indicated. As she walked along the corridor, she allowed herself to think for the first time of what exactly she wanted to ask Sophie. She didn't want to upset her too much – but on the other hand, Sophie ought to be kept up to date with what was going on, and she might have things to contribute to solving the mystery. She might have some idea who the nurse who was involved might be.

Room 202. This was it. Angel rapped softly on the door and peeped round it. 'Sophie? May I come in?'

A high pitched squeal interrupted her. 'Angel! Come in at once, darlin' girl! I'm so happy to see you again! Thanks so much for visiting me so soon!'

Sophie sprang out of bed with unexpected agility and darted across the room to fling herself into Angel's arms. The two staggered for a moment, then, laughing, regained their balance.

'Oh, Sophie, it's so great to see you!' Angel said.

'Come and sit down, pet,' Sophie said, leading Angel by the hand to the two comfortable chairs placed by the French windows. 'I've been hearing bad news since I saw you yesterday. Tell me – what's been happening? I can't believe what I've heard!'

It hadn't occurred to Angel that Sophie might know about the shooting. But it was a small island. Probably news travelled fast. She was glad she had come. Her reason had been to find out if Sophie knew anything helpful and also to explore the nursing home and see if she could track down the nurse whom she had half recognised. But now she was glad that she could put Sophie's mind at ease by telling her exactly what had happened.

Quietly, holding Sophie's hand and rubbing it from time to time, she outlined the events of the shooting, taking care to minimise the hurt and to explain that both Marge and Josh were recovering well. 'Hamish has brought a live in nurse to look after them both,' she finished. 'A Dido Marinas. She seems very competent.'

'Dido!' exclaimed Sophie. 'I wondered why I hadn't seen her since yesterday! Yes, I'm sure she's competent enough.'

Her voice expressed some of the doubt Angel had felt herself about Dido.

'You know Dido, then?'

'Oh, yes, Dido worked here up until yesterday. As I say, very competent, no doubt. But –'

'Wow, that's just exactly what I think about her!' Angel exclaimed. 'Very competent, I'm sure, but –! I don't know what I think the problem is. Just a – well, a coldness? Is that what you felt, Sophie?'

'That's it exactly, Angel!' said Sophie eagerly. 'I don't mean to criticise her nursing skills. But I just feel I wouldn't want to be dependent on her care, with no one else to give me support.'

'There's some more stuff I need to tell you, Sophie,' said Angel slowly. 'I found the tracks of a moped near the pool, just outside the villa grounds, but in the direction the bullets came from. And I found a bit of cloth from what seemed to me like nurse's uniform, the sort the carers wear here. And when I looked into the matter of moped hire, the nearest place for that belongs to a guy called Alex, and he showed me the list of people who'd hired mopeds recently. And one of them had dropped a photo from his wallet and Alex had found it afterwards. And it was, I'm pretty sure, one of the nurses from here. And she was wearing your sapphire necklace.'

Sophie said nothing.

'And I wondered if I could have another look at your photo of the necklace, Sophie, just to be sure it's the same?'

Still speechless, Sophie got up, went over to the drawer where she kept her photographs, and took out the album with the snap of herself wearing the sapphires and thrust it at Angel. Angel, allowing for her upset, said nothing, in return, but opened the album and turned the pages until she found the photo.

Yes, there was no doubt it was the same necklace she'd seen on the throat of the woman in the photo Jason Horowitz had dropped from his wallet.

Chapter Eighteen

But equally certainly, it wasn't Dido Marinas. This was a fleeting thought which had drifted through Angel's head since Sophie had told her a moment ago that Dido had worked at the nursing home up until yesterday. But, no. The sight of the necklace refreshed her memory of the photo Alex had shown her.

No, it definitely wasn't Dido. But all the same, Angel decided, she wouldn't be too surprised if it turned out that Dido was involved in the robberies in some way. Pure prejudice, since she disliked Dido, probably.

'So, this is definitely the same necklace, darlin',' she said. 'And the next thing, Sophie, is to see if you can identify the woman as one of the nurses here if I describe her.'

'Well – I'll try. The thing is,' said Sophie ruefully, 'I'm not that good at visualising. My creativity is all poured into singing and song writing. The visual arts seem to have been bypassed in me! Pity you don't have the photo for me to look at.'

Yes, it was a pity, Angel realised. Why hadn't she been firmer with Alex and managed to borrow it from him? But looking back she remembered how definite he'd been about keeping the photo safe for its owner. He'd hardly let her look at it for more than a few moments.

'Okay, we'll have to do out best, Sophie,' she said. 'Dark hair. Probably a lot of your nurses have dark hair?'

'At least 60%, I'd say at a guess, Angel love.'

'So – age between twenty and thirty – this is a guess too, mind you! Might be well on in her thirties but not showing it.'

'Well, that rules out a few. There are quite a few nurses in their forties or fifties. Leaves maybe three or four.'

'Great! So, good figure, I'd say. Certainly not too fat or too thin. And probably what most people would call good looking.'

'Well, that rules out poor wee Nurse Helena – for someone with the name Helen – like Helen of Troy, the most beautiful woman in the world in her day! – she just doesn't live up to it. Really overweight, poor lamb!'

'Anyone else?'

'Well, Nurse Ianthe is a bit on the opposite extreme. Thin as a rake. If anyone can be too thin in these days where thin is beautiful, then Ianthe's done it, I'm afraid. So not her, in my opinion.'

'So, how many does that leave?'

'Only two or three.'

'That sounds hopeful. So, can you give me their names?'

'Okay, there'd be – let's see – Nara – yes, she'd definitely fit the description. Then there's Barbara. Well, I suppose so. And Rena. Well, yes, maybe – dark, good figure – a bit unpleasant, actually. Not what I'd call good looking.'

'I suppose that might depend on whether she was happy, smiling, or not?'

'Well, yes, I suppose.' Sophie sounded doubtful.

Just then there was a knock on the door and a woman dressed in nurse's uniform sailed in.

'Time for your check up, Mrs Papodopolous,' she said, with an attempt at a smile.

'Oh, is it, Nurse Rena?' Sophie said, obviously thrown at the sudden interruption.

Nurse Rena, whom they'd just been discussing. Dark, good figure, possibly good looking if she was smiling properly.

Angel stared at her. This was, without any doubt, the woman in the photograph!

Pulling herself together, she regained her poise. 'Do you want me to go, nurse?' she asked.

'If you don't mind.' Rena spoke politely but with no real warmth.

'Wait outside, Angel darlin'. This will only take a few minutes!' Sophie said urgently. 'We've still lots to talk about.'

'No problem, Sophie.'

Angel slipped quietly out of the room and began to pace up and down in the corridor outside. She could have wished that Sophie had been a little less blatant in her comments. 'Still lots to talk about,' sounded a bit too important if Rena was on the alert for suspicious conversation.

She must have already overheard Angel's previous conversation with Sophie, and that had led to the shooting, and the message, *'Go home, Irish. Keep your nose out of our affairs, you and your boyfriend.'* Angel shuddered as she remembered the words, which were imprinted on her heart. She hoped some day soon to be able to forget them.

Supposing Nurse Rena had been listening again today before she burst in? She'd have learnt way too much about the photo and about Angel's suspicions, and above all about the probable identification of herself as the woman in the photograph who was wearing Sophie's necklace. So what would this lead too? Another shooting, more successful this time? Angel seriously hoped not. She had no desire to end up on a mortuary slab as a victim of gunfire. Or for Josh to end up there either.

She waited impatiently, and presently Sophie's door opened and the nurse came out.

'Okay if I go in again now, nurse?' Angel asked. 'Are you all finished?'

Nurse Rena smiled coolly, accentuating her likeness to the woman in the photograph, whose smile had been so much happier, but nevertheless similar.

'Certainly, miss.'

'Okay, thanks.' Angel went past her and into Sophie's room. She went right up to Sophie, who was now back in bed.

'Sophie, that's her! I'm certain of it!' she said softly, only too aware of the possibly listening ears. She put a finger to her lips. 'Hush,' she hardly breathed. 'Let's keep this really quiet!'

Sophie nodded tremulously.

'There's really nothing more to say right now, Sophie. I want to slip out when I'm sure Rena isn't watching me and see what I can find out about her from the admin here. Who should I talk to, do you think?'

'I suppose the Matron, her name is Washington and she's actually an Englishwoman, an ex-pat. Or maybe you'd get more out of the receptionist – also the secretary – Lydia Alanis. She's very friendly and I've always found her helpful.'

'Okay.' Angel came over and gave Sophie a warm hug. 'I'll head off, now, darlin'. Look after yourself! See you again soon. And not a word to Rena, mind!'

Angel opened the door cautiously and peeped round the edge. There was no sign of Rena. She breathed a sigh of relief. Rena must have gone to carry out her other duties. After all she couldn't spend all day eavesdropping on Sophie and her visitors. Slipping quietly out, she headed in the direction of the reception desk.

Chapter Nineteen

Lydia the receptionist seemed the best bet for a first try. The Matron would probably be much less ready to give away information about her staff. Lydia must be the girl she's already met, with long black hair and huge dark eyes.

Approaching the desk Angel saw that she was there.

'Hi, Lydia!' she greeted her. 'It is Lydia, isn't it? My friend Sophie Papadopolous gave me your name.'

'Yes, I'm Lydia.' The young woman looked at her cautiously.

'I'm wondering if you can help me. I need a nurse for an elderly aunt of mine who lives here – I've out here partly on holiday, but partly to visit her and check that she's okay. And it turns out that she could do with a live in companion who was a qualified nurse. Now, Sophie says a lot of the nurses here are very willing to take on that sort of work, and she recommended a Nurse Rena. I should have got her other name, but Sophie wasn't sure of it. But maybe you know who I mean?'

'Yes, that would be Rena Serkos. I'm sure she'd be happy to work for your aunt. To tell you the truth, the wages here could be better. Private nursing is usually much better paid. If you offered her a good salary, I'm sure she'd accept at once.'

'Good. But, you understand, before taking her on, I'd need to know a bit about her. Do you see what I mean, Lydia?'

Lydia frowned and then said, 'Yes, I understand. You would not want to trust your aunt to just anyone.'

'That's it, exactly. So, can you tell me something about her?'

'I don't really know very much,' Lydia said uneasily.

'But you must have some records here,' Angel said with a friendly smile. 'If you looked them up, you could give me some information about her background, her qualifications, her references, that sort of thing.'

'Surely she could tell you this herself?' Lydia frowned.

'Probably. But it would be more reliable, less likely to be made up, if you understand me, if it had already been checked out when she applied here.'

'Yes, I see.'

'And I'm sure she'd want you to supply it to me – she'd hate to lose this opportunity, wouldn't she, and I'm afraid if I can't get the info from you, Lydia, I'll have to forget about her and look elsewhere for a nurse for my aunt.'

'What you say is true.' At Lydia's words, Angel had the grace to blush. 'All right, I will look up her records.'

She turned away went through the opening behind her desk into a small office, and began to hunt in the filing cabinets which Angel could see vaguely against the far wall. Presently she returned with a file which Angel could see was labelled with Rena Serkos's name.

'This is her personnel record,' Lydia said. 'But of course it is in Greek. You would not be able to follow it, no?'

'No,' agreed Angel sadly.

'But I will tell you as much as I can.' Lydia began to leaf through the file, reading out and translating the relevant information as she went.

Apparently Rena had a qualification in nursing and one in midwifery. She had worked in London at Guy's Hospital and had returned to Corfu two years ago. Her references were from Guy's and from a private patient for whom she had worked for the first year of her return. She had started in this nursing home just under three months ago. Her home address –

Lydia hesitated. 'She lives in at the nursing home. Do you need her home address? She is only there in her off duty hours.'

'It would help,' said Angel firmly.

'Very well.' Having decided that giving Angel the information was helping Rena, Lydia seemed ready to go the whole hog. 'She lives in Corfu town. Here, I'll write down the address for you.' She scribbled on a slip of paper and passed it across the desk to Angel, who stuck it in the pocket of her yellow shorts. 'An apartment, I think. She may share with someone.'

'That's great, Lydia! She sounds as if she'd be the right person. I'll probably try to contact her at her home address to save embarrassment here, okay? Don't mention it to her, will you, in case I change my mind? I'll head on now. Thanks again!'

Angel smiled, and strolled out of the front entrance in a leisurely way.

What would be best to do next? She could check out Rena's address in Corfu town – but it was a fair distance. Or maybe she should try to track down Jason Horowitz. Might he even be the one Rena was sharing with? It was certainly a possibility. She glanced at her watch. It was still early, only three thirty. Corfu Town it was, then!

She walked at her usual fast pace round to the area where she had parked her scooter and climbed on board. There seemed to be something strange about it. It wasn't quite in the same place as where she had left it, she thought. And there was something on the ground beneath it, she didn't know what. Not oil or petrol, certainly. Oh, well. Angel shrugged. She'd see first of all if it started, and if it did she was probably imagining things.

She kicked the starter and felt the motor purr into action beneath her. No problem there, it seemed. Angel drove down the entrance drive and steered the machine carefully out onto the minor road where the nursing home was situated.

She felt the same uplifting of her spirits as before, and the same urge to sing, as she whizzed along the road in sole control of her journey.

'On Raglan Road on an autumn day
I saw her first and knew
That her dark hair would weave a snare
That I might one day rue.
I saw the danger and I passed
Along the enchanted way
And I said: 'Let grief, be a fallen leaf
At the dawning of the day,'

sang Angel, the words as always moving her almost to tears. The melancholy mood of Irish folk always stirred her emotions to the extreme, and in particular this song, with its words by the poet Patrick Kavanagh and its traditional folk tune.

The wind stirred up by the moped's movement rushed through her own long fair hair and she lifted her face to enjoy the warmth of the sun. In spite of all the bad events, she was really enjoying this holiday.

There was a small hill curving down towards the main road, and Angel was aware that she needed to brake as she got closer to the place where the roads joined up. She began to brake slightly in what should have been good time.

This was strange. Nothing was happening.

Angel braked harder. Still nothing. It became obvious that something was wrong with her brakes.

The major road loomed ahead. Angel looked to her right and her left. On her right was a wall of rough stones. On her left a bank covered in wild flowers, blue hyacinths, pink cyclamen, white daisies, gold orchids.

It was clear to Angel in the split second she had left to think that since the brakes weren't working, she needed to take some action. Twisting the handle bars furiously, she steered the moped as hard as she could towards the bank, which at least, she seriously hoped, should be soft. Then, at the last moment before crashing into it, she leapt from the saddle and aimed to land front down on the soft bank just beside the moped, her hands up to protect her face.

A second later she was lying, winded but undamaged, in the midst of the wild flowers, the scent of their crushed blossoms all around her. The moped, its wheels still spinning, lay beside her. Angel raised her head and breathed a sigh of relief. Hard as it was to believe it, she had survived and was still alive. Someone had wanted her dead, but they hadn't, once again, succeeded. But how long could they go on failing?

Angel shuddered. Her eyes closed and suddenly everything was dark.

Chapter Twenty

Bright lights were spinning round. Angel was at a fun fair, riding high on the big wheel, spinning high above the earth, colours dazzling her from every side. Red stars, green stars, purple stars. Yellow zigzags, blue streaks. Then she was falling from a great height, from the top of the big wheel –

Angel forced her eyes open and the fun fair disappeared. Instead, a face was hovering anxiously over her, a face vaguely familiar, although for a moment she couldn't put a name to it. Then reality rushed in.

'Jason Horowitz!' she murmured.

'Yeah, yeah, it's me. Angel are you okay?'

'Probably,' Angel said with a laugh. Her voice was shaky, she realised. 'My brakes didn't work.'

'Yeah, Rena cut them and drained out the fluid.'

'What!'

'She told me what she'd done and I rushed after you to try to catch you before you drove off, but I was just too late and I came after you.'

'That was kind. That must have been brake fluid I saw on the ground beneath the moped, then.' Angel tried to sit up, and found that her head was still dizzy. Something was trickling down her forehead and on down her cheek. She put up a hand cautiously to feel what it was, and then brought the hand back into sight. Blood. Looking down, she saw that her yellow shorts were filthy and there was a long graze and scratch on her left leg. Nothing serious, though. Except for her head.

'Why did Rena tell you anything about what she'd done?' was the first question that occurred to her.

'Ah. Well. Well, she thinks we're working together. Actually, that's not how it is. But she sort of trusts me, see?'

'So, why does she think you're working together if you aren't?' Angel really wanted to get this confusing situation clear.

'Aw, eff it, Angel, why do you have to keep asking these questions? I might have been better leaving you to crash on the moped, see? I'm not supposed to tell anyone this stuff!'

'Well, I'm certainly glad you didn't leave me, Jason. So, tell me more.'

'I guess I'll have to. Okay, here's how it is. I'm working undercover to catch a gang of crooks operating here on Corfu. A bit of a surprise, right? Not the sort of place you expect this. But you've heard of the jewel robberies – hell, that's why Rena was after you, she knew you'd heard stuff from Sophie that made you suspicious of Rena, though I don't think she knows quite why. She overheard some stuff, but nothing about the photo, I'm glad to say.'

'Ah, yes, the photo.'

'You saw it, I think. Alex told me so.'

'Alex did?'

'Yeah, I went back up there earlier today, just after you'd left, it looks like it musta been, and Alex gave the pic back to me – I gave him a sob story about it being a snap of my best girl and how heart broken I'd been when I thought I'd lost it. And he mentioned that you'd seen it and you'd said some stuff about it being evidence of grand larceny – I don't think he believed you, he was ready enough to accept my story instead – '

Angel groaned. 'I should have made him give it to me. I could have explained more, about the robbery and Sophie's necklace. I don't really know why I didn't. Just being over cautious, I suppose.'

'No harm done. I have it safe.'

'You! And just who are you? Someone working undercover, you say! A likely story.'

'Okay, here's my ID.'

Jason took out a folder from his pocket, opened it, and held it out for Angel to read, nevertheless holding on to it firmly.

Angel, her head still dizzy, managed all the same to read the details of Jason Horowitz's Scotland Yard police card, and the note seconding him to Interpol. She gulped. Jason, whom she'd thought was the villain in the piece, was actually a colleague of Josh Smith. But why had Josh not recognized his name and told her so?

She realized that she had no way of telling if the information Jason was showing her was accurate or forged. It didn't matter right now. She decided that she would behave as if it was genuine. She wouldn't give anything away, of course. Later, she could check it out with Josh. There wasn't anything she could tell this guy Jason that he didn't know already, and maybe she could pick up some info from him which she needed to know.

'So, Jason, you probably know far more than I do about what's going on here,' she began. 'Suppose you begin telling me some stuff?'

'No problem, Angel. But, hey,' he added, showing concern, 'you're shivering! What am I doing, letting you sit here on this bank with an almighty bruise on your head and blood trickling down your face? The first thing is to get you to the nearest doctor, girl!'

Angel, a sudden wave of weakness sweeping over her, realised the truth of Jason's words. 'Okay, boyo,' she said. 'So – what do you think we should do?'

'I think I should take you into Corfu Town to the hospital,' Jason said.

'Great. So, do you have a car?'

'Well, no. But I have a moped. Here. Let me help you up.'

He bent down solicitously and put an arm under her shoulder, helping her to stand upright. Angel, weaker than she had realized, allowed him to raise her to her feet. She brushed at the dust on her shorts and top without much success. A thought occurred to her. 'What about my own machine? Do we just leave it lying there? Alex won't be too pleased.'

'Well, I don't see what else we can do right now,' Jason said philosophically. 'We can't very well hoist it onto the back of mine, or even tow it unless you were riding it – which you're definitely not fit to do just yet. We can find someone in Corfu Town to fetch it in and return it to Alex. It's only the brakes that need fixed, not too big a problem.'

'Thanks, Jason,' Angel murmured. 'That sounds the best idea. So, now I get on your moped?'

'Well, if you can manage, Angel.' Jason climbed onto his machine and waited until Angel succeeded in to getting up behind him. She knew she would have to do this by herself.

Jason needed to be already seated in order to keep the moped upright.

At last she found herself settled safely behind Jason, clinging on with all her might, with her arms round his waist. It reminded her of the Superman movie, the bit where Lois Lane said, 'You're holding me – but who's holding you?' as Superman floated through the air carrying Lois in his arms. But Jason seemed safely anchored. With a kick at the starter, he headed off down the path, toward the main road and Corfu Town.

Chapter Twenty One

'Do you know where the hospital is?' Angel ventured to ask after a while.

'What?' yelled Jason against the wind whistling past both their ears.

'DO YOU KNOW WHERE THE HOSPITAL IS?'

'YES!'

Angel gave up the hopeless attempt to converse.

Presently the wide road became lined on each side with buildings, mostly commercial, shops, cafes, offices. Looking in both directions Angel remembered coming past this way with Josh on the previous day. There were houses with huge cactuses planted in their minute gardens, their spiky leaves painted pink and blue and white. How strange they looked. And there were shops with ice makers for sale, and bars with special liqueurs advertised in their windows, and other shops with arts and crafts of all sorts which were appropriate to Corfu.

Awnings hung over cafes where cool drinks, both alcoholic and soft, were for sale, and food ranging from cheeseburgers to lamb kebabs could be bought. There were upmarket restaurants and many of the cheaper takeaways. The smell of olive oil and garlic and various spices permeated the warm air. And everywhere the heat poured down.

It was exciting, enthralling. This was Greece. This was the real thing. Angel had been to mainland Greece before and to Crete, but this, Corfu, was something else. She forgot for a few minutes about the pain in her head as she gazed around her.

Presently Jason skidded to a stop at a crossroads and then turned off, presumably in the direction of the hospital. For a crazy moment Angel wondered if she was mad, if the accident and the bang on her head had affected her common sense. Why was she letting this suspicious stranger, on the basis of an ID card which might easily be forged, take her to who knew where?

Before she could make up her mind to leap off the moped and run for it at the next red light, a large white building swam into view and Jason shouted. 'THIS IS IT!'

It certainly looked like a hospital. Jason swung in through the entrance gates and pulled up before a sign which said 'Accident and Emergency' in English as well as in Greek. Angel breathed a sigh of relief. Whatever might be the truth about Jason himself and his ID card, this was certainly the right place. Once she'd had some treatment for her head, and, she hoped, some pain killers, it would be time enough to worry about how far she could trust this man.

They sat for a while until eventually a nurse came and led Angel into a small cubicle, leaving Jason in the waiting room.

The doctor, a young Greek man with the usual dark hair and moustache and a beaming smile, spoke English, to Angel's relief.

'This doesn't seem too bad,' he said after a thorough examination. 'I'll put some ointment on it and a bandage, and you must keep this in place for the next two days – then come back and see me again. I'll give you an appointment.'

He called the nurse and told her to put Angel down for three days' time in the afternoon. The nurse wrote in her appointment book, then gave Angel a card with the date and time on it.

'Thanks a lot. How much do I owe you?'

'Oh, it's covered by the reciprocal Health services between EC countries,' the doctor said cheerfully. 'So don't worry! Bring your passport with you next time and we'll be able to sort it out.'

Angel, who hadn't realised this, was quite pleased. She'd envisaged an expensive bill, and had reconciled herself to it, feeling that it was necessary. This was a lot better.

Emerging from the cubicle, Angel found Jason waiting for her on the seat where she had left him.

'Okay, Angel?'

'Okay. But I must look a rare sight in this bandage.'

'Not at all – it suits you. You look like a nineteen twenties woman tennis star – Little Mo, maybe.'

Angel laughed. 'Now, do you know any breakdown places we could get to fetch my moped and deliver it to Alex? Preferably one that won't charge a fortune?'

'I know just the guy. And he's round the corner from here, what's more – we'll head there now, and then I'll take you home.'

'But not until you've explained a bit more clearly just what's going on, Jason boy!'

'Ah. Well. I suppose I'd better do that thing. But let's get your moped sorted out first. Then I'll take you for a drink –

orange juice if you're not allowed alcohol with that head – and tell you as much as I can before I get you home.'

They left the hospital, retrieved Jason's moped, and whizzed round a couple of corners until they reached Cosmo's Breakdown and Rescue service. Again the sign was in English as well as Greek. Cosmo, apparently a good friend of Jason, came out and was welcoming and eager to oblige, and the price he quoted Angel for picking up and fixing her moped seemed reasonable enough, to her relief. It had been starting to look as if this holiday was going to cost her every penny she had and then some.

Then Jason took her arm, led her back to his own vehicle, and whizzed round a couple more corners until they were at the coast, where Angel remembered that they'd seen a number of restaurants as they drove into the town. Pulling up, he parked along the edge of the road and led her to a small but attractive restaurant with tables set out in the open air.

'We could buzz on into the centre, but this is a good enough option and it'll save us time,' he said. 'Another time, I'll take you into one of the upmarket places along the Liston, and give you a really good evening, gorgeous. Now what are you drinking?'

'The doctor didn't tell me to keep off alcohol,' Angel said cautiously, 'but maybe – '

'Well, if he didn't, no need, then. I'll get you some wine.'

One of the waiters came over just then, and Jason ordered for them both.

'Now,' said Angel, 'thanks for the lift, and the help and the drink, Jason. But you've circled round this story enough. Time to get on with it, boyo!'

Chapter Twenty Two

'Okay. Here's the story.'

Jason sighed, leaned his elbow on the table and his chin on his elbow, and began to talk. He had been sent out, it seemed, from Scotland Yard to work with Interpol and the Corfu police a month or so after the first few robberies, back in April.

'It was a bit of a shock to the guys here – they'd never had to deal with anything as serious before. They reckoned they needed help, and they used their wits and sent for some. They already had a few clues and links, and they put me onto this nurse Rena. Seems she's worked for several of the families robbed – they were mostly elderly people with a lifetime's accumulation of money and jewellery. The money would be in the bank, but the jewels tended to be kept in their houses so the lady could wear some when she had a big night. At least, that was the way of it with the ones who were robbed.

'Rena was suspected of being the inside stand, the one who got up the info and passed it on to the actual crooks who broke in. In a couple of cases she opened a door for them, but mostly she kept well away from the actual robbery. Arranged to be on leave at the time, that sort of stuff.

'Anyway, she was fairly small potatoes. What we wanted was the names of the guys who were paying her, especially whoever the big cheese was, the boss who planned and organised it. Rena might not know him, but she must know the next link up the chain from her, the guys who break in. And if we knew who they were, or even one of them, they could give us the boss with a little persuasion.

'So I picked up Rena at a nightclub where she often hangs out, got friendly, and managed to get one of the names out of her – the only one she knows, she said, her own contact. She introduced me to him, and I managed to get quite friendly with him. He even borrowed my moped yesterday. All this took a bit of time, right. I claimed to be part of the gang, and I knew so much about it that she and her contact had to believe me. She'd been handed some of the jewels to look after until they could be got out of the country and fenced, and one night recently I got her to put on the necklace you recognised, and then I took a photo on my mobile before she realised what I was doing. I meant to use it to pressurise her for info. I pretended I'd deleted it when she kicked up a fuss, but actually I printed it out as soon as I got a chance. I hadn't picked the right opportunity to show it to her and see what I could get out of her, when you came busting in, Angel. And that's the story.'

'So, you lent Rena's contact your moped yesterday – but you weren't with her when someone shot Josh and Marge McPherson?' Angel asked slowly.

'Who, me? No way! I don't believe Rena was there, any-way. She's not the girl to get involved in a shooting, you can take my word for that!'

'So it was just a coincidence that you hired a moped from Alex just before the shooting and lent it to a crook, and there were marks of one near where the hit man must have stood?'

'Hey, this is all news to me! Do the Corfu cops know this stuff?'

'Well, no, I haven't told them yet. But they should have found the tyre marks for themselves, okay?'

'Angel, you're not dealing with super 'tecs here, sweetheart. They might have missed the marks easy enough.'

'I suppose I should pass on the info, then.' Angel spoke reluctantly, and wondered why. But she knew why, really. It was because she wasn't sure how much she should trust Captain Doukas. Gregor.

'Yeah, you're right. I'll give them a ring when I get back. Or you could tell them, since you say you're working with them.'

'Since I say? Sounds like you still don't quite believe me?'

'Well, I only have your word for it, Jason!' Angel retorted. ' But how about that story you fed me back at the airport? That you were importing things from the UK which were cheaper to buy there in bulk, bring in, and sell to ex-pats and shops and restaurants? Was that just a load of rubbish, then?'

'No way. I do really import stuff like that. But, hey, it's my cover story as well, see?'

'Okay,' said Angel slowly. 'Okay, I'll accept that. Weird as it may seem. Look, you've been very kind, Jason. I do appreciate your help with the moped and my accident. I don't know what I'd have done if you hadn't come along, so I owe you one, right? And thanks for telling me your story. I won't spread it around, don't worry. But if you don't mind, I'd like to get back now. Is that okay with you?'

'No problem, Angel,' Jason said promptly, sounding his cheerful self again. 'Come on, let's hop on the moped and I'll have you back in no time. I reckon I'd better get hold of Rena tonight – she should be off duty and coming down here to Corfu town to her apartment – and I'll show her the pic, and sort of persuade her to work with me to catch the gang. I'll promise her that she'll get off, herself, see?'

'The sooner the better, Jason, far as I'm concerned. Then maybe she'll stop trying to knock me off.'

Jason grinned. 'I get you, Angel. Okay, then, let's get going. You'll need to direct me, mind – I don't know where you're staying except that it's North somewhere.'

And Angel wondered if he really didn't know, or if this was just some more of the cover up.

Chapter Twenty Three

Josh was still in his room when she got back. She slipped quietly into the house without being seen and tiptoed up the stairs. Knocking quietly on Josh's door she heard his voice call, 'Come in,' and opened the door just enough to put her head round it into view. Josh looked round at her and gasped in horror. He was sitting on his balcony, relaxing on a lounger and reading, but when he saw Angel's bandaged head he sprang to his feet, dropping the book.

'Snap!' Angel said, pointing first to her own bandage and then to Josh's.

'Honey! What happened?'

'Aw, nothing much, Josh,' Angel replied airily. 'A bit of an accident with the moped. The doctor said it was nothing to worry about.'

'What did you do?'

'Hey, listen to the male chauvinist assumptions! It wasn't anything I did, mister! That nurse, Rena, the one who was wearing Sophie's necklace in that photo I told you about, cut my brakes and drained the fluid while I was still inside, first of all talking to Sophie and then checking Rena out with the receptionist. But, as soon as I realised there was something wrong, I steered into the bank at the edge of the road and jumped clear, Had a lovely soft landing in a bank of wild flowers – must have been a pretty picture.' Angel laughed, then shuddered as the memory overcame her again.

'Hey, sit down and tell me all about it,' Josh said in a voice of concern.

He placed Angel in the lounger he'd been occupying himself and dragged up another soft chair beside her, and Angel obediently repeated for him the events of the afternoon. 'So, what I'm wondering, Josh, is if you know anything about this guy Jason Horowitz who claims to be working with Interpol?'

'Can't say the name's familiar,' Josh said, frowning as he tried to remember. 'But I don't know everyone who happens to be seconded there, right? He could well be genuine – why not? Is there anything in particular that makes you doubt him?'

'Apart from the coincidence that he hired a moped just before the shooting? I tend to think that's plenty!' Angel said drily. 'But, no, nothing else, really. He has explanations for everything except that, and he claims that's a coincidence.'

'Well, lots of people hire mopeds in Corfu,' Jason said sensibly. 'You did yourself. It's a pretty popular way to get around.'

'I suppose so.'

'But, hey, I meant to ask much sooner, except you started me off explaining what happened. How are you? How's the arm? And what about Marge?'

'I believe Marge is well on the mend, from what Hamish told me when he called in earlier. And I'm fine. The arm's much better. In fact I'm getting really browned off spending my vacation in this room, sun balcony or not. Tomorrow I'm going to take you sightseeing, honey.'

'And what about my investigation?' Angel demanded indignantly. 'And, by the way, how can you take me? I don't think you're arm's going to be fit to drive just yet. It'll be me doing the driving and taking you, more likely.'

'Not at all. I'll be well able to drive by tomorrow,' Josh said firmly. 'Now, how about going downstairs and seeing what's happening about an evening meal? On second thoughts, you'd better take a shower and change out of those clothes – you look like a tramp, if you don't mind me saying so.'

Angel aimed a punch at his head, but he ducked out of the way and grabbed her instead. A minute later they were kissing seriously.

Angel pulled away eventually and caught her breath. 'Wow, let me come up for air! Okay, I'm going for that shower. See you in fifteen mins or so.'

As she headed for her own room, she realised that she still wasn't too sure about getting into a really serious relationship again, after her disastrous marriage to Micky Murphy which had ended when she finally realised that she shouldn't put up with his violence any more, and walked out on him. She was fond of Josh, but did she love and trust him enough to risk a full commitment? Angel just didn't know. But the idea of a day relaxing with him and exploring Corfu tomorrow sounded good.

When she appeared downstairs about half an hour later in a short blue skirt and white patterned top, Josh was waiting for her in the kitchen. Hamish had called in with him to say that Marge wasn't up to coming downstairs just yet, but hoped to make it tomorrow. He wanted to eat in their room with her, but the cook had left food which just needed a quick heat up in the microwave. There was moussaka as a main course, stuffed vine leaves which didn't need heated as a starter, and ice cream in the freezer for afters, if they wanted it.

'Sounds great!' said Angel enthusiastically. 'I love moussaka!'

They settled down with the stuffed vine leaves and a chilled bottle of golden white wine, in the late evening sunshine which would soon turn into velvet darkness, while the moussaka heated quietly in the microwave. The ping came just at the moment they were ready for it.

'So, Josh,' said Angel conversationally, 'where were you thinking of taking me tomorrow?'

'Well, I thought you might like to see the Kaiser's Throne?' Josh suggested. 'It gives a view of most of Corfu, and there's a restaurant beside it where they do a mean iced coffee.'

'The Kaiser's Throne?'

'Yeah, Wilhelm of Germany – Kaiser Bill of World War 1 – he used to love Corfu. He had a home here and he used to love to climb up to this place and watch the sunset. There are easy steps up, so no problem there.'

'Sounds great, Josh! The Kaiser's Throne it is, then! Unless it's raining, of course.'

'Raining? You must be joking!'

'Well, of course I am! But that's what we always have to say back home in Ireland, see?'

Josh laughed. 'Well, if it rains here in Corfu tomorrow, I'll fly you to the moon instead.'

He leant over to kiss her, but Angel happened to be getting up at that moment. She yawned. 'Time for beddy-byes.

We're both invalids right now, and we'd better remember it! See you tomorrow, Josh.'

'See you tomorrow, honey,' Josh said wryly, as Angel left the kitchen and made her way upstairs.

Chapter Twenty Four

The next day, as soon as lunch was over, Angel and Josh went out to his car.

Angel was still worried about Josh driving, but she buttoned her lip and said nothing. If he thought he could manage, better to let him do it.

She had taken off her unsightly bandage, and saw when she examined the damage underneath it that there was little to be seen apart from a scrape. No need to worry about it any more, she decided as she picked up a sun hat instead to wear with her green top and white shorts.

They drove off towards Corfu Town, the sun beating down on the car windows. Angel was very glad to have the air conditioning.

'Phew! It's hot!' she said, fanning herself with her sun hat.

'I'll turn the AC up if you like.'

'No, Josh, it's fine now it's starting to kick in.'

The road plunged downwards and took them to the main highway to the town. They turned right on it, driving along with the sea miles beneath them and only a tiny wall protecting them if they happened to slip over to that side. Angel was mercifully free from vertigo or else she might have been screaming as Josh increased the speed. On the other side the hills rose, covered in sparse grass and wild flowers in varied colours ranging from white, pink, blue, or yellow to the bright scarlet of poppies.

The turn off for Pelekas was clearly signposted and they turned right, up into the hills, climbing higher and higher through silvery olive groves until they reached the diminutive village.

Winding their way through steep streets with amazing views down over the sea, with white houses crowding in on every side in rising steps, they gazed in delight at the villas and cafes mostly covered in purple bougainvillea, the green leaves and the masses of flowers producing a wonderful effect of beauty and brightness, with the blue, blue sea, beneath them.

'Wow!' Angel said. 'Isn't this something?'

'This is only the start of it,' Josh murmured. 'Now we head on up to the Kaiser's Throne.'

'Wouldn't it be nice to have a cold drink in that lovely little taverna up those steps?' Angel suggested, but Josh shook his head.

'Not unless you're really dying of thirst already, honey. There's a taverna up at the Throne – we can get iced coffee or whatever up there.'

'No problem.'

They drove on up an even steeper track and emerged at the entrance to the Kaiser's Throne, where there was a small car park. Josh found a parking space and pulled into it.

There were quite a few cars already parked, but enough empty spaces to make parking easy. Josh and Angel walked across towards the stone steps which led up to the Kaiser's Throne, and stood aside to allow a number of people to come down and head back to the car park.

'It gets really busy later in the day,' Josh told Angel. 'People come especially to see the sunset, which was what the Kaiser himself liked to do. In a couple of hours this park will be crammed. But just now, although you can never have the place to yourself, it's not as busy as it might be.'

Having crossed the park, they went in through an old looking stone gateway. There was a steep path, and then they found themselves climbing a set of stone steps carved out of rock. The steps allowed them to climb up a huge rock, with nothing much all around it. At the top, as Angel looked up, she could see a stone platform with a metal rail surrounding it on three sides, forming three quarters of a circle.

There were rails to hold onto as they climbed, and they had to squash to one side more than once to allow other sightseers to descend. Then all at once it seemed that they had the place to themselves. They came out onto the empty platform and Angel drew in her breath.

'Wow, Josh, this is something else! Thanks for bringing me here!'

On all sides were views of Corfu, east, west, north and south. They could see the sea surrounding the island. There were spreading plains where groves of olive trees waved their silvery leaves and branches, tiny villages, hills and bays and golden beaches. And down below, not too far, was Corfu Town.

'You can look through these binoculars, if you like, honey,' Josh suggested, pointing to large set of binoculars fixed to a pole for the use of tourists. 'It's amazing how close up everything seems when you do that.'

'Great idea!'

Angel fiddled with the binoculars to bring them into focus with her eyes, then peered in all directions, emitting gasps of amazement at the sights revealed. Last of all she focussed on Corfu Town and was awestricken at the details she could see. Suddenly an exclamation burst from her lips.

'Josh!'

'What is it, honey?'

'I can't believe it! Jason Horowitz, that nurse Rena Serkos, and Gregor Doukas, drinking coffee and with their heads together talking, at an open air café on the Liston!'

'What? Here, let me see!'

Josh took over the binoculars. He had to adjust them to his own eyes, but a moment later he was seeing what Angel had seen.

'But it may mean nothing,' he said after a moment. 'Horowitz and Doukas are probably working together, from what he told you. And they might both need to get more info from this nurse Rena.'

'Maybe. But I don't believe it,' Angel said sceptically. 'I think this needs looking into.'

'But not right now,' Josh said sensibly. 'By the time we get down there, they'd almost certainly have broken up and gone their separate ways, right? No point in rushing down.'

Angel could see the sense of this but was reluctant to agree. 'We could at least try, Josh.'

'No, honey. What would be the point? If we did by some miracle catch them still together, they'd have some explanation. We'd never be able to sneak up and hear them talking, would we?'

'No, I suppose not,' Angel agreed reluctantly. 'Okay, Josh, you win.'

'So, how about you give me a nice smile and I take a pic of you?'

'Just as long as you let me edit it before you post it on Facebook or anywhere!'

Josh laughed, and began snapping away. Several photos later, he began to zoom in on the view rather than just on Angel. Then it was time to move on and allow the new arrivals at the top their turn with the binoculars and the platform.

'How's about that iced coffee you promised me, Josh?' Angel said as they headed back down the steps.

'Good idea. Let's go for it, honey.'

They sat at a table looking out over the stunning view and Angel sighed in delight as she sipped the ice cold coffee. 'This is heaven, Josh.'

'Maybe not quite, honey. But near enough,' Josh said, as he gazed at her lovely face and wondered what the future held for them. He knew Angel had been badly hurt. He wasn't about to rush her into anything.

Some time later, he said, 'Would you like to go down and wander round Corfu Town? And end up with a meal on the Liston?'

'Sounds perfect.'

'I'm not suggesting that we might run into Doukas and the others, now,' Josh warned her. 'This is purely for fun.'

'Right.'

'And maybe tomorrow, or some time soon, we might come back and explore the citadel. Not today, I'd think – we've done enough sightseeing for now, right?'

'Absolutely correct, master!'

'Hey, I'm not trying to boss you!'

'No, I know – just joking! Okay, darlin', let's head back to the car, then.'

And so they did.

Chapter Twenty Five

It was still warm and pleasant as they parked the Audi and wandered down to the market where the bright stalls sold bags, purses, clothes and snacks varying from stuffed vine leaves to fried cheese balls. The lovely smell of olive oil and garlic wafted through the air.

'That would suit you, honey,' Josh said, holding up a pale blue top embroidered with sparkling beads against Angel.

'Maybe.'

'Well, would you like it?'

'Depends if it fits! Seems like a one size fits all set-up.'

'I don't think you can try them on.' Josh looked dubious. A Greek woman, probably younger than she looked, bobbed up beside them and said, 'Lovely! Try it on back here,' and waved Angel into a small curtained space behind the booth. Smiling, Angel dodged in behind the swinging curtains, stripped off her apple green top, and slipped into the pale blue one. There was a mirror tilted at an angle on one side of the small space. As far as she could see, the top looked good with her white shorts.

'Josh? What d'ye think?' She emerged, still smiling, from behind the curtains.

'Fantastic, honey! We'll get it, then – you like it, don't you?' he asked Angel anxiously, and when she nodded, he turned to the woman and negotiated the price with her.

A few moments later, they left the stall and wandered on, Angel still wearing the pale blue top, her green top in a bag provided by the stall-owner.

Presently, having added a purse with Corfu written on it, two hair combs, an embroidered silk wrap in dark green, and a narrow leather belt for Josh, to their purchases, they emerged from the market area, and strolled, hand in hand, in the direction of the Liston.

A string of restaurants, all with outdoor tables and chairs under canopies, stretched along the edge of the square, with its dusty grassy space where cricket was still played in its season. Horses wearing straw hats with their ears peeking through pulled carriages around the town, starting at the top of the Liston and including a journey round it.

'We'll do that tomorrow, in daylight, if you like, honey,' Josh said. 'It's more fun if you can see where they're taking you. And after that we might go up the citadel. Unless there's anything you'd rather do?'

'No, sounds like fun, Josh. You know your way around here, so you can make the suggestions.'

'Ideal wife material,' Josh said lightly, then wished he hadn't as he felt Angel stiffen beside him. 'Whoa! Just, joking, honey!' he added quickly.

Angel laughed. 'You'd better be, mister!'

'Time we found a restaurant and grabbed something to eat,' Josh said. 'There are so many here, it's hard to choose, but I remember a specially good one from last time I was here. Not too far down now, I think.'

He led Angel on a little further, then stopped. 'Yes, this is it. Taverna Chloe.'

The place didn't look all that different from the other restaurants they had passed, but it had a bright, clean air to it, and the sparkling lights hung along the outdoor tables added a touch of romance. Angel loved it at once.

They made their way to an empty table under one of the great trees which lined the place and sat. At once a smiling, bright-faced waitress approached them with menus printed both in Greek and in English. Josh smiled at her and thanked her, and ordered a bottle of white wine to drink while they choose their meal.

'So, honey?' he asked presently as they sipped their ice cold wine.

'I'll start with stuffed vine leaves, yet again – but I do love them,' decided Angel. 'And after that – the trouble with Greek food now is that you can buy the more familiar dishes anywhere. It isn't a novelty any longer. I love moussaka, for instance, but I can get it in lots of places at home – even in the supermarket as a ready meal – and after all, we had it last night. Do you know what I'd love, and what I've never seen at home – Greek green beans in the special sauce they cook it in, fried onions, tomato and garlic. I really love that.'

'Get whatever you want, honey. I think I'll join you in the stuffed vine leaves, and then I'll have the roast lamb. Some places don't cook it for long enough, and it ends up tough, but I seem to remember that this place is an exception.'

Josh poured another glass of wine each as they waited for their stuffed vine leaves, and they sat quietly, listening to the music drifting through the air and watching the moon lighting up the leaves on the tree above them. The green beans, when they arrived at that stage of the meal, were everything Angel had remembered from her last visit to Greece.

'This is so beautiful, Josh,' sighed Angel eventually. 'The moonlight and the music. It reminds me of the meal we had in Athens when we first met.'

'Well, let's hope it'll be different in one way,' joked Josh, 'and we won't go back to your room to find a dead body lying stabbed on the bed there!'

'Heavens, yes! That was a terrible experience. But we managed to deal with it.'

'Right. But once is enough for that sort of stuff.'

They ate and drank and were happy. Presently Josh said, 'Would you like to go somewhere to dance, now, honey?'

Angel snapped out of her dreamy, romantic mood and sat up briskly. 'No, thanks, Josh. I'll tell you what we're going to do now. We're going to call on Rena Serkos, the nurse from Sophie's care home, and see what we can persuade her to tell us. That is, if she's here and not still on duty.'

Josh gaped at her. 'We're – what?'

'I have her address here. If she's in, we'll use a mixture of bribes and threats. You being with Interpol and sort of official, even if you're not actually supposed to be working on this case, will be very helpful. And I can always threaten to break her arm – or her neck.'

'Angel!'

'You think I'm joking? Look what she and her mates did to you, boy! Darlin', I can't allow that sort of thing to go on – we need to put a stop to it.'

'But, honey, we can't just bust in and threaten this woman.'

'Well, see here, Josh Smith, if you don't want to come with me, no problem – I'll go on my own. I can always get a taxi back to the MacPherson's, I suppose.'

Josh frowned. 'Angel, you're talking rubbish and you know it. How do you think I'd feel, leaving you here on your own to deal with a villain and possibly her mates while I head off back to the Villa Callidora? You know, honey, this is straight blackmail.'

'Is it?' asked Angel sweetly and innocently. 'I don't see it. Anyway, boy, there's no question of busting in. I have Rena's address. We go there, knock on the door, and go in when she opens it. Of course,' she added thoughtfully, 'if she's not in, I would have to use my trusty picklocks. We might easily learn more by exploring her apartment when it's empty than we would learn from Rena herself.'

'Angel!'

'Aw, c'mon, Josh, don't be so straight! You know you're dying to try it!'

Josh laughed. 'Well, okay, I'll go there with you. But if she's not in, no promises about the next step. We'll stop at that point and think, okay, babe?'

'We'll see!' retorted Angel. She gathered up her packages and they strolled back, in the romantic moonlight, to where they had parked the car. But whatever plans Josh might have had, based on that same romantic moonlight, were no longer in the picture, at least not as Angel saw it.

Chapter Twenty Six

Rena Serkos lived in a new looking apartment block at the other end of Corfu town. Angel and Josh drove there and parked as near as they could, in the next street. Then they got out and approached the building.

'So, we'll see if we can get into the block first,' Angel said.

The door to the apartment block stood half open, so that answered the first question.

'Rena's on the third floor,' Angel said. 'We might as well get the lift up.'

'Won't she hear it and be warned that we – or somebody– is coming? What's wrong with the stairs, where we can approach much more quietly?'

'Okay, Josh,' Angel acknowledged. 'She'll know we're here as soon as we ring the bell, mind you, but why give her advance warning? You've got a point there.'

She ran lightly up the concrete stairs, bare of carpet, which were all the building offered. On the fourth landing she pushed open a wide door, Josh close behind her, and they found themselves on a landing with four doors set into it at intervals on opposite walls. Apartment 4 A, where Rena lived, was directly across the landing from them. Angel went forward and rang the bell.

They heard movements inside, someone coming towards the door. Then a voice.

'Hullo? Who's there?'

The voice spoke in Greek. Angel knew just enough Greek to understand it. But the sooner they switched to English, the better, she decided.

'Is that Rena?' she asked.

The fisheye in the door opened and an eye peered out at them. Josh was deliberately standing well to one side, so that Angel was the only one on view.

'Who are you?' Rena asked sharply.

'Angeline Murphy. Known as Angel. A friend of Sophie Papadouplos. We've already met, remember? I'd like to talk to you about Sophie – I'm worried about her.'

'Okay.' The fisheye closed, then there were sounds of a chain being released, and the door opened cautiously a few inches. Angel stepped forward, pushing it further open, as Josh came up behind her. Rena promptly responded by trying to shut it again. Apparently she'd changed her mind as soon as she saw Josh there as well.

'So,' Angel said loudly to Josh as she held the door in its open position against all Rena's efforts to shut it again, 'should I begin by giving her a display of some kick boxing? Straight to the chin, maybe? Or would you rather start by letting her see your Interpol card?'

Josh's mouth dropped open.

'Angel, you're joking, aren't you?'

'I'm joking, Josh.'

But before Josh could do more than sigh with relief, she continued with a straight face, 'Kick boxing wouldn't work. A bit of Judo would be better.'

Pushing harder, she opened the door to its full width, and Rena backed away. As they advanced into the room, she turned and ran from the hallway into the main room. Angel and Josh followed her without hesitation, only to pull up quickly as they saw Rena take something from the drawer of a desk and turn to point it at them. It was a large, powerful looking gun, a .45 Angel guessed, its blue steel facings gleaming in the apartment's wall lights.

'Jason!' she called out in a high wailing voice, 'come quickly! It's that girl again!'

Someone came rushing out through the door which led to the next room. Jason Horowitz, of course.

'Rena!' he shouted as he saw the gun in Rena's hand. 'What the eff are you doing?'

'She's going to attack me, Jason!' Rena panted. 'I heard her, talking to her friend outside before they pushed in. She's going to kick box me or do judo on me!'

'It was a joke,' Angel said coldly. 'I was talking to Josh, not you. If you eavesdrop on other people's conversations, you should expect to misunderstand what you hear. Mind you,' she added, 'it may not stay a joke if you keep pointing that gun at me.'

'Rena, for Gawd's sake! Put the gun away! Where on earth did you get it?'

'I'm looking after it for a friend of mine.'

'Must be a nutter, to let you have it, babe! C'mon, put it away!'

'No, Jason, I don't trust her.' Rena turned her head slightly to look at Jason.

Angel took a deep breath, jumped forward while Rena was still looking away from her, and kicked the gun from her hand. It exploded as Rena's finger jerked on the trigger, but the kick had already sent it off target and the bullet whistled harmlessly towards the ceiling, crashed into the overhead light fitting, and brought the shade hurtling to the ground. The bulb exploded and there was no more light.

Angel was near enough to Rena to be able to seize hold of her before she could recover. Taking hold of her by the right arm, she twisted the arm up behind Rena's back and pushed her over so that she was leaning forward, helpless. The gun was now somewhere at their feet. If she were surer where it was, she would grab it. Light, that was what she needed.

Just at that moment the necessary light appeared. Josh had switched on the torch which he always carried, even on holiday. Stepping forward, he picked up Rena's gun.

'Hey, guy, are there any other lights in this place?' he drawled to Jason, who was standing thunderstruck at the swift turn of events.

'Yeah – yeah, there are wall lights. Give me a tick and I'll switch them on.'

Jason fumbled his way over to the wall and quickly produced a low level flood of light, then, making his way across the room, found another switch and with it more light.

'Okay, man?'

'Okay.'

'Rena,' Jason said sorrowfully, ' are you nuts or what?'

Rena glared at him from her bent over position. 'I think it's you who are nuts, my friend! These people are dangerous!'

'Not to us, they're not, Rena. Only to the crooks who're doing these robberies. You and I are trying to catch them, right? We agreed about that last night, didn't we? We should be glad of some help.'

Rena hissed something in Greek which Angel didn't catch. Probably just as well, from the apologetic look Jason sent her.

'C'mon, Rena, don't be daft. And watch the language, girl! Sorry, Angel. She's pretty upset – she doesn't understand. Maybe if you let go of her? You have her gun now, after all. She can't do much, now can she?'

'I suppose not,' Angel admitted. 'Hey, Rena! Are you listening to me? If I let you go, will you behave?'

'Okay.'

'Right. I want you to go and sit down there, where I can see you, and listen to what we want to say – right?'

'I guess so.'

Angel released her hold on Rena's arm, allowed her to stand upright again, and waited while the nurse hobbled slowly over to the upright chair Angel indicated, and sat there carefully.

'So, I want to know more about this gang than I do right now. And I hope you realise that my partner has your gun – so don't start any dirty tricks.'

Josh winked at Angel and slid the gun into his pocket.

'I know you have a lot more info to give me, Rena,' Angel began. 'So, tell me. Who runs this gang? And who else is in it?'

Rena gaped at Angel in horror.

'How should I know? I'm working with Jason to find that out! I've done some small stuff for them, passing on info about rich patients and their houses to get well in with the gang, but the only one I know is my own link, Costas Bakis. He passed on my info to the boss. I've never known who that is. I can't help you – the one you should be talking to is Costas.'

'Okay. Where can I find this Costas Bakis?'

'If I tell you, he'll kill me!'

'But how would he know you had told us – unless you tell him yourself?' asked Angel reasonably. 'I can promise you he won't hear it from us.'

Rena looked at her, doubt and hesitation in her face.

'Well – okay. I'll give you his address. But if you let me down – it's my life in your hands!'

'We won't let you down, Rena. Come on, tell us his address.'

And slowly, reluctantly, her voice faltering, Rena finally told them.

Chapter Twenty Seven

Costas Bakis lived not far away from Rena, as it happened. It would only take them a few minutes to get there. But suppose Rena warned him, and he was expecting them?

'Hey, Jason,' Angel said. 'A word in your ear. This friend of yours is clearly loony-tunes. I'd watch out for her if I were you. Tie her up or something – hey, Rena, that was another joke, by the way!'

Rena glared at her. 'Why should you say such a thing about me?'

'Well,' said Angel reasonably, 'you've only tried to kill me twice now, once by cutting the brakes on my moped at the care home, and just now by pulling a gun on me – I suppose I should let you away with it until the third time –'

She stopped suddenly.

'Anyway, Jason,' she resumed quickly, 'don't let her phone this guy Costas Bakis, okay? Or you could both be in big trouble.'

'Why should I phone him?' Rena scowled. 'I don't want him to know I've told you about him, do I? I'm not crazy, whatever you may think!'

'Fair enough – if you can think reasonably about it.'

Josh touched Angel's arm. 'C'mon, honey – let's get weaving.'

'Right,' Angel muttered back to him. 'Got that gun?'

'Sure thing. I'm not leaving it with this dame. Loony-tunes is right, about her.'

They backed out of the room and then on out of the apartment, making sure there was no final attack from Rena or even Jason – Angel still wasn't sure how much she trusted Jason, and Josh never had.

When they had closed the door behind them, they belted for the lift and since it was already at the landing they travelled down to the ground floor at quick speed.

Once outside the apartment block, Angel breathed a sigh of relief. 'Whew! Josh, do you know what I'm thinking?'

'Maybe, honey.'

'What, then?' Angel challenged him.

'Why, that maybe Rena hasn't just tried to kill you twice. Maybe the total adds up to three times. Maybe Rena was with the guy who fired at us at the pool, maybe he's the one who asked her to look after his gun, and maybe we should get this gun checked by the police against the bullets that hit me and Marge. Right?'

'Right.'

'And one more maybe – maybe it was this guy Costas Bakis? The one we're going to see?'

'Do you know something – I should have asked Jason if it was this Bakis who borrowed his moped, shouldn't I?'

'Yeah, we tripped up there, honey. But I think we can be pretty sure of it, anyway,' Josh said. He grinned cheerfully at Angel. 'Didn't Jason say he leant it to Rena's contact – and we know now that that's this guy Bakis? Hey, we seem to be really getting places, finding out what's been going on. So, let's get back in the car and get over to where Bakis lives, quick as we can. Maybe he can tell us something worth hearing. Especially since we still have this gun.'

'Oh, so you've changed your mind? You're happy to use threats against Costas Bakis? Although you were way against me threatening Rena?' Angel smiled at him as they ran towards the car.

'There's a place for everything, honey.'

'Fair enough, darlin'. You win!'

They piled into the car and Josh started up. The journey was short.

'Okay, Angel,' Josh said as he parked as near as possible to the apartment block where Costas Bakis lived. 'So, we just go in, do we? Or should we be a bit more cautious about this?'

'Well, what do you think, Josh?'

For once, Angel was prepared to take advice.

'I think we should go right in, honey.'

'Great! Just what I think!'

Angel got out of the car, full of enthusiasm. But when they stood before the apartment block where Bakis lived, there was an immediate problem. The street door was locked, unlike the outside door of Rena's apartment block.

'We're going to give him warning if we use the answer phone,' Angel said dubiously.

'True. But, sure, what other way is there to get in?'

'Let's see.'

There was a list of names for the various apartments. Angel chose one at random and lifted the phone.

'Georgias Simoniades?'

'Ne, Simoniades.'

'I have your wallet here, found it in the street, I'll bring it up to you if you'll open the door.'

A startled exclamation, and the buzzer was pressed to allow Angel to push open the door, before Simoniades could realise that his wallet was safely in his pocket.

'A mistake –' he began in halting English, but Angel had replaced the phone and she and Josh were standing in the entrance hall.

'Bakis is on the second floor. We'd better get up there quickly before this guy Simoniades alerts the security or the cops.' Josh made for the stairs.

'Right. And yes, better to take the stairs, again. The lift would give away where we went if anyone's trying to check out intruders.'

They hurried to the top of the second flight and turned left for Apartment 2b.

Angel rang the bell.

'Yes?'

'I think this must be your wallet I found? Costas Bakis, it says on the card.'

'No, you've got it wrong – my wallet's here. Let me see what you've got hold of – someone who knows me, if they have my card.'

They heard the sound of the door being unlocked, and then it opened slightly on the chain. Angel held up her own wallet for want of any alternative. Josh stood back out of sight.

Possibly it was the sight of Angel, young, sexy, attractive, that made Bakis unfasten the chain and open the door wider. Before he had time to change his mind, Angel, closely followed by Josh, was inside. Angel put her wallet back in her shoulder bag.

'Sorry about the little trick, Costas, but we need to talk to you.'

Costas Bakis was a small dark man, thin but wiry, with the usual Greek dark moustache. To Angel's eye, he didn't look like a match for her, let alone for Josh, and it seemed that he thought so too. He backed away across the entrance hall and into the huge sitting room. A gentle push from Josh landed him into one of the soft leather sofas.

'What – what do you guys want?'

His English remained good but his voice was quavering.

'Oh, not a lot, Costas,' Angel told him blithely. 'We're looking into the jewel robberies and shootings that have been going on here over the past short while. We've been told you know a lot about them?'

'Me! You must be dreaming!'

Josh produced the gun they'd taken from Rena and flourished it under Bakis's nose. 'Dreaming? More like a nightmare, man. So, tell us what you know, okay? Just wondering if you recognise this gun, for instance?'

'But I don't know anything! Why should I recognise this gun?'

'That's not what we hear. Okay, forget about the gun right now. But we've been told you are someone who could contact the big man. That means you know who he is – or how to get to him.' Angel noted the flicker of Bakis's eyelids as she spoke. He definitely knew something.

But he wasn't saying. Short of physical intimidation, which neither Josh nor Angel were into, there seemed no further way of forcing him to speak.

'Whoever told you was making it up.' He spoke earnestly. 'I guess they wanted to get you off their back, so they picked on me to throw to the lions. I'm not involved at all, really! Okay, I've heard some gossip, and I could probably give you the name of the fence the gang most likely use – though that would only be a guess. But that's as far as I can help!'

Neither Angel nor Josh believed him. They exchanged a look, then Josh put the gun back in his pocket.

'So, give us the name, then.'

'Franco Marcelli – he's an Italian, but he's lived here for a long time. Has a jewellery shop down at the Liston, but he wouldn't be there at this time of night, and I don't know his home address. But you could catch him there tomorrow. Franco's Treasure Chest – you'll find it dead easy.'

'So, Angel?'

'Yeah, that seems to be it, darlin'. Let's head.'

They backed out of the apartment and this time took the lift to the ground floor for speed. Neither spoke until they were outside the apartment block.

Then Josh said, 'Are you thinking what I'm thinking, honey?'

'Sure, I'd guess so, darlin'. Thon one's a lying toad. Likely this Franco has nothing to do with it. And if we could just tap dear Costas's phone right now, I bet we'd pick up something worth having. He'll be ringing his boss, or I'm a monkey's uncle.'

'Well, you're certainly not that, sweetie. But even if we can't tap his phone, there's something else we can do.'

'Wait to see if he comes out and heads off to meet up with the big man? And then follow him?' Angel brightened up at the thought.

'You took the words right out of my mouth, honey. Let's get back to the Audi and find a good place to keep watch until he comes out.'

Chapter Twenty Eight

The first thing was to identify the car park in use for the Apartment block, and its exit. It wasn't difficult. There was no underground car park – it would have been unusual in Corfu if there had been.

But a sign outside the block pointed off to the left with the words, '**Car Park. Visitors and residents.**'

They followed it around the next corner and found a half empty site with a number of cars presumably belonging to residents of Bakis's apartment block.

Josh pulled their car in and paid the man on duty for a couple of hours parking. Then he said, 'We'd better have some excuse for parking here, Angel. If you don't mind?'

His arm went round her, and he pulled her down against him.

As it turned out, Angel found she didn't mind at all.

In fact, it was hard not to let her attention slip, and when Josh whispered in her ear, 'Here he comes,' it was as much as she could do to come to the surface again in time to register Costas Bakis approaching a Seat car parked not far from their own Audi.

As Angel sat up to peer out at Bakis, Josh pulled her face down again unto his shoulder and used her as shelter for himself as he managed to keep an eye on Bakis's actions. It wasn't until Bakis was pulling out of the car park that he quickly released her, sat up himself, and started the car.

'Okay – we don't want to lose him now!'

'No way,' Angel murmured sleepily.

'Wake up, honey – we're going!'

They took off at top speed and just managed to see Bakis's dark blue Seat turn the corner in front of them. After that it was a question of dodging in and out of traffic, not getting too close in case they were seen, and making sure they didn't lose him – a fine line. Presently they found themselves on the main road north, heading towards the coast.

Angel suddenly remembered to fasten her seat belt, and nudged Josh to do the same. They left the town and its lights behind them and began to be dependant on the head-lights of the cars in front or coming towards them to light up the route. The moonlight gleamed on the water as they ran alongside it, adding little to the visibility, but a lot to the beauty of the night.

Josh was still keeping fairly close to Bakis in his Seat. Suddenly it served off to the left with no signal. Muttering curses to himself, Josh slowed down and followed suit. 'Just as well there's nothing coming up close behind us,' he said half to Angel and half to himself. 'The trouble is, turning after him like that at a moment's notice may have given us away. I need to drop back a bit, out of sight of his rear view mirror if possible.'

He slowed almost to a stop, then proceeded cautiously.

'Good that it's a twisty road,' Angel said. 'Means you can keep back and be behind a bend most of the time.'

'Yeah.' Josh was concentrating on his driving, not willing to talk. Angel decided to keep quiet.

The road began to run uphill, still with many twists and turns, and the two cars followed it in procession. It was hard to believe, in spite of all Josh's efforts, that Bakis hadn't spotted them.

The Seat took another turn to the left, and this new road, really only a lane, grew even steeper. It wasn't a road on which speed was possible. They found themselves crawling through small villages, with narrow streets hard to negotiate. It was in the third of these villages that the Seat drew to a halt just down the street from a low building with a lit up sign in front of it saying, 'Taverna.'

Josh drove on past, then pulled up round the next corner. 'Stay here,' he said to Angel. 'I'll slip back and see what's going on.'

'Hey, hey, now wait a minute, boyo! I'm coming too.'

Josh shrugged. 'Harder for both of us to keep out of his sight. Still, up to you. Come on, then.'

They moved back towards the taverna.

It was a small building with one room filled to capacity by four tables, a kitchen at one end down a few stone steps and a bar to one side selling Metaxa brandy, kumquat liqueur, very cheap whisky, vodka and gin, and of course the inevitable ouzo. Wine would certainly be available also, Angel knew, but it wasn't in evidence at the bar.

Peering in from one side of the open doorway, Angel and Josh saw Bakis making for one of the small tables. The other three tables were already occupied with what seemed to be a party of Greeks, apparently all part of the one family.

'There's no way we can go in there and not be seen at once, honey.'

'Sure, Josh, we'd be mad to try.'

They watched as Bakis opened his mobile phone and began to text a message.

They backed away from the door and moved off along the village street.

'Best we can do is keep watch. Someone must be joining him. When they leave, we can follow his contact, trace him and identify him if all goes well.'

'Sure, Josh, he may have been texting them a warning – don't come here, I'm being watched.'

'Could be.'

'Maybe the best we can do is see if someone turns up, and if they don't, then keep following Bakis.'

'Yeah.'

They waited, well out of sight behind the corner of a white-walled house. Presently they spotted Bakis coming out of the taverna, wiping his mouth with the back of his hand and looking more relaxed. He stood for a few moments, looking all round, and taking the opportunity to light a cigarette. Then he strolled casually down the street in the direction of his car. Angel pinched Josh's arm.

'Let's wait – give him a chance to think he's dodged us, or was maybe just imagining that someone was following him,' she breathed.

'Okay.'

They waited, standing close to each other in the shadow of the wall, until they heard the Seat starting up.

'Okay,' said Josh again. 'Let's run for it.'

It was just as well that there were no turnoffs in the main street of the village. Josh and Angel reached their car, dived in, and were away in record time, following the now distant sound of the Seat.

'We'll keep further behind this time,' Josh decided.' I don't know if he rumbled us or just felt like a drink while he sent his text, but better take no chances.'

The road wound higher and higher. The moonlight was brighter now and its help was valuable. Josh kept his headlights off and drove on sidelights only. The red tail light of the Seat glimmered before them, now far, now nearer. When it grew nearer, as the Seat slowed round a particularly difficult bend, Josh promptly slowed down and kept his distance.

'What a pity we aren't in an American cop movie,' sighed Angel, 'where we'd have a link to headquarters and they could tell us what Bakis just texted on his phone.'

'Yeah? Certainly need to be in a movie for that, rather than real life,' Josh said sceptically. 'We'd do better to guess. 'Think I might have been followed here. Don't come. Meet instead at – ' And the rest we'll find out when we get there.'

'Hey! Look out! He's pulling off down that track!'

There was a narrow, rough track off to one side of the road between a few scattered olive trees, which was even less suited to a car than the one they'd been on for the past while. Josh wondered if he should risk his car on it, and thought that Bakis must be desperate to keep out of sight if he took his Seat down there. He drew to a halt, listening to hear if the Seat was still moving. The night was still. The only sound was a bird singing in one of the trees.

'Okay, Angel. I think we get out now.'

Chapter Twenty Nine

'We should see if we can hide the car first. There's no sign of another car, so probably the guy Bakis is meeting isn't here yet. Too bad if he sees our car when he arrives, and takes off again.'

'Good point, sweetie. Okay, we'll keep to this side road and I'll drive on a bit and see if we can turn off into the trees further along.'

About a couple of hundred yards along the road they found a good spot. Josh backed his Audi carefully under the branches until it was out of sight of a casual passerby.

'Okay now?'

Angel climbed carefully out of the car, regretting that she had worn sandals with a slight heel for what had begun as a day's sightseeing with Josh, instead of her more comfortable trainers. They made their way back through the dark night lit faintly by occasional gleams of moonlight until they reached the top of the rough track where Bakis had turned off, and began to descend.

'We need to keep to the side and be ready to duck off into the trees,' Josh said. 'I don't think he can have gone much further. We should see the Seat soon. But we need to look out for the boss man's car arriving from the road.'

Angel nodded, then, realising that Josh probably couldn't see this, she murmured, 'True.'

Keeping to the side was no joke for Angel in her heels. The path was really just a cart track, and the ruts, dried out in the fine weather, were hard to negotiate. It was the faint smell of cigarette smoke which told them they were nearing Bakis and his car.

Josh grasped Angel by the arm, but there was no need for him to warn her to stop. They needed, now, to circle round to the rear of Bakis's car, somehow, and be ready to overhear whatever Bakis had to say to his contact.

Moving slowly, Josh went further off the track, into the trees by its side. Angel slipped off her sandals, carried them in one hand by the straps, and followed him.

There was silence all around, except for the occasional scurry in the undergrowth of some little animal, possibly a marten seeking its prey or a hedgehog escaping from its hunter. Angel held her breath as they drew nearer to the Audi and crept up to the rear window.

Bakis was standing in front of the car, which he had reversed into its position for a quick exit. He hadn't heard them, it seemed. All his senses were focussed on the cart track he had driven down, in expectation of the new arrival.

A car engine sounded like an explosion out of the stillness as someone drove down the track, headlights glaring. The brightness of their light made it impossible to see past them to identify the car or the driver.

Bakis darted forward, pitching his cigarette to one side. 'Took your time, boss!' He exclaimed. Then he pulled to a halt.

'Why are you here? Where's the boss?'

'He couldn't make it – sent me instead.'

It was a woman's voice, low and hard to make out. Angel thought she'd heard it before, but it was difficult to be sure.

'So, what does he want me to do? These nosy English have found out too much.'

'Irish and American, actually.'

'All right, all right, so what? What do we do about them? They think I'm involved. I tried to put them off – but what if they come back looking for more info?'

'Then you tell them nothing.'

'Yeah? Okay for you – they don't know you're in it. I need to cover myself somehow – give them something to keep them happy.'

'Give them what?' The voice was suddenly sharp.

'Oh – nothing important.' Bakis's voice made it clear that he knew he'd stepped out of line.

'I don't like the way you seem to be thinking, Costas. And I'm quite sure the boss won't like it either.'

'I didn't mean – ' Bakis's voice broke into a whine.

'You'd better not 'mean' anything. You're walking on thin ice, Costas.'

The woman's voice was growing more and more familiar, the more Angel heard it. And more and more threatening.

'No – you got me wrong!'

'I hope so, Costas.'

There was a sudden sharp crack from further back in the woods. Bakis screamed and toppled over, clutching his chest. The woman laughed. Then she got back into her car, stepping over the silent body at her feet, and drove away.

'Okay, follow me if you can, honey. But I need to find out where that shot came from!' Josh said. He took off through the trees. Angel moved forward and knelt on the rough ground where Costas Bakis lay still.

A few moments convinced her that he was dead. There was no pulse either at neck or at wrist. Blood had poured at first from the wound in his chest and the larger exit hole in his back, but already that was stopping, as his heart no longer pumped it around his veins and arteries. Angel shuddered and stood up.

She should try to follow Josh, if possible give him some help against the gunman. It seemed likely that the woman who had come in the second car was long gone.

It wasn't easy to make her way through the trees in the faint moonlight. Angel did her best. She hadn't gone far when she heard a crackling noise to her rear, too large to be a hedgehog, a marten, or any other of the nightlife of Corfu. She spun round, too late. Arms were twisted round her in a fierce grip, and there was hot breath against her neck and cheek. Fingers and thumbs pressed against her neck muscles. Before Angel could recover enough to take defensive action, her senses began to swim, bright lights made a dazzling picture before her eyes, and then everything went dark.

Chapter Thirty

Angel came to herself in the darkness of a small, cramped space. A noise in her ears alarmed her, then made her feel sick. Minutes later, her head still swimming, she realised that she was hearing the engine of a car. Not a very large car, she thought. Not much room here in the back.

She was curled up in the car's rear seat, pressed against soft upholstery, liable to be thrown around as the car speeded around bends and straightened up again. She struggled to sit upright and realised that she was tied in a bundle, her hands fastened in some sort of handcuffs, her arms and legs bound with thick rope against her body, making her into an unpleasant and uncomfortable package. At least her mouth was free – no gag. Good news.

Angel looked round, trying to see out of the car window to identify her current whereabouts. In the faint moonlight she just could see that the car was high up on one of Corfu's roads which led across the island, a modern road but one which mounted up by twisting round bend after bend. On either side awesome heights and depths warned drivers to stay safely between the white lines marking out the secure lanes.

Angel was glad she wasn't driving. The car seemed to her, wrapped up and helpless as she was, to be moving at a horrendous speed.

Twisting her head uncomfortably, she could just see forward enough to enable her to see the person driving.

Only the back of their head. But that was enough, she thought, to see that it was a woman. Although lots of men still wore their hair long. Ah, well, it didn't really matter. She had just thought it might help to know if this was the woman who'd talked to Bakis, rather than his murderer. It might be that the woman would be easier to deal with.

A sudden jerk, and the car drew up. Now what?

The driver got out. Angel could see the person's outline, and felt even more convinced that this was a woman, presumably Bakis's interlocutor.

Were they somewhere public, somewhere that would allow Angel to alert an impartial audience to her plight?

But it seemed not.

She could hear the curiously familiar voice whispering to someone. It wasn't clear to Angel if it was someone on the end of a phone or not. Yes, probably it was – why would anyone come out here to such a remote place to meet the driver?

The woman's voice was speaking in Greek as far as she could make out, which made it even more difficult for Angel to make out what was being said.

The driver got back in the car, and the uncomfortable journey continued.

But by now, as her head began to clear slightly, Angel realised that she had had enough of it. Time to take some direct action. She squirmed around until she was sitting upright instead of crouched in a heap. The risk of falling to the floor of the car was always there, but she had to ignore that. She began to wriggle against her bonds.

One blessing was that there had not been much time for the woman to tie her up. Which meant that probably she hadn't been able to make a thorough job of it, and the bonds might not be too difficult to undo. She hoped.

Angel found herself praying. She remembered her friend Mary Branagh, back in Belfast, who ran a retreat centre on the Antrim Road. Mary had told her, 'Whenever I need help, I know there's someone who can sort everything out. So I just ask him to do it.'

Angel prayed, 'Help me now, Lord. I really need you to!'

As she wriggled, she was certain that she could feel the bonds begin to give way. Just a little more effort.

Suddenly she felt the ropes begin to move. Then they shifted some more, and her arms were free.

But not her hands, which were still handcuffed.

Angel looked round.

There was nothing she could do about the handcuffs. But she should be able to undo the ropes around her legs. It didn't take too long. Angel cautiously flexed her leg and arm muscles.

So.

She'd done this sort of thing before. The handcuffs, carefully wielded, would act as a weapon. But not while the car was being driven at reckless speed on a dangerous road. As soon as it slowed down enough for safety, that would be the time. But if she left it too late, and they had already arrived among other members of the woman's gang, she would be helpless against them.

Angel drew her breath in and waited for her moment. The darkness gathered round her, stifling her. She wished Josh was here. Then she caught herself on, despising the weakness which had led to that thought. She'd put all that sort of thing behind her when she walked out on Michael, her husband, now dead. She was on her own and could manage her own life.

The noise of the engine changed. Was it slowing down? Peering out of the window, trying to see what was happening, Angel saw by the headlights shining before the car that the road was flattening out. Were they coming to a main road? Would the driver have to stop and give way? Only if there was no traffic coming. Angel prayed for a flow of cars which would make it essential to stop. She sat up straighter and prepared herself for action.

The driver cast a glance into the rear mirror, seeing Angel motionless. She seemed satisfied with what she saw. The quick glimpse hadn't allowed her to see that Angel's ropes had fallen to the floor. Driving slowly now, she took the car up as far as the give way sign, and drew to a halt.

This was Angel's chance. Raising her hands above her head, she brought the heavy handcuffs down with a crash on the woman's head. Then, as the driver groaned and slid down in her seat, Angel leaned over her and grasped the wheel.

The important thing now was to get the car parked safely. Angel clambered over the seat into the front, pushing the unconscious woman out of the way, and managed to steer round the corner into the main road, where, to her relief, she could see that there was a break in the traffic just then. There was a wide band of dry earth along the roadside. Angel pulled in, and used her feet to brake. Manipulating the handbrake was difficult enough, but she managed it.

The next thing would be to get rid of these handcuffs. The woman should have a key for them somewhere. Angel tried to search her pockets, finding it hard to get one hand inside each, and eventually was rewarded with the clink of something metal. Result!

She extracted the keyring, fumbled with it, and decided that the smallest of the keys looked like the right one. Then it was a case of manoeuvring her wrists into position so that she could fit in the key with one hand. Not an easy task. It was some time, slow, dragging time, before Angel heard the reassuring click of the key turning successfully. She breathed a sigh of relief. After that, releasing the other hand was easy.

Her wrists ached from the strain of turning them round enough to fit the key in the lock with one of the trapped hands. She rubbed at them, hoping to bring some comfort.

Then she sat up. Time to take stock. Where was she? Above all, who was the woman?

Chapter Thirty One

So far, Angel's main concern had been to get free before the woman recovered. For the first time, she took a good look at her. There was little enough light to see by – some faint moonlight, an occasional flash from a passing car. Angel lifted the woman's head and turned it to face her. She couldn't see much. Taking her mobile phone from her pocket, she switched it on. By its light, she could see the face more clearly.

Not entirely to Angel's surprise, she recognised her. It was Dido, the nurse whom she had met at the McPherson's villa. For whatever reason, Angel had never either liked or trusted her.

Time to move on. She had choices. She could ring someone – either Josh or the police. Probably the wisest option. But it might be a while before they got to her. And meanwhile, if Dido recovered consciousness?

Or she could drive the car to somewhere safe, the nearest hospital was one idea, and leave it to the people there to deal with Dido.

She hesitated, then held up her phone and checked for a signal.

Nothing.

Angel got out of the car, hoping reception would be better outside. She walked about, and finally got a faint flicker. Yes.

A noise behind her, from the stationary car, warned her to take note of what was happening. She spun round, and saw that Dido, apparently recovered, was sitting up in the driver's seat, switching on the engine.

Angel sprang for the car and hauled open the front passenger door. A moment later she was standing on the opening of the door, while it swung to and fro behind her. But by then, the engine was fired up, and Dido was steering out into the traffic lane, such as it was.

Angel climbed further in. She leaned across and began wrestling the steering wheel from Dido. The road was still fairly empty. But as Angel succeeded in grabbing the wheel, a car roared round the nearest bend, and missed them by a hair's breadth. The driver hooted angrily at them as he disappeared into the night. Angel became more aware that she needed to be careful.

Dido had relinquished her grasp on the wheel. But she had other ideas. Before Angel knew it, Dido's left arm snaked out, and Angel felt the fist punching her hard in the gut. She was winded for a few moments and swayed backwards and forwards, trying to recover her breath while holding on to the wheel.

Dido's hands were free. Without a moment's hesitation, she took advantage of Angel's temporary breathlessness to lash out at her neck. The blow wasn't very successful, but coming on top of the previous punch it was enough. Angel found herself leaning backwards. Her hands slipped from the wheel. The passenger door was still swinging open. Angel needed to recover her balance. She pulled herself upright. As she did so, Dido lashed out again, her left elbow making contact with Angel's stomach. Angel gasped.

As the car went round the next bend at speed, she knew that she was falling. There was just time to pull herself round to face the door. Only one option left.

With an immense effort, Angel relaxed her body, and jumped for the wide verge, as the car went plunging on into the night, gathering speed with every minute.

Angel landed on her hands and knees, rolling over as she did so. She was okay, she thought. She could see the tail lights of the car as it raced down the straight piece of road ahead of it. There was a bend not far in front. Dido was driving far too far on the wrong side of the road, hoping to corner at the same speed. Angel could hear an engine and see the reflection of headlights just round the bend. A second later, the car was there. Also on the wrong side of the road by a mile. Angel held her breath and watched helplessly as the two cars met.

It was catastrophe. The noise of the crash as the two cars, despite all the efforts of their drivers to pull away to the safe side of the road, locked bodywork and concertinaed into a crumpled mess of what looked like squashed tinfoil, echoed in Angel's head for many nights afterwards.

Springing to her feet, she raced down the road. Dido's car was nearest to her. She tried in vain to pull open the passenger side door. She could just about see through the smashed window.

Dido lay in a broken heap half in the driver's seat, half on the floor. She hadn't had time to fasten her seat belt, Angel realised.

Angel was too far away to be able to try Dido's neck for a pulse. But the angle of the woman's neck told its own story. Dido was dead.

Chapter Thirty Two

It took Angel only moments to recover from the shock. This was no time to be thinking about herself and her own feelings. She moved quickly round to the other car and peered in turn through its window.

The driver, a middle aged man, was lying back in his seat. Angel noted the fastened seat belt and the inflated airbag. He had, she hoped, at least a chance of surviving. Time to call for help.

She took out her mobile phone and checked for a signal. Yes. The emergency services, first.

On arriving in Corfu, one of the first things Angel had done at the airport had been to find out what the number was for emergencies and to make sure she entered it on her phone. So she was able to ring it straightaway and give the necessary details, in as far as she knew them. Looking around her to see if she could recognise something to help the emergency services to find her, she realised that they had come back out unto the main road northwards out of Corfu town. Or so she thought. She gave this information, explaining at the same time that she couldn't be really sure, since she had been driven there with no idea where she was being taken. Then she tried to ring Josh, but got no answer. For the first time since he had left her to chase after whoever had fired the shot that killed Bakis, Angel began to worry. Where was Josh by now? Why wasn't he answering his phone?

Since she recovered consciousness tied up in Dido's car, Angel's attention had been concentrated on escaping from her own problems. Now she had done that, she had time to begin worrying about Josh. Josh had been chasing a murderer. Supposing that murderer had realised Josh was after him? Supposing he had caught Josh and taken him away somewhere? Or simply shot him?

Angel knew that as soon as was realistically possible, she had to get back to the place where she had last seen him and try to track him down from there.

She wasn't even sure where she was right now, but when the emergency services arrived they would be able to help her. In spite of the scantiness of the information she had been able to give them, they had seemed confident that they would find her.

Sure enough, not many minutes later, she heard the sound of several vehicles approaching, and saw by the headlights that the first was an ambulance and the next a police car. Angel breathed a sigh of relief and went forward to meet them.

Explanations took some time. Angel kept it to the minimum, saying nothing about the shooting of Costas Bakis or their previous interviews first with Rena and then with Bakis, and eventually found herself free to go. She was glad to be told that the driver of the other car hadn't been badly hurt, and should recover easily. He would be kept overnight in hospital, but probably not for longer. But, as she explained to the policeman who had been taking her statement, she herself had no way of leaving the scene, since she had been abducted from her car.

'Any way you could drop me off near to it?' she asked beguilingly, giving the young policeman her best smile. 'Or at least, give me a lift to town where I can hire a taxi to get me there?'

'I think we could give you a lift,' the policeman grinned. Like many Corfiots, he spoke very reasonable English. 'Come on, hop in.' He led the way to the patrol car, and Angel followed.

As it turned out, the Audi Angel and Josh had come in was still where Josh had parked it, untouched. It occurred to Angel as she left the police car, thanking them again, that Josh might easily have driven it away in pursuit of the killer. The fact that he had not worried her even more.

The first thing to do, when she had waved goodbye to the police car, was to head down to the trees where she had last seen Josh as he took off in the direction of the shot which had killed Bakis. Angel went as quickly as the rough ground would allow her down the track towards the spot where she and Josh had stopped to overhear the conversation between Bakis and the woman – Dido, Angel now realised. No wonder her voice had sounded familiar, even in a whisper.

Josh had gone off into the denser trees to the left hand side of the track. Angel set out to follow.

There were signs of where he had left the path. Broken branches where he had crashed into them, grass, scanty as it was, showing marks where it had been trampled underfoot. Angel moved cautiously along the clearly marked track Josh had left. She could smell the bruised leaves of various herbs which were growing between the olive trees and which Josh had clearly trampled on in his progress – she could recognise mint, sage, and thyme, and there were others less familiar. She was reluctant to make too much noise just in case the killer, or one of his henchmen, was still lingering in the near vicinity. Moving softly, she made her way along the route Josh had followed.

She hadn't gone far before she tripped over something and saw with pleasure that it was her sandals. She would have dropped them when Dido attacked her. It must have happened about here, then. Hastily she put the sandals back on. Walking in the woods had been no joke without some protection on her feet. Heels or no, she was going to wear them this time.

The moon was brighter now, which helped her to follow the signs. Angel could have used her phone as a torch, but was unwilling to do this because it would use up the battery. Instead, she relied on the moonlight filtering through the trees, and saw that she could make her way along, still seeing the traces Josh had left, without too much difficulty. Presently she came to a small, trickling stream of water – part of the irrigation arrangements, she supposed. As she stepped carefully over this, her eye was caught by a silver glint reflected in the rays of the moon. She stopped and bent down.

A rectangular object, gleaming silver in the moonlight, lay half buried between two of the larger stones on the river bed. Angel bent further to retrieve it. As she worked it out carefully from between the stones, she realised something. The silver gleams came from the casing someone had added to make the object doubly secure. It was a mobile phone. One that Angel knew and recognised at once. Josh's mobile phone.

Being dropped in the water had put it out of order. No wonder it had been dead when she'd tried ringing it. So much for twenty-first century communication. Back to the foot slog, it seemed. Angel wiped the phone down and slipped it into her pocket. Maybe Josh would be able to retrieve something from it. She went on following the traces he'd left as he'd crashed on after the killer.

Chapter Thirty Three

Josh, like Angel, had been taken by surprise. He plunged through the woods, avoiding twisted roots and trailing bushes, following the crashing sound of the killer in front of him. He splashed across a small stream, almost tripping on the rocks, and dropped his mobile phone without realising it.

Concerned with making as much speed as possible while keeping upright, he hardly noticed that the noises ahead of him had ceased. Just as he had begun to realise that the only sounds in the wood were the ones he was making himself, he heard a light crackle of twigs behind him. As he spun round, hands seized his throat and fingers squeezed his neck. Blackness came down on his senses like a blind shutting off the light, and he fell heavily.

It must have been not too long afterwards that he opened his eyes with a struggle and saw that he was lying on a primitive single bed, very narrow, in a scarcely furnished room whose walls were of rough wood. A farmer's hut, perhaps? He began to sit up and felt his head spin. A rattle of hinges told him that the door was opening and he lay back and closed his eyes again. No need to give away that he was conscious. He might discover something if his captors didn't know he could hear them.

Two people came quietly into the room. Josh, listening intently, could hear that both were men. And both strangers

175

to him. More members of the gang, clearly. They spoke in Greek, which Josh had no problem in following.

'Still out.'

'You'd better check.'

'Okay.'

One of the men came over to Josh and put a finger on the pulse at his neck.

'He's alive, anyway. Should recover soon.'

'Does he have any identification?'

'None. I already looked.'

Josh, lying quietly, allowed himself to feel surprised. What had happened to his wallet? It occurred to him that the man who was speaking, who seemed to be the junior of the two, might have pinched it for the money and didn't want to say. Josh had been carrying a reasonable amount of money, to cover the day out with Angel, and still had much of it left. A prize for the junior gang member.

'Okay. We'll question him when he comes to. But I can't think why you had to grab him, Christos. All you had to do was get away after you'd shot Bakis. You must have mucked it up thoroughly.'

Christos's voice took on a whining, defensive note. 'He kept following me – he was getting closer all the time! I had to stop him.'

'Yes, okay, but why did you have to bring him here with you? Why not just leave him where he fell?'

Christos was silent. Then he mumbled, 'Seemed the best idea at the time.'

'Leave it. Let's go into the other room and have a drink. You can look back in on him presently.'

Josh heard the door again, and the two men were gone.

Josh reckoned he had between five and ten minutes to sort out some way to escape. He sat up, ignoring his head, which was in fact feeling a lot better by now. He looked carefully round the room.

There was a minimal amount of light which he now saw came from an oil lamp on a high shelf just inside the door. There were no windows. The door was shut. Swinging himself off the bed, he went over to the door and found, as he'd expected, that it was locked.

Apart from the bed there was a rickety chair with a jug of water on it. That was the lot.

Josh worked out his options. No windows, and the only door led to the room the two men had gone into. No point in trying to break out through it.

So. He could break a leg off the chair. It looked as if that wouldn't be too hard. Then wait behind the door and hit Christos over the head with it. Probably the other man would hear something and come to see. If so, he would likely have a gun, and he would come carefully. Not so easy.

Josh's gaze fixed itself speculatively on the oil lamp. It should be possible to do something with that.

He stiffened as he heard the rattle of the key in the lock once more. Christos was coming back sooner than he'd expected. Josh sat down on the edge of the bed, swung his legs up, and began to groan.

Christos pushed the door open and came in. Josh regretted that he hadn't had time to break off a leg of the chair. The plan would have worked out perfectly.

Christos began to speak to him in Greek as soon as he was through the door. 'Back with us again? Time to answer a few questions, then, mister.'

Josh looked at him with an expression which he hoped looked bewildered, and answered in Polish. 'I don't understand. What are you saying? My head hurts.'

'What's that gibberish?' Christos snarled. 'Speak Greek, fool!'

'I'm not Greek. I don't know what you're saying.'

'This is impossible! Don't talk nonsense – say something I can understand!'

Christos came rushing over to the bed, his fist raised. Then, as Josh stood quietly to his feet and Christos realised that this man was towering over him and looking threatening, he lowered his fist and backed away.

'This is no good. I'll have to get Marios. What did he want to go over to the house for just now? And why did he take the gun? How does he expect me to manage this brute on my own?'

Josh watched as Christos backed slowly out through the door. He heard the key click in the lock.

Things were looking up. It seemed that the other man, Marios, had gone over to 'the house.' Would Christos be stupid enough to go after him, leaving the way through the front room unguarded? Or not?

Josh listened, but could hear no sound of Christos going out. He could hear the man moving about, and a splosh that sounded like a drink being poured out into a glass. Maybe Christos wasn't so stupid after all. Or maybe he knew Marios would be angry with him if he didn't stay as, Josh was sure, he had been ordered to do.

Back to plan B.

Josh pulled the chair across to the high shelf above the door, and reached up to lift down the burning oil lamp.

Chapter Thirty Four

Angel went on through the woods. The sound of the stream she had crossed continued in her ears, and the night birds called to each other through the trees.

She was still in an olive plantation. The trees were low, straggly, with silvery leaves which shone in the faint moonlight and made a rattling noise as she brushed past them. Nets were spread across the ground to catch the falling olives as they ripened. Angel found it hard in the growing darkness, as clouds began to throw a soft covering over the moon, to avoid tripping over these nets, and found herself going more slowly and carefully.

It had been an exhausting evening. She realised suddenly how tired she was. Should she sit for a while and recover her strength before going on?

But, no. She was determined to find Josh as soon as she could. While she had every confidence in his ability to look after himself and deal with the killer who had shot Bakis, she couldn't help wanting to be with him, to lend a hand if he needed it – as he well might.

A murmur of voices came to her ears. There was someone else nearby – more than one, unless he was talking to himself. Angel stopped moving.

It was so dark now that she was confident no one would be able to see her. But she was glad that there was a fairly substantial tree in front of her, giving extra concealment.

However, by the same token she would find it hard, if not impossible, to see these people or recognise them. She listened instead, straining her ears to try to make out what was being said.

'Well, we're rid of him now.' It was a man's voice, hard and resonant. He was speaking Greek. Angel tried hard to make out some of the words with her scanty knowledge of the language.

'Your decision, Marios.'

'Not mine, Christos. The boss's.'

'Oh, yes.'

'And he's not too pleased with you, Christos. Why you had to grab him in the first place, I'll never know.'

'Didn't want him giving us away to the cops.'

'He had nothing to give away at that stage. Now he's seen us. Far too dangerous. And your fault.'

Angel froze. The few words she had understood had told her that they must be talking about Josh. Were they? Had to be. What had they done with him?

The man called Christos had grabbed him, apparently. And it was 'far too dangerous.' And she had also made out something about 'got rid of him'.

To Angel, the words could have only one meaning. Was Josh dead? Had these murdering brutes added him to their tally?

As she stood motionless behind her tree, the voices grew fainter and she realised that the men were going.

Should she try to follow them? What good would it do? If Josh was dead, there was nothing she could do for him. But at least she could try to catch these evil men.

Pulling herself together, Angel began to make her way through the trees in the direction she thought the men had taken. It was hard going, especially as she wanted to keep her pursuit silent. No need to give them warning of her approach. She found that the need for stealth was making her go more and more slowly.

Presently she realised that she had lost track of the men. The clouds had moved on and there was some moonlight again. She was in a wide area now, with fewer olive trees and a dark shape looming up directly ahead. Angel approached it cautiously.

She knew very little, so far, about Corfu and its trade. But she remembered Josh telling her, as they drove up to the MacPherson's villa along the coast road, that olive oil was one of Corfu's main products, and that when the olive oil had been poured out into tubs to be sent for bottling, leaving the huge press empty, the press would be flushed out with water which would flow down into the bay, leaving the sea water smooth and lovely because it was now mixed with what remained of the olive oil. It made the waters around Corfu a pleasure to swim in, like a bath to which special oils had been added to improve the consistency of the water.

It might well be, Angel considered, that this looming darkness was a press for olive oil, produced from the olive trees she had been making her way through. So was she nearing the buildings of a farm where olive oil was the main produce? Probably. She moved on past the press. She could see some small buildings and a larger house not too far away. Was this where the men had gone? And was Josh somewhere near here, dead or alive?

The acrid smell of burning came to her nostrils as she moved nearer. She could see that one of the smaller buildings has been burning recently.

Angel retreated.

She was back in among the trees now. Should she just go back to the car, and get the help of the police to arrest these men she had heard talking? Or should she try to find the men and discover more about Josh first?

As she hesitated, still moving back into the shadow of the olive trees, the moon gleamed more strongly through gaps in the olive grove, and an eerie light shone down on her through the branches. Angel saw by this light that she had been following a track through the trees, one created by the workers who came to gather up the ripe olives from the nets. She hadn't realised that there was a track. In the semi-darkness in which she had been moving until now, the occasional glimmer of moonlight had shown very little. She moved on along the track. Was this the way she had come? She could see the odd broken branch, some wet marks left by her feet where she had crossed the stream. Yes, this must be the way. It wouldn't be too far to the car now that she could see where she was going. Angel decided to hurry back there and contact the police.

Suddenly she froze where she stood. Ahead of her something dark was spread across the path.

She knew without thinking what it was. The body of a man.

Angel moved forward.

The moon shone down through a wider gap in the trees. Its light showed her the man's face. She looked and went on looking.

It was Josh Smith. He was lying quite still, his face white in the moonlight.

White, Angel thought, with a pallor that could be nothing but death.

For a moment she stood motionless, unable to move, unable to feel, unable to think.

Chapter Thirty Five

When Josh had lifted down the oil lamp he set it carefully to one side, then inspected the back wall. It was, as he'd already noticed, wooden, and not very strong. It might be possible to kick it in. That would be noisy, though, and would probably bring Christos running.

Normally, Josh would have dealt with Christos easily. But the combination of things in the last few days, starting with the shooting by Hamish's pool and ending with the attack which had left him unconscious, made him realise that he wasn't as fit and strong as usual.

Instead, he lifted the chair and inspected it. It was a rickety, spindly thing, with narrow legs and a back consisting of a few thin struts with a bar across them at the top to hold them together. First Josh twisted two of the legs off the chair, then pulled off some of the resulting splinters. When he had a small pile of splinters, he positioned them against the back wall and rested the two thin chair legs across them.

Next he undid the chimney of the oil lamp and set it to one side. Then he took a fairly sturdy splinter from his pile and poked it carefully into the flame of the lamp, being careful not to put the lamp out in the process. When he was sure the splinter was well alight, he knelt down by the pile and, shielding the flame of the splinter with one cupped hand, he set fire to the rest. A welcome crackle rewarded him and presently the splinters were well alight. As soon as he was sure they were not about to fizzle out, Josh nudged one of the chair legs into the blaze and was happy to see that it was soon on fire. He added the other chair leg, and began to pull the chair back apart. When he had a number of thin struts detached, he heaped them criss cross onto his fire and sat back to watch.

It was pleasant to see the fire catching hold. The wall didn't resist for long. Presently the blaze was travelling upward, burning a sizeable gap. When he was sure that the gap was big enough for him to get through, Josh moved into the second stage of his plan. He lifted the jug of water, kicked the remains of his original bonfire aside, and splashed water carefully on the burning wall. There was a hiss and considerable smoke. There wasn't a lot of water, but enough, Josh hoped, to do the job if he was quick. Seizing the rough blanket from the bed, he wrapped it round himself, making sure to cover his face and hands, and used it to force a way out through the smouldering gap. Then he ran.

He had heard nothing from Christos since the sound of him pouring a drink five or ten minutes ago. He rather thought the man had gone out after Marios, but had no way of telling. Alternatively he might be sitting comfortably in the front room, downing drink after drink. It didn't matter now which of these ideas was true.

Josh reached the shelter of the nearest outhouse and thought out his next move. He wanted to know more about these men. Where did they fit into the picture? One of them – probably Christos, from what he had heard Marios say– had shot the man Bakis who was Rena's contact. Marios must have taken away the gun Christos had used. Probably he was afraid of Christos using it irresponsibly. Christos hadn't got a gun now as far as Josh had been able to tell. Were they part of the gang, getting rid of a dangerously weak link? Or were they part of some rival gang?

It seemed to Josh that he should make his way carefully over to the house, see if he could find Marios, and possibly find some information one way or another. He was quite prepared to wring the necessary information out of Marios by force if that was what was needed.

He slipped quietly between the various buildings until he reached what was clearly the main house. There was a light glimmering from behind the carelessly drawn curtains in one of the rooms in the wall facing him. Josh looked about him for a way in. Since Marios had come over here not much more than twenty minutes ago, he probably hadn't locked the door behind him. There was a door on the same side as the window with the light, not too far along. Josh turned the handle and pushed gently. To his satisfaction, it opened, and he went in.

He was in a large kitchen, stone floored and tidy. There was no one there, he was glad to see. A voice sounded faintly through the farther door which opened into the rest of the house. Josh went across to it and pushed it gently open.

The voice sounded louder, now. He was pretty sure it was Marios.

There must be a land line somewhere near. Marios wasn't using his mobile, but maybe that was because reception was bad up here.

Josh advanced cautiously.

'But boss,' he heard Marios say. He sounded worried. 'It wasn't my fault. It was all Christos's doing.'

A crackle on the line.

'Well, yes, I know, boss, I know I was responsible for him.'

Crackle crackle.

'Boss, I had him shoot Bakis while he was talking to Dido, and then we had to get away. I didn't realise Christos was lagging behind.'

Crackle Crackle.

'Boss, first I knew, he appeared, dragging this guy. He said the guy had been following us. So I helped him to carry him here – what else could I do?'

Crackle crackle.

'Yes, Christos pinched his wallet – he hid it in his own room – I found it easily. The guy's some sort of cop – Josh Smith.'

Josh heard sounds over the phone as if someone had exploded.

'Okay, boss, I know we don't want trouble with the cops.'

Crackle.

'Let him go? But boss, he'll know us!'

Crackle.

'Spin him a yarn? Like what, boss?'

A prolonged crackling. Josh strained his ears but could hear nothing distinctly.

'Okay, boss. If you say so.' Marios sounded resigned. A moment later, he put down the phone and turned away.

Josh wondered for a split second what he should do now. If they had been told to let him go, should he let them find him before they knew he had escaped? Or what?

Chapter Thirty Six

It took him less than a minute to make up his mind. Then he was racing back to the outhouse where he had been held prisoner, and bursting into the front room where Christos was snoring in a comfortable chair, drunk out of his skull.

The door was easy to kick open. Josh loomed over Christos and seized him by the throat.

'Not a sound out of you, mister!' he hissed in Greek. Christos came to himself and stared at Josh, his eyes goggling.

'I thought you didn't speak Greek?' was his first remark.

'Yeah, well, that's where you were wrong,' Josh said. 'I speak Greek and a ton of other languages, but what's it to you? When Marios comes, you say nothing about me, right?'

Christos nodded his head feebly.

'Or I'll break your neck before Marios or anyone else can stop me, okay?'

'Okay.'

There was the sound of approaching feet. Marios pushed open the door and stared at them. Josh had one of Christos's arms twisted behind his back and his other hand was at the gangster's throat. Marios gaped at the tableau presented to him, and said nothing for a moment. Then he moved forward and spoke.

'Hey, no need for this, okay?'

'No?' Josh asked grimly. 'You let me go or I break his neck, understand?' He stared at Marios, making no move to let Christos go.

It was the first time Josh had seen Marios properly. He was a big man, much the same size as Josh himself. Josh knew he would recognise him again. He had a thin, distinctive face and a narrow mouth, unshielded by the usual Greek moustache. But it was his eyes which were unforgettable – narrow, yellow eyes which gleamed like the eyes of a wolf.

'Come on! It was all a mistake! Christos thought you were a guy who'd been causing us a lot of trouble, who shot our friend Bakis earlier tonight. But I've just been looking at your wallet and I see that you're Josh Smith, and you're a cop, right?'

'Right.'

'So Christos got it all wrong. Hey, he often does! I was coming over to let you out and I run into this! No need for it, Inspector Smith. No need at all.'

Josh looked at him coldly. 'I wish I could believe that.'

'Listen, I'll walk you out now – direct you back to your car, wherever it's parked, will that do?'

'It'll do,' said Josh slowly, 'provided we take Christos here with us, and I hold onto him until I'm sure you mean what you say.'

Marios stared at him. Then he shrugged. 'Hey, whatever. Let's go, then. And no hard feelings?'

'None, if you keep your side of the bargain.'

'Oh, I will, I will.'

Marios turned and led the way out through the door. Josh followed him, holding Christos's arm still twisted up his back, and with his hand at Christos's throat.

The little procession made its way down into the grove of olive trees and along the track towards where Josh had left the car. When they had gone a certain amount of the way, Marios stopped.

'I think you'll be able to find your way from here,' he said.

Josh shrugged. 'Probably. I'm parked up not far from the back road from Corfu town.'

'Oh, no problem, then,' Marios said cheerfully. 'Just keep going for a bit, cross the stream, and you'll be nearly there. Okay?'

'Okay,' Josh agreed. He knew he was being released on the boss's instructions, although Marios had made a good job of spinning him a yarn with a different reason. Still, it was good to get away without further violence. He would puzzle it out later.

Marios gave him a causal wave, and turned away. Josh released Christos, waited to see him follow Marios, and moved away in his turn. There was a sudden rushing sound behind him. Christos landed on his back, pushed him energetically forward, and caught his ankle with one foot. Josh fell headlong. His head banged against a protruding tree trunk, and he knew no more.

He lay there for some time.

And it was so that Angel, coming through the woods, saw him, and froze where she stood.

Then, with a sound which was neither scream nor cry, she ran to him, moving as swiftly as a hare fleeing from the hounds, desperate to escape from the terror which had come upon her. Casting herself down upon Josh's body she began to weep helplessly, and the anguished sounds of the grief which filled her heart poured themselves out as she did so.

Her arms wrapped themselves round him and her mouth showered kisses on his quiet face.

'Josh! Josh!'

Time went on.

Angel felt an ever increasing pain. What was she to do?

Then the moonlight shining down on Josh's face showed her a small movement.

Josh was opening his eyes.

Angel gasped. Her arms went round Josh more tightly than ever.

She found it impossible to speak.

Josh looked at her, and she saw that he was smiling weakly.

The words which expressed her feeling burst out from Angel's heart.

'Josh, Josh, Josh! I thought you were dead!' she cried out. 'I thought you were dead, Josh! I thought you were dead!'

'I'm not,' said Josh faintly.

'Oh, Josh, I love you so much!' Angel said.

'And I love you, Angel.'

Then his arms went round her, and they were hugging each other and kissing with an unbelievable intensity.

Chapter Thirty Seven

It was a long time before they were able to sit up and talk sensibly.

'Josh, what did those people do to you?'

'It's a long story,' Josh said wryly. 'Okay, it was like this.'

When he had finished, Angel sat up alertly. 'So, they come from that olive farm nearby. Do you want to go back and see what more we can find out about them?'

'Maybe not right now. I think I need to get home and sleep for a while before we plan any more action.'

'Of course. I'm a fool. We should get back to the car and take off.'

'Yeah. We need to report Bakis's murder, too.'

'Do you think we need to? I didn't tell the cops about that.'

'When were you speaking to the cops?'

'It was when they came out to the accident.'

'Accident?' Josh said sharply. 'Angel, it's your turn to fill me in – what's been happening to you?'

Angel talked for some time. When Josh had finished asking her questions, they stood up, holding on to each other as much for support as anything else.

'Okay,' Josh said. 'I think what we should do now is go back to where we left Bakis, and check that he's dead –'

'He is. I checked at the time,' Angel interrupted. 'Sure, do you think I wouldn't have told the cops if there was any chance that he was still alive and needing help?'

'Fair enough, honey. But let me go on. I think we can be pretty sure by now that it was Bakis who shot Marge and me, and then passed his gun to Rena until he was sure no cops would come looking for him and find it on him. It would have been clear evidence of what he'd done, right? So I'm suggesting that we leave the gun beside him, and then ring the cops anonymously to report seeing him there. Okay?'

'Sounds like a plan,' Angel agreed.

It wasn't far to the place where Bakis had been shot. His body lay where they had left it. There was no sign that anyone else, cops or otherwise, had been near him.

They went up to Josh's car and retrieved the gun from the glove compartment. Josh wiped it carefully. Then they returned to Bakis, and Josh clasped the dead man's fingers round the butt and trigger.

'Let's hope I've done that well enough to be convincing,' Josh said cheerfully. 'Okay, honey, let's go before I collapse completely.'

'Sure, we're a right pair,' Angel said. 'Let's hope at least one of us is fit to drive. And I think it had better be me, darlin'!'

They staggered back again to where Josh's car was still parked, and Angel drove.

The Villa Callidora was dark and silent when they reached it. Angel checked the time on her phone. Three thirty. They would all be in bed and asleep hours ago.

A side door had been left unlocked for them, and they crept quietly up to their rooms.

It was a while before Angel slept that night. There was something that Josh had said that had rung a bell. But she wasn't just sure what it was. Maybe it would come to her in the morning, if she left it for now. Things often did.

There was something else on her mind. Something that mattered a great deal. When she had walked out on her abusive husband Michael, Angel had made a promise to herself, that nothing on earth would ever make her give any other man the power to hurt her which her husband had had. Not simply by his violence. But by the pain he had caused her at a deeper level, the pain of betrayal and of the cruelty of hateful words from someone whom she had thought loved her. And the hurt caused by his unnecessary anger, which sprang out so often after their first few honeymoon months, and the cruel things he regularly said.

Never, and never, and never again, she had sworn passionately.

Was she about to break her promise? Was Josh really different?

Angel shivered. Yes, she was sure he was – but suppose it turned out that she was wrong?

Yet when she had thought he was dead, and then found that he was alive, she had felt a joy, a happiness, unlike anything she had ever known.

She didn't want to lose that joy. Did she dare risk another commitment, another trust? She had no problem taking physical risks. She had done it again and again over the last few years since she'd been on her own. Life had thrown up some dangerous situations which she'd had to deal with.

But an emotional risk? Was she too great a coward for that?

The hours went past, and still Angel wondered.

Chapter Thirty Eight

Breakfast next morning was difficult. Going downstairs, Angel wasn't sure how much Hamish knew about Dido. Had the police been in contact with him to let him know she was dead? Surely they had. She hoped they'd accepted it as a straightforward accident, and weren't going to investigate further.

It seemed that they had. The police had rung Hamish not long after the accident, looking for information about Dido. As her current employer, they expected that Hamish would know Dido's next of kin. They hadn't suggested that it was anything but an accident.

But, as Hamish told Angel, he hadn't been able to help them. All he really knew about Dido, he said, was that she was a good nurse, recommended by his doctor, and as such he had employed her on several previous occasions, and had thought of her first when Marge was shot.

'And dreadful of me as it may be, lassie,' he said ruefully, 'my main concern now is that I'll have to find someone just as good to replace her. Och, I'm certainly upset that she should have been killed in this car accident, poor wee girl, but what am I to do now about Marge?'

'Probably the doctor can suggest someone else?'

Hamish brightened up. 'Yes, of course. I'll talk to him about it.'

Josh came downstairs a little later.

'What are you doing out of bed, darlin'?' Angel asked him severely. 'He took far too much out of himself yesterday,' she told Hamish. 'First day up, and he did far more than was wise.'

Hamish seemed happy to accept this without further detail.

'Honey, you worry too much,' Josh said. 'I'm fine now that I've had a good sleep. A big breakfast now will finish the trick – I'll be fighting fit in no time!'

'These Interpol cops are tough as old boots, Angel,' Hamish laughed. 'You won't find this laddie staying in bed unless he's tied down.'

Orange juice, an omelette and a stack of toast worked miracles for Josh, to Angel's relief.

'Now, what plans have you for today, Josh?' Hamish asked presently, when he came back from phoning the doctor about a new nurse. 'You need to make sure this lady gets a thorough all round view of our lovely island. Plenty more to see yet!'

'We thought we'd get the maps out and plan a route later, after a swim,' Josh said. 'Okay by you, honey?'

Angel, who was well aware that they needed to talk, and not in front of anyone else, even Hamish, smilingly agreed.

'Let's go down to the beach to swim,' Josh suggested abruptly. 'We could drive over to Agios Georgios. It's not too far, and you'll love it – one of Corfu's most beautiful bays.'

They set off in the car, Josh driving this time. And this time Angel made sure to wear her trainers, after last night's experience.

'Are you sure you're okay, darlin'? You looked like something dragged through a hedge backwards last night.'

'Honey, you really encourage me. Thanks a million! Sure, I'm fine now. A good sleep and some breakfast. Like Hamish says, we cops are tough!'

Angel sat back to enjoy the beautiful drive across the top of the island from the East coast to the West. Not as far as that sounded.

'I think we need to sort out what we know so far,' Josh said presently. 'Things were happening so fast yesterday that they're all a bit of a jumble in my mind. But swim first, I think. After that, we can sit in a private corner of the beach and talk it all through.'

'Sure, that's fine by me, darlin'.'

They pulled up at the top of the road to look down on the fine sparkling sand, the dazzling blue of the sea, the black rocks edging the bay, and Angel breathed a sigh of pure enjoyment. Then Josh drove down the sloping lane and found a place to park. They changed quickly and ran down the beach together to the water's edge where small lazy waves trickled round their feet, and then waded in.

The water was warm but invigorating. Angel swam ferociously across the bay, then turned on her back and floated happily with the heat of the sun lapping her round, and felt bliss flooding her. She felt that she could have stayed there forever.

All too soon, it was time to move out of the direct sunlight. They made for the shore and found a sheltered place beside some rocks where a shadow gave them protection for their talk.

'Now, then,' Josh said.

Angel, lying full length, propped herself up on one elbow and turned towards him where he lay stretched out beside her on his beach towel.

'There was something you said last night, Josh, that rang a bell with me,' she said. 'But I still can't think what it was.'

'It may come back to you. If not, I'll try to go over what I said in the hope of reminding you. But, meanwhile, let's make a note of the stuff we've found out so far. First of all, a list of the people involved. Quite a long list. But some of them are dead now.'

'Okay. Well, we saw Doukas talking with Jason and the nurse Rena. But Jason claims that he's working undercover with Doukas, and that he's brought in Rena so as to have someone on the inside.'

'Right. Don't know how much of that's true. Then, Rena put us on to her contact, Costas Bakis.

'Who's dead now.'

'Yeah.'

'And although we found out that Dido the nurse Hamish hired to look after Marge was part of the gang, she's dead, too.'

'A lot of dead ends, in a manner of speaking.'

Angel grinned.

'So, that leaves us with the toughs who grabbed you, Josh darlin'. Christos and Marios, right?'

'Right.'

'And Marios seems to be able to contact the Big Man directly.'

'Yeah. That's important.'

Josh rolled over onto his front and propped himself on his elbows while he thought.

'So, babe. Looks like Marios is our main link. And maybe Christos, too, though I'm bettin' he doesn't know as much as Marios does.'

Angel sat up suddenly. 'Josh, you described this guy Marios to me last night. Sure, I can't remember just what you said, but I reckon there was something important there. Tell me again about him.'

Josh began. 'He was a big man, much the same size as me. I told you I knew I'd recognise him again. He had a thin, distinctive face and a narrow mouth. You could see it clearly because he didn't have the usual Greek moustache. But it was his eyes which were unforgettable – narrow, yellow eyes. It may seem daft, but I couldn't help thinking his eyes gleamed like the eyes of a wolf.'

'Got it!' Angel exclaimed triumphantly. 'I told you something you said last night rang a bell with me!'

'So? What was it then?'

'Marios's eyes! When poor Sophie was telling me about the men who broke in and held her up and stole her jewellery, that was what she said about one of them. He was wearing a mask, but his eyes showed through the slits, of course. She said they were yellow – they made her think of the eyes of a wolf!'

Chapter Thirty Nine

'Wow,' Josh said thoughtfully. 'Okay. We knew these two guys came into the picture somewhere. Now it looks like they may be the main operators.'

'I'd think so.'

'It doesn't take us too much further, though, does it, babe? We can say there's a big boss, and that Marios knows who he is, and that there are several others involved – two of them dead, now. Looks like the team's shrinking.'

'So maybe it'll be easier to catch the ones who're left!' Angel said enthusiastically.

'Yeah.' Josh sat up to think better. 'What we do need to do is to be careful not to end up getting the links we know about, I mean Marios and Christos, eliminated – shot or whatever – before we get all the info we can out of them.'

'Right.'

'We have to go real careful.'

'Right. But we're going to do something, Josh?'

'Yeah.'

'And today, okay?'

'Today, then, honey.'

'So let's start by heading up to that olive farm where they live and seeing what we can find out there.'

'Makes sense. But we really do need to go carefully, babe.'

'Sure, darlin'! Hey, do you have a gun?'

'I don't usually carry. But today I thought it might be smart. I have a gun in the car. In fact, I have two. One in the glove compartment and one in the pocket of my shorts.'

'Two gun Smith!'

'Yeah, yeah. You can have one if you need it, sweetie.'

'Good. Then, when we get there, you can burst in and say, "Freeze! Police!"'

'No way!'

'Oh, all right then, I'll take the other gun, and I'll burst in and say, "Freeze! Not the police!" How's that? Even more scary, right?'

Josh laughed. 'If I didn't know you were joking, sweetie, I'd say you were loony tunes. C'mon. Let's have a final quick swim, then head off.'

He reached out a hand to pull her to her feet, and they ran helter skelter down the beach and into the cool refreshing sea.

When they had swum, dried in the sun, and dressed again, Josh said, 'Time for some lunch. There's a really swell taverna just back along the beach a bit.'

'Cool,' Angel said, following him happily.

They choose a table outside where they could watch the ripples of the waves gently stroking the sand, and sipped white wine under the shelter of a large umbrella which canopied their table. Small fish cooked in a special sauce with Greek salad made a light but attractive lunch for Angel, while Josh opted for a more substantial meal of lamb kebab with what he referred to as 'French Fries,' although to Angel they were simply chips. And very nice, too. She couldn't resist pinching one or two from Josh's plate, and was threatened with Josh's fork for it.

'So, we'll begin by heading back to the farm and seeing if we can pick up anything there about Marios and Christos and the big man, right, babe?' Josh suggested, pushing back his chair and standing up.

'First, I'll check out their ladies' room here,' Angel said.

'Good idea. I'll pay the bill, then, and wait for you out front.'

Presently they were strolling back to where Josh had parked the car. Angel was glad to get in and feel the cool blast of air conditioning. The midday heat was beginning to get a bit overpowering.

'I guess we're hoping for something that will lead us to the boss, right?' she commented.

'Well, that would be the ideal. But any more info about Marios would be good. We don't even know his second name.'

They meandered at their leisure through the lanes until they came out on the familiar road which ran along the east coast of the island. Angel felt as if she'd driven up and down it a hundred times already, although she'd only been in Corfu for a few days. They headed southwards, passing the turn off for the Villa Callidora, turned off up into the hills of olive groves, and presently came to the area where Josh had parked the car out of sight the previous evening.

'This is where we get out and walk, I guess, honey. Down the lane, through the trees, and over the stream. Easy enough to find our way.'

In the clear sunlight, as golden as the wine they had sipped at lunch, the way lay open before them. Angel, remembering the dark and difficult route she had followed last night, hardly recognised the clusters of olive trees as the same confusing wood.

'We should try to be as quiet as we can,' Josh said. 'So none of your wild shrieks or noisy singing, right?'

'I'll ignore that,' Angel said. 'You're the one likely to make the most noise, you loud mouthed American!'

In spite of the jokes they both knew that it was seriously important to approach the farm as silently as possible. They were dealing with dangerous men. It would make life simpler if they had no idea Angel and Josh were tracking them down.

'Do you think the police have found Bakis yet?' Angel said. In mutual, though unvoiced, agreement they took care to avoid the place where Costas Bakis had been shot.

'No sign of police activity. But maybe they've taken the body away long ago. Hope so. I rang and reported it anonymously, early this morning, as I told you I would.'

'Good. If we hadn't stayed anonymous, we'd have been held up and dragged into the whole business,' Angel said. 'Much better to get on with finding the gang ourselves.'

Josh shrugged and said no more.

They reached the stream sooner than they had expected, and by daylight saw that there were stepping stones which would allow them to cross with fairly dry feet. Last night in the dark they had each splashed their way through.

A little further on, Angel looked round her and shuddered. 'This is where you were lying when I found you, darlin'. Sure, my heart nearly stopped beating.'

'The guys brought me as far as this and then said it wouldn't be much further. Cross the stream and then keep to the track. Marios went on, but Christos sneaked back as soon as I'd turned away from them, tripped me up and knocked me out. A bit of revenge, nothing else. I told you that, didn't I?'

'You did. Hateful man!'

'Not the best,' Josh acknowledged with a wry grin. 'Never mind, honey, when we catch him you can demonstrate your kick boxing on him. This time I won't try to stop you – at least, not just straightaway!'

As they moved on through the olive grove, they could see, coming nearer, the outbuildings of the farm.

'Okay,' Josh said. 'This is where we work out our plan. Do we head straight for the farm itself, the house where Marios did his phoning, or do we explore the other buildings first? Any thoughts, sweetie?'

Chapter Forty

'Let's scout around first, see where the guys are. And see if anyone else is here – people running the press and stuff like that.'

'Okay.' Josh took Angel's arm and steered her towards the nearest outbuilding. As they approached it, walking as silently as they knew how, they began to hear a murmur of voices from nearby.

As Angel had guessed, people were working at the olive presses, some offloading the olives they had gathered, others directing and starting up the presses when they were full enough, and seeing that the oil produced ran safely into the huge tubs waiting for it. As each load of olives was delivered, the gatherer went back to the olive groves, possibly to collect more olives or perhaps to carry out some other work on their plot of ground.

Angel and Josh listened to the conversation for a while, but learnt nothing of value. Most of it was joking between the men and the women, of the type Angel was used to hearing in Belfast, as far as she could tell, from the pushing and laughing which went on. She was able to pick up bits and pieces, and Josh translated some of it for her in a whisper, but mostly she was guessing from the expressions on the workers' faces and the actions as they pushed each other, laughed, and sometimes pelted each other with a handful of olives.

'Okay,' Josh whispered presently, 'this isn't telling us anything. Let's move on. Up towards the big house, okay?'

Angel nodded, and they headed in that direction.

Josh knew the way, but Angel also remembered it from the previous night. A long, squat house, white and shining in the sunlight, with vines climbing round the verandas and bright geraniums in boxes along its front steps, the farmhouse gleamed attractively in the early afternoon light. Josh and Angel crept quietly up towards it.

'Okay, honey. What we want is to get within an easy distance so we can overhear what these guys are saying, right?' Josh murmured in Angel's ear.

'Right.'

Angel made sure she kept very quiet as she followed Josh towards the rear of the house where it would be easier to get close without being seen.

About halfway there, something occurred to her. 'Josh!' she whispered.

Josh stopped and turned towards her.

'Not being able to understand more than a few words those guys at the olive press said made me think – there's no way I'll understand much of what these Greek speakers up at the house happen to be saying. Maybe it would be better if I stayed on guard where I can see if anyone's coming, and then I could warn you? You can tell me after if you hear anything useful, right?'

'Very sensible, honey. Okay, you find somewhere around here to hide and keep a lookout, and I'll go on up to the house and round to the back, and see if I can find out any-thing.'

Putting his arm round her shoulders, Josh gave her a quick hug, then moved quietly on.

Angel looked round, and noted a tree beside one of the outbuildings near the main house. She slipped over to it and positioned herself carefully out of sight of anyone approaching from either direction, and waited.

Josh walked on up to the house. On the previous night he had noticed that Marios had phoned from the land line set up in the passage just outside the kitchen. The door had been unlocked then, and Josh had had no problem in getting in. He hoped it would be as easy today. He came cautiously up to the door at the back of the big whitewashed house which he knew led to the kitchen.

Before pushing it open, he listened for a moment or two, and was very glad he had done so. Inside the room he could hear voices. One, he was pretty sure, was Christos, the other Marios, and as Angel had expected they were speaking Greek. It was hard to hear much distinctly.

Taking his hand from the door which he had left as it was, Josh moved along the back wall until he found a window which he was pleased to see was partway open. Standing beside it, he could hear much more clearly, well enough to make out what was being said. Josh listened carefully.

'So, are we going to meet up with him?' Christos was demanding in his whiny, uncertain way, waiting for Marios to give him a lead.

'We'll see,' Marios replied curtly. 'I'm expecting to hear from him sometime soon. Then we'll have a better idea what to do.'

'If only those fools like Bakis and the rest hadn't started demanding a bigger cut. They were doing all right for the lowlife scum that they are. They probably never before in their lives saw the sort of money the boss was handing out to them. And they had to go yapping for more! No wonder he wasn't having it!'

'Yeah, yeah, past history, Christos. I heard you complaining a time or two yourself, don't forget. Anyway, the boss has shown them they can't get away with it. The point is, what are they going to do now? Accept his terms or go on fighting?'

'So, do you think he'll want us to bodyguard him if he sets up a meeting?'

'That's what we're waiting to find out. He's going to let us know.'

'But after what they did, I shouldn't think he'd be in a mood to let them off lightly, Marios.'

Meanwhile Angel, keeping well out of sight between her tree and the building beside it, suddenly stiffened. That was a car coming, wasn't it? She peered out carefully and saw a big maroon Mercedes heading up towards the house. She knew Josh had gone round to the back, and this car would certainly make for the front entrance by way of the tarmac drive, but he needed to get out of there before it was too late. Giving the Mercedes just time to get out of sight, she ran in the direction Josh had taken.

Josh, standing by the open window and listening with all his might, jumped as he felt a soft hand on his shoulder. Angel's voice whispered in his ear.

'There's a car coming. It's gone round to the front. Let's get going!'

Chapter Forty One

Josh turned round. Moving very quietly, he steered Angel away from the open window until he was confident whispers could not be heard from inside the room.

'Honey, thanks heaps for warning me. But the very last thing I want to do is leave now. If this car has gone round the front the guys who get out of it won't see me here at the back. They'll go in at the front, through to the kitchen, and start talking to Marios. And that I need to hear, see?'

Angel nodded her understanding.

'So, honey, what I'd like you to do, if that's okay, is to make tracks back to the car as quick as you can, and I'll join you there when I've heard all I want to. Then we'll be ready to follow whoever looks most interesting.'

Angel nodded again, not risking further whispers, and glided quietly off towards the olive grove and the path back towards their car.

Josh looked after her with a half smile. He was surprised that she had done as he asked without questioning it. Still, it was obviously the best plan. And Angel wouldn't have wanted to make any noise by discussing it. Josh moved back to the open window.

He was in time to hear Marios welcoming the new arrival. Just the one man, it seemed. The voice was strange to Josh. Was this yet another member of the gang, one he hadn't yet come across?

'Timon, good to see you,' Marios was saying. The name rang a faint bell in Josh's memory.

'No time to waste, Marios,' Timon snapped. Josh didn't think he had heard the voice before, with its harsh, aggressive tone, full of anger and authority. 'You and Christos between you have made a complete mess of things. Okay, past history. The boss wants to see you as soon as possible to talk face to face. Clearly he couldn't come here. This place is known, now. Anyone might see him and be suspicious. So he says he'll be in the café at the top of Pantokrator in an hour from now. Get there, right?'

'But, Timon –' Marios wailed, 'I can't just drop everything here and walk out! The boss has been a businessman himself, he knows the importance of being on the spot when the workers are supposed to be working – otherwise they slacken off and nothing gets done.'

'You can leave Christos in charge, can't you?'

The argument continued. Marios was very reluctant to trust Christos. Josh's face grew grimmer and grimmer as the talk went on. At last Timon raised his voice and said, 'Enough! Do you want me to tell him that you don't feel like obeying his instructions?'

The next few sentences were harder to hear. Both men had moved away from the window and out of the kitchen, as Timon prepared to depart and Marios trailed after him, still arguing his case. But Josh had heard enough.

Before the men finally separated – and Josh was in no doubt that Marios would keep the appointment that had been made for him – Josh was sprinting back towards the olive grove, and was in between the trees. Then it was a matter of hurrying back along the track until he came out where the car was parked and saw that Angel, on the look-out for him, had swung open the car door.

Tumbling in beside her, Josh gasped out, 'Okay! This is where we head for the Pantokrator! Get going, sweetie!'

'Josh, I can get to the main road, but you need to tell me more before we get there quite soon, okay? Like which way to turn, left or right?'

As she spoke, Angel was putting the car in gear and turning towards the road.

'Turn right, honey. I'll have a quick look at the map and tell you when I'm clear myself.'

Angel turned right and drove along the now familiar coast road at the northern end of Corfu in the direction of Corfu town, while Josh frowned over the map.

'Okay, honey,' he said presently. 'I think our best bet is to turn off presently for Perithia. Pass Kassiopi and turn inland and you should see the sign. The map seems to be telling me that there are two possible ways up Pantokrator. The first by a new road from Perithia. The other by an older road. It seems to me to be more direct, but I'd rather not go for it. It might be dangerous, and we'd be pretty likely to get a flat tyre at some point. Too big a risk. We could do with getting there before either Marios or his boss, so's to get a good position for ourselves to hide and see what happens.'

'That sounds like the right idea, Josh,' Angel agreed. 'But now, are you going to tell me what you overheard? Something about Pantokrator, right? But sure apart from that, you realise I'm in the dark. So what did they say?'

'Sorry, honey. I was rushing so hard to get there first I nearly forgot I hadn't told you. Okay, Marios is to meet the boss in a café at the top of Mount Pantokrator, the highest mountain in Corfu, in an hour's time. It'll push him to do it, I should think, and it'll push us to get there first, especially as the boss may plan to be early. We'll need to make sure neither of them see us.'

'Fair enough, Josh.' Angel concentrated on her driving for a few moments. Then she said, 'Josh, darlin', I know you well enough by now to realise that you have something on your mind. Something you heard up at the house has upset you. Don't try to fool me – I know. So are you going to tell me what it was?'

'Angel, I probably should tell you. The trouble is, I'm not entirely sure if I heard it right. I need to think about it first. Do you mind, honey?'

Angel drove on in silence. Then she said, 'Josh, darlin', I've been trying for the last couple of days to make up my mind to trust you completely. It's hard for me. You know a lot about my first marriage. I've told you things that I've told nobody else. So you understand what I mean when I say how hard it is for me to trust again. But I'm nearly there, sweetheart.' She hesitated, and glanced round at him. 'Okay. But if I need to learn to trust you, then you need to trust me, too, don't you? So are you going to trust me to hear what you heard and try to work out what it means, just as you're doing yourself? Or not?'

'It's not a question of trust, honey. At least, that's not how I see it. I don't want to be unfair to the person I thought was being mentioned. I may have got it well wrong. But listen, Angel, if it matters so much to you, I'll tell you exactly what I thought I heard, and you can work it out for yourself, like you said, okay? After all, two minds are better than one, especially if they're brilliant ones like ours, baby.'

'Thanks, Josh.'

'It was Marios I heard first. He was saying, "He was pretty sharp with me on the phone last night about that young American cop." Then the other guy, Timon – I'm sure I've heard that name before – he said – ' Josh broke off abruptly. 'Look out, Angel, you should be turning inland here!'

Angel looked round. They had passed Kassiopi, and she had managed also to pass, without noticing it, a sign pointing to 'Mt. Pantokrator'.

'Wow! Sure, I'm a right eedjit!'

Braking quickly, she began to reverse, watching in the mirror to make sure she wasn't about to back into an approaching car. Suddenly they heard the noise of an engine roaring just behind them, out of sight round the last bend in the road.

'Look out!' Josh shouted.

Chapter Forty Two

Angel reacted instantly. There was only one thing to be done. She braked, changed gear, and began to move forward again as quickly as she could propel the car. It worked. She drew in as far as she could to the side of the road while moving swiftly forward. A few seconds later, a huge powerful car, a BMW she thought, went racing past her, skimming her side so closely that she almost felt its nudge. Then it was roaring on out of sight.

Angel slowed down, shuddering.

'Are you okay, honey?'

'Yeah.'

'Better not try backing on this road again. Drive into the next village and we'll find somewhere there to turn.'

'Yes, that's what I thought!' Angel retorted. She concentrated for a few minutes on driving on carefully along the twisting road.

'Josh,' she said presently, 'did you recognise the driver of that car?'

'Well, no, honey, I didn't really take time to look at him. Why?'

'It was Captain Doukas. The policeman who came to the Villa Callidora after the shooting at the pool. The one I met on the plane and who you saw in the airport, remember? He claimed to know you, but you didn't seem to like him too much. And what's more, the one I saw through the telescope, talking to your woman Rena and Jason Horowitz.'

'I know the man you mean. So he was in that car? That makes me think, honey.'

'Me, too.'

'Listen, baby,' Josh said presently, 'I've changed my mind about telling you what I heard just yet. For one thing, I'm not sure I picked it all up right. They were moving away from the window – it was hard to make it all out. For another, I reckon we need to concentrate on the road right now. We want to make sure we find the right way to Pantokrator. I really think we want to get there before anyone else, see?'

'Fair enough, Josh. To be honest, I'm still recovering from the shock of that near accident just now. I don't want to risk a repeat. Let's just drive and make sure we get there as soon as we can.'

They drove on in silence for ten minutes or so, passing through a small village and heading on down the coast road without seeing either an opportunity to turn or another sign. Suddenly Angel gave an exclamation.

'Look, Josh! Mt Pantokrator! On that signpost!'

The sign pointed upwards along a small, rough looking track which turned inland from the coast road as they had expected.

This time Angel made sure she didn't miss it. Twisting the wheel violently she left the main road and headed up onto the path on the right hand side, and kept going.

'But, honey!' Josh expostulated. 'Do you think this is really the way? It's certainly not the main road shown in my map!'

'No, we missed that miles back, remember, Josh?' Angel retorted. 'But if we don't want to lose time trying to find a place to turn back to that road, then this looks like a good option to me, okay?'

'Okay, honey. You win. We'll give it a go, then.' Josh spoke grimly. His car bucketed on along the rough track, much to his dismay. But there didn't seem to be any other choice for him, short of wrestling the wheel away from Angel, which he was certainly reluctant to do.

As they climbed steeply onwards, the track grew rougher. Every now and then there was a division in the track, but Angel plunged on, taking the turning which led higher. At last Josh ventured to speak.

'Are you sure this is taking us the right way, Angel? There haven't been any signs for quite a while, and we've made choices at least twice.'

'Sure, we have to keep making choices, Josh. But we can tell we're going upwards.' Suddenly she brightened. 'Hey, look! There're two guys with a map, checking that they're taking the right turning at this next division. Let's ask them if we're right for Pantokrator.'

The two people were dressed for hiking, in shorts to allow for the heat, but with rucksacks on their backs and long sticks to help with the climb. The boy held a map and the girl was peering over his shoulder as he held it spread out to see better.

'Hi, guys!'

Angel pulled the car up alongside them. 'We want to get up Pantokrator,' she said, smiling pleasantly. 'Are we on the right track?'

'Ja – Pantokrator.' Clearly the couple were German. Not unusual with tourists in Greece, Angel remembered. 'We go there. We walk for pleasure.' The boy spoke in a stilted, careful attempt at English.

Angel pointed at the road ahead. 'Up there? Pantokrator?'

'Ja, ja. For a delightful walk.' The girl was obviously quoting from something she'd read or seen on the Internet. 'Right way.'

'Danke, guys!' Angel said, smiling more brilliantly than ever. 'Auf Weidersen!'

Putting the car into gear, she released the clutch and took off in the direction of the pointing hands.

'Angel,' Josh said carefully, 'you realise those tourists told you this was a track for walkers?'

'Oh, I'm not stupid, Josh. I caught on to that okay. But it goes the way we want to go. As long as it's wide enough for the car – and so far it is – it's a bit of a short cut, isn't it? Let's go!' She pressed hard on the accelerator, and the car bounded forward. Josh groaned to himself, but said nothing. Clutching his head in his hands, he hoped for the best.

'Of course, what we really should have for this route is my moped. Pity it's still in being fixed!' Angel remarked cheerfully.

Josh realised that he had something to be thankful for. The journey in a safe, reliable car was bad enough. On one of those moped things it would be plain murder.

The car charged on round twisty bend after twisty bend on the rough rutted surface. Angel was pushing it along at the fastest speed she could make.

Suddenly Josh saw something in front of them.

'Angel!' he yelled.

It was the back of a hiker, in fact the backs of two hikers, plodding up the steep track with sticks in their hands and rucksacks on their backs.

Angel jammed on the brakes, and immediately the car started to slide back down the hill. There was nothing else for it. Jerking the gear stick into neutral, Angel tugged on the hand brake and a moment later found that the car had stalled. Getting it started again on that steep slope was going to be a nightmare.

The indignant faces of the two hikers glared at them through the windscreen. Angel jumped out.

'I'm so sorry!' she cried, turning on her most charming smile. 'We're obviously on the wrong road, but we were told this was the way to Mount Pantokrator!'

'It is,' said the man grimly. He and his companion were middle aged and clearly English, with accents which could be nothing else. 'But not for cars.'

'Oh, I know! I'm such an eedjit! But I couldn't see what else to do, once we'd come part of the way up and were starting to realise that it was wrong. We couldn't reverse down a hill like this, sure, could we?'

'She's right, Peter,' the woman hiker said. She was a sturdy, tweed clad figure, thin but strong looking, obviously very healthy. 'That would have been far more dangerous than going on. So what are you planning to do now? I'm Jessica Naylor-Jones, by the way, and this is my husband Peter. We're on a walking holiday in Corfu, following the Corfu trail. We always enjoy this climb up Pantokrator, but I must say this is the most exciting thing that's happened to us so far.'

Josh left the car and approached the couple. 'I'm Josh Smith and this is Angel Murphy,' he drawled. 'My, you guys are taking this really well. You've every right to be real mad at us!'

By now both the Naylor-Joneses were smiling. 'Never mind,' Peter said briskly. 'I think the best thing we can do is give you a push up this steep bit to get you started uphill again – then you can get to the top and make sure you go back by the main road!'

'Would you really?' Angel asked gratefully. 'Thanks so much! You're both darlins'!' And she gave both of them an impulsive hug which brought blushes to their weather beaten faces.

'Well, let's get going!' said Jessica. 'You can help too, young fellow, while your girl friend drives!'

Angel and Josh both felt that it wouldn't be appropriate to mention Josh's damaged arm and other recent injuries. 'Don't push too hard, darlin', I don't want you hurting your arm any more,' whispered Angel as she passed Josh on her way to get back into the car while the other three went to the rear.

Angel got back into the Audi and started the engine, engaging first gear and the other three began to push as the car moved upwards sluggishly. Eventually the track grew less steep and as the car began to accelerate Josh, abandoning the Naylor-Joneses, dived for the passenger side door and managed to scramble in without slowing the car's forward motion. With shouts of thanks and with hands waving goodbye, they shot forward out of sight round the nearest bend.

'Wow! Let's hope we don't run into any other hikers further up, Josh.'

'We didn't actually run into them – you got her stopped in time, honey.'

'You're so funny. And just as well – if I'd damaged them they'd never have been able to give us that push.'

Chapter Forty Three

Although the journey seemed to have been going on forever, a glance at her watch told Angel that they had left the coast road to follow the sign to Mount Pantokrator less than fifteen minutes ago. They might still be ahead of Marios. Well, it was possible.

'We'll need to be very careful when we get to the end of this track, Josh,' she said. 'We have to make sure neither Marios nor this boss he's meeting sees us.'

'It's not something we can plan for in advance, honey,' Josh said sensibly. 'It'll depend on what sort of cover there is, if any.'

Then, as they came round the last twist in the track, they saw that they were about to emerge onto a large, flat area, where a scattering of cars were parked.

'Whoa!' Josh said.

Angel spun the wheel and turned the car in among the trees at the end of the track. They were out of the way of any hikers coming up the path, but not quite out in the open. She parked carefully.

'This is where we get out of the car and explore, trying to keep out of sight, honey.'

'Lead the way, Josh darlin'. We're looking for a café where these guys are meeting up, didn't you say?'

'Yeah. And that looks like a possibility, right over there.'

At the edge of the open space, where the ground went down into a slight hollow, was a large, sturdy looking building with tables and chairs laid out on its wide veranda. No one else seemed to be about. Angel and Josh ventured hopefully towards it.

'Do you think we should risk going in?' Angel whispered.

'Probably be okay. But we shouldn't stay – just ask a few questions, right?'

They climbed onto the veranda and looked around the empty place. 'No one about. Maybe they're closed,' Angel said.

But they must have been heard, for just then a youngish man, slim and with hair receding slightly from his forehead, came bustling out from the back of the café where the kitchen must have been, and greeted them exuberantly.

'Hullo! Hullo! Great to see you! And what can we do for you? A meal? A coffee? Just give it a name, guys!'

He was obviously not Greek, and in fact he reminded Angel strongly of Jason Horowitz, so much so that she couldn't help asking, 'Are you any relation to my mate Jason Horowitz? You remind me of him so much!'

'Funny you should ask. Actually Jason and me are brothers. Small world, eh? As Bertie Wooster says, I've never known a smaller.'

Angel, a long time PG Wodehouse fan, laughed, while Josh looked faintly puzzled.

'This is great!' Angel said. Ignoring a tug from Josh, she asked, 'Do you know anything about a meeting set up here this afternoon? Just between two fellas – not a big get-together, I mean. Did anyone book? And is this the only café on top of Mt Pantokrator?'

'No one booked with me', replied Jason's brother promptly. 'I'm Terence, by the way. But, yeah, there are other cafes, but they're closed until the evening, when they get people driving out for a special meal with a view. Over there.' He pointed vaguely across the parking area, and added, 'Down below on that side is the old village of Perithia, a real tourist attraction. You should have a look.

There are two Perithias. The new village, on the main road leading up here – I expect you came through it on your way here? And the old village – very, very old, with mostly ruined houses and a few restored buildings, a B&B and a couple of tavernas. You'll enjoy looking round it, I'm sure – most tourists love it.

Then, if you come back here, I could have hot food ready for you – anything on the menu.' With a flourish, he produced two enormous red backed menus with tassels hanging from them and handed one each to Angel and Josh, who were rather taken aback.

'Um. Yes.' Josh said. 'We were thinking more of coffee, actually, if that's okay. And I think maybe we'll drift down and look at this old town first, and then come back for the coffee presently. Right, Angel?'

'Right. But thanks anyway, Terence.' She gave the café owner a bewitching smile which seemed to be enough to leave him happy, and followed Josh down off the veranda and along to the side of the flat area and down a sloping path.

'So, what do you think, honey? Suspicious, or what? A brother of Jason Horowitz, who we know is well mixed up in all this? Is that why the boss chose this place for his meeting with Marios? Or is this guy Terence actually the boss?'

'Agh, no, Josh, he was sweet!' Angel protested. 'And so is Jason, who I bet was telling us the truth about trying to track down the villains.'

They headed on down to the old town of Perithia.

There was a scattering of ruined buildings, and, as Terence had said, a few restored ones. There was the Merchant's House and the Butcher's Shop, both well worth seeing, reflecting the lifestyle of Corfu hundreds of years ago, and many ruins of houses where the inhabitants of this old village had once lived. The rough stone walls were covered with plants clinging to their surface, and wild flowers grew between the arches. Angel and Josh wandered round, enthralled.

'Isn't this amazing, Josh?' Angel breathed. 'I'm so glad we've seen it, aren't you?'

'Yeah. It's really something. But Angel, we need to be finding somewhere to hide where we can see who arrives.'

'Sure, that's right, Josh. But how do we know which café they plan to meet in? There are two more down here.'

'Yeah, but they're both shut, as Terence Horowitz told us.'

'Sure, so they are. Okay, so unless they plan to use one anyway even if it's shut, we can guess the meeting's in Terence's.'

'Yeah, and if we keep out of sight down here, we'll be able to see all the possibles, honey. When we know which one it is, it'll be time enough to get closer and see if we can hear what they say. Anyway, the main thing is to see who this boss guy is.'

'Sure, that's right. Well, how about staying down here, but hiding in the ruin nearest to Terence's café, where we can see without being seen?'

'Sounds good, honey.'

They wandered over to the ruined house nearest the edge of the village, trying to look casual, then climbed up to the centre of the ruined stone walls and found themselves places where they could see out, and would know when people arrived above them on the level of Terence Horowitz's café.

Angel found herself leaning against a stone wall where a beautiful, sweet smelling pink flower trailed its narrow stem down past her ear. She thought it might be a cyclamen but wasn't too sure. The little white flowers growing beside it were clearly daisies, and over on the other side of the wall she recognised white wild garlic flowers with their fascinating smell which always reminded her of an upmarket restaurant.

They didn't have to wait long.

The sound of a car engine alerted them, and then the noise of a car drawing up in the parking level not far above them.

Chapter Forty Four

Peering out carefully, Angel saw a man she didn't recognise getting out of the car. Josh whispered in her ear. 'It's Marios.'

'Okay, so one of them. Good. We're in the right place,' Angel murmured back.

Then it was a matter of waiting for the boss.

It didn't take long.

A powerful maroon car, a Mercedes as far as they could tell from that distance, drew up on the far side of the car park, and they saw a man climbing out of it. Josh recognised the man whom he had seen talking to Marios at the farm. This couldn't be the boss. Why hadn't he given Marios whatever message he had earlier? And where was this boss?

'We need to get closer, now, honey,' Josh whispered.

'Sure, we need to be able to hear what they say, darlin', so we do,' Angel agreed.

Moving silently, they made their way upwards, out of the ruined house, until they were within sight of Terence's café. Then, still on the lower level, they edged slowly closer to the two men sitting with cups of coffee at the front of the café.

'So, why didn't the boss come himself?' Marios said, as they drew gradually nearer. He was speaking Greek, to Angel's annoyance. Once again she was left out and could only pick up a few words, relying on Josh's explanation later.

'Why don't you ask him?' the other man replied sharply. 'No doubt he has his reasons. He changed his mind, that's all I know.'

'Okay.' Marios sounded disgruntled. 'So, why didn't you give me your message earlier?'

'I didn't want to risk Christos hearing. I don't trust him.'

'Okay, so what's this message?'

'It's this. There's been far too much disruption lately. We used to have a good team, all working together. But recently, instead, we've had nothing but trouble. A divided gang, half of them trying to take over – as if they could run it better than the boss! Well, Bakis got what he deserved, and before long the rest of them will, too, if they don't settle down. And that includes you, Marios, if you don't tow the line. You're not on their side, are you, Marios?'

'Me? No way! You know that, Timon, don't you?' Marios sounded nervous, unlike his usual competent self. 'And I don't understand why you don't trust Christos. He was the one who shot Bakis, after all.'

'Oh? I thought that was you?'

'No. But if you thought it was, why ask me if I'm on their side?'

'There are complications. Double crossing, right?'

'Oh.'

'What about Jason? Do you know where he stands?'

'You should ask Terence that one.'

'Do you really think he'd tell me? I don't think so!'

'Hush, he's coming over.'

Angel and Josh heard footsteps above their heads as Terence crossed the floor of his restaurant and approached the table where Marios and Timon were sitting.

'Everything all right, folks? Are you ready to order?'

Timon switched to English, to match Terence, much to Angel's relief. 'Forget about that, Horowitz! We need to ask you about your brother!'

'Jason?'

Terence Horowitz was obviously taken aback.

'Yeah, Jason. How many brothers have you got, here in Corfu? What do you know about him? Is he involved in this plot against the boss?'

'How would I know?' Terence gasped. 'I only do small jobs – pass messages, that sort of stuff. Jason asked me as a favour to help him out that way from time to time. I'm not involved in the big time, and I haven't a clue how it works for Jason.'

'Okay. Maybe not.' Timon sounded sour. 'So do you know where he is right now?'

'No idea.'

'And if you had, you wouldn't tell me, huh?'

'Listen, it's nothing to do with me! I don't want to get involved!' Terence's voice ended in a squeak, as Timon apparently grabbed him by the throat. Angel risked looking out carefully round the edge of a projecting piece of rock and saw that her suspicion was correct. Timon's big powerful hands were squeezing Terence's neck dangerously. After a moment, the grip slackened, and Timon allowed his victim to slump onto the nearest chair, while still holding him by one arm and shaking him.

'That was just a little warning, Horowitz! You're involved all right, stupid! So where is your brother?'

'Last I heard he was in Corfu Town!' Terence squeaked, 'I don't have an address for him!'

'Okay.' Timon released the café owner and stood back, dusting his hands as if to remove the dirt of contact with Terence Horowitz. 'Marios, time we headed off. I'll report to the boss and see what he wants to do next about this rebellion in the ranks.'

The two men headed off towards their cars, while Josh and Angel backed further out of sight, staying silent in their hiding place at the front of the café.

'We should follow Timon, if we can,' Josh murmured when they were out of earshot. 'I guess he'll lead us to the boss, if we can manage it.'

'Sure, it sounds like it,' Angel agreed. 'So let's get moving, okay?'

Cautiously they crept away from the café and headed back to where they had left Josh's car. Up above, Terence Horowitz was still too shaken up to notice them.

They sat in the car, ready to leave at a moment's notice, and saw Marios and Timon get into their separate cars and pull out of the car park in the same direction, towards what Angel guessed was the main road, the one Angel and Josh had by passed on their way up. A minute later, Josh, who was driving this time – Angel thought he was probably determined not to risk any more of her shortcuts – started the engine and followed them cautiously.

With no idea where the road led, they followed blind. Presently they found themselves passing through a small pretty village, which to Angel's surprise was signposted Perithia.

'Wow! This is a bit different! Are there two of them, then?'

'Yes. This is the modern Perithia, the one we should have headed for when we were coming, instead of taking that awful track to the old village,' Josh pointed out.

'Well, I still think it was quicker,' Angel said defiantly. 'After all, we got there before either Marios or Timon, didn't we?'

'Got to give you that, honey,' Josh acknowledged. 'The question was if we'd get there at all?'

Angel grinned at him, and said nothing. She knew, or hoped she knew, that Josh wasn't too serious.

They drove on, keeping well behind the other two cars, but making sure not to lose them. Presently, when they emerged onto the main road, the car driven by Marios took a left turn, heading back towards the olive grove where he ran the farm. Timon, however, went to the right, continuing on a different route in the direction of Corfu Town, and Josh followed him perseveringly. After a good few miles Timon slowed down and turned right off the main road and up into the hills. Josh drove on past the turning, then as soon as possible he pulled in to the side of the road, did a highly illegal U-turn and came back.

The car was almost out of sight round a bend in the narrow road. Josh put on a spurt and raced after it. He needed to make sure he didn't lose it. At the same time, he had to keep far enough back not to be seen by Timon. Tricky enough. However, Josh's police training and experience had taught him how to manage this sort of thing.

They were drawing near to a village. Josh pulled back. The narrow streets of a typical Greek village would make it impossible for him to keep out of sight of Timon when they got closer to the houses and tavernas of the main street.

He could still see the car in front. Then, to his relief, it pulled to a halt outside the main taverna.

Josh drew up just out of sight round the corner.

'Will you stay in the car, honey, ready to start up again in a hurry if we need to?' he asked Angel. 'I'll get out and see if I can get some idea of who Timon's meeting, even hear a bit of their talk, okay?'

'Sure I will, Josh,' Angel smiled. 'Off you go!'

Josh slipped out of the driving seat and Angel slid over to take his place. To tell the truth, she was looking forward to the chance to drive again. It wasn't in her nature to enjoy being a passenger.

She watched as Josh slipped quietly along the main street until he reached the taverna. Luckily Timon had gone inside, so no one was on the look out to see Josh.

However, this also meant that although she hoped that Josh, peering round the door, could see whom Timon was meeting – the boss? – she herself could see nothing.

As the minutes went on, Angel grew more and more impatient. What was happening? Josh had disappeared inside. He must have felt that he could find somewhere to sit or stand out of sight of Timon and his companion. Even, Angel hoped, to hear what was being said. She wished he would come back and tell her what was happening.

Then suddenly Timon came out again hurriedly, and sprang into his car. He drove further up the street and round the corner, where she could see that there was another door to the taverna. She could just about tell that someone else was sliding into the car.

Josh came hurrying out of the front door and waved to her. She could make out that he was mouthing, 'Start up!' Obediently she started the engine, expecting Josh to sprint up and get in.

Certainly Josh was sprinting. But far from getting in, he was slipping on the uneven cobbles of the street and Angel saw him fall and groan in pain. She began to get out of the car to go to his aid, but Josh was shouting. 'Go on, honey! Follow them! I'll be okay!'

'Right!' Angel shouted to him. She put the car into gear, released the clutch and started off down the village street in pursuit of Timon and his passenger.

Chapter Forty Five

It wasn't hard to catch up with the car in front. It wasn't really possible to move at any great speed through the narrow streets with the houses crowding in on each side. Angel's main problem was not to be seen, and that was almost impossible. She pulled back as far as she could and kept following Timon in his Mercedes.

It was still hard to see who the front seat passenger was. Angel couldn't help thinking he looked familiar. But perhaps she was just imagining that.

The Mercedes roared on, now that they had passed the narrow streets of the village. Angel, making sure she kept up with it, was very aware that the narrow, winding road with its steep sides over chasms dropping from the hills, was no place to drive so fast, but she wanted to be sure that she wouldn't lose Timon and his Mercedes, and above all, his boss – if that was who it was in the front seat beside him.

Using all her skill to keep Josh's car on the road, she whirled round bends, made sure she didn't go over the edge of the road and down into the deep ravine beside her, and kept up the necessary speed to prevent herself from losing the Mercedes.

Then they were out on the main road to Corfu town again – heading towards the town, not back up north. Angel pulled out into the stream of traffic, and found it easier there to keep not too far behind the Mercedes without being obvious.

It was getting late. She noticed the clock on the dashboard, and realised that a lot had already happened that day. Soon it would be getting dark, and not the gradual dusk that she was used to at home, but the sudden blanketing dark of Corfu. At least there were plenty of headlights to drive by, from the traffic along the main road.

Suddenly the tail lights ahead of her swerved to the right. The car was pulling off into a side road, rather than heading straight on to Corfu Town as Angel had been half expecting. She pulled up, turned right in her turn, and dived into the side road after Timon and his passenger.

It was another of the narrow, steep, twisting roads she was getting used to in Corfu. Angel refrained from looking too often over the edge and concentrated on keeping to the road. As she had expected, darkness had swooped down on her, and here, off the main road, there was nothing but her own headlights and the lights of the car in front to show her where to drive. Angel became aware that Timon, by now, must have realised that she was following him. In the traffic of the main road, he might not have thought of it, but now, with no other cars around, it would be fairly obvious.

Well, she could only keep going and see. If he was planning anything, any attack on her or simply a trick to let him escape her, she would know all about it soon enough.

Carefully, keeping most of her attention to the road, Angel reached over and felt around with her left hand in the glove compartment of the car. Her hand felt something cold and hard. Josh's gun, she hoped. Stretching further enough to get a firm grip on the object, she pulled it out unto her lap. Yes, it was Josh's gun. Angel breathed a sigh of relief. At least if Timon tried anything she wouldn't be completely defenceless. She slipped the gun into her shoulder bag.

Just as she was sighing with relief, the car in front braked suddenly. It was as much as Angel could do to stop in time before crashing into him.

'Lunatic!' she shouted, as she trod on the brakes. Before she could get herself together any more, she was aware of someone racing towards her, and a second later the car door beside her was jerked open, so that she almost fell into the road. A hand grabbing her shoulder helped her the rest of the way.

The gravel was hard against her face. Sticking out one hand, she tried to protect herself from its impact. She instinctively retained her clutch on the shoulder bag which swung from her left arm, where the all important gun nestled. Then she was jerked to her feet and out of the corner of her eye she saw a silver coloured metal object darting towards her right arm. She had just time to recognise that it was being propelled towards her by the hand of the man called Timon. Then there was the cold sharp impact of the needle thrusting into her shoulder, and Angel felt herself losing control, as everything swam around her in a bright firework display, and then went black.

'Quick!' she heard a strangely familiar voice say just before she went under. 'Get her into the car before anyone else comes this way!'

She was aware of hands half dragging, half lifting her away from Josh's car and into the Mercedes. She was pushed into the back seat. Then she collapsed completely and knew nothing else.

Chapter Forty Six

Josh watched ruefully as his car, driven by Angel, speeded away from him in pursuit of Timon.

It had been the only possible decision, to let Angel go on. They had a chance here to find out who the mystery boss was. He supposed Angel was heading into possible danger, but he knew she would cope with whatever came up. He wasn't worried, any more than he would have been worried if she had been his partner at work. But he was pretty sickened at being left behind.

Would it be possible to hire another car and follow in his turn?

It was worth a try – although by the time he managed it, he would probably be too far behind to catch up. There was a garage just down the street from the taverna where Timon and his companion had met. Josh hurried over to it.

No cars. But the owner had a moped which he sometimes hired out, if Josh was interested?

'Yeah,' Josh said. 'Great!'

He paid the deposit and jumped onto the moped. Then he was away, driving at top speed, hoping to catch a glimpse of his car before it had gone out of sight.

Since both cars had of necessity driven fairly slowly through the village, he did, in fact, manage to get a fleeting view of his Audi as Angel increased speed on the open road past the houses. He in turn tried to move more quickly, but the moped was already going as fast as it could. Josh sighed in frustration, and pushed on, hoping that one way or another he could keep on their track.

He knew the island well enough to tell that the cars in front were heading for the main road to Corfu town, and wondered if it might be a good idea to take one of the many shortcuts that he was familiar with. But then, if the Mercedes turned off somewhere, he would have lost them for good. No, better just continue to plod after them and hope for a miracle.

It was at that moment that the rough road proved his undoing, and his front tyre burst with a loud noise. Josh managed not to turn the moped over, and himself with it. He pulled in to the side of the road and regarded his vehicle in annoyance.

'What am I going to do now?' he wondered.

A sudden blast from a horn as a car pulled up behind him, unable to get past, made Josh realise that he was taking up too much of the road. He looked round. The driver stuck his face out of the window, and Josh exclaimed aloud.

'Doukas! What are you doing here?'

It was the cop they had bumped into several times, and most recently had seen driving along the main Corfu Road as they looked for the sign for Mt Pantocrater.

'My job!' replied Captain Doukas tartly. 'Catching this gang of jewel thieves, remember? And in particular, catching the people who shot you and Mrs McPherson.'

'Well, you've come to the right place,' Josh began. Then he hesitated. He'd had his doubts about trusting this man in the past. But, nevertheless, there was no real reason not to trust him. And if he was on the right side, then he'd turned up just in the nick of time. Josh decided that no harm could come of telling Doukas some of what he and Angel had found out so far. But only some.

'Hey, look,' he said, 'I'll tell you all about it as we go along, but right now I need a lift. I'm trying to follow two guys who are mixed up in the robberies and shootings. Let's go!' He pushed the moped further off the road and scrambled into the car, and Captain Doukas released his hand brake and roared off down the road.

'All right, Smith,' he said, 'tell me your story.'

Josh picked his words carefully. He was reluctant to tell Doukas too much, but clearly he had to tell him something – he couldn't simply demand a lift and give no reason.

'Okay,' he began, 'Last night Angel and I saw a man being shot, and we followed the guy doing the shooting to an olive grove nearby. We had to run for it, in the end, and just about got away. This was just off the main road to Corfu Town, not far from where we're staying. So this afternoon we thought we'd try to go back to the farm, listen in and see if we could find out who he was working for. We heard him arrange to meet someone and we followed him, ending up in that village back a few miles. I went in to the taverna where the guys were sitting talking, to try to overhear more, and that meant that Angel had to follow them on her own when they came out – if she'd waited for me we'd have lost them. So I hired that moped and it let me down. They aren't too far ahead. Making for the main road, I guess. The guys are in a Mercedes, and Angel's driving my Audi.'

He was aware that he'd left out a lot of important stuff, but thought he'd made a smooth enough story of it.

Doukas shot him a sharp glance. He was still driving fast, and Josh had hopes of catching up with Angel, at least, before long.

'Okay, Smith. I'll concentrate on catching up with them. Then, I'm going to expect you to tell me a lot more, because I know you've kept so many things from me.'

Josh grinned. 'Doukas, we'll see about that when you catch them, okay?'

The car roared on through the late evening.

At the main road, the darkness came down with a rush. They were about five minutes behind Angel, if they'd known it. There was nothing to do but continue along the road. If they didn't see Angel in front of them, they were lost. It wouldn't be possible to do anything except keep going on the main road, and hope that the two cars they were following hadn't turned off.

'Hey!' exclaimed Josh a few minutes later, 'what's that I see ahead?'

It was the taillights of the Audi, his car which Angel was driving, he was pretty sure. It gleamed in the lights along the main road, easy for Josh to recognise. And it was turning off to a side road on the right.

'Quick!' Josh shouted. 'That's them! Turn off after them!'

Doukas braked abruptly. Too abruptly, as it turned out. A second later, the car was skidding across the road. Doukas pulled desperately to a stop. He was just in time to prevent the car from crashing into the edge of the road.

Chapter Forty Seven

Angel stayed unconscious for some time. When she came to herself again it was hard to know where she was or what was happening. She lay still for a while, listening.

The familiar voice said, 'Can't you put on a bit of speed, Timon?'

'Doing my best,' grumbled Timon.

Angel, still not fully aware, wondered if it would be wise to open her eyes yet, or if she should stay as she was and let them go on talking, not knowing that she was listening and able to take in what they said. Better keep still, probably.

'We have to get rid of her,' said the first voice. 'She knows who I am – I can't have her telling the cops.'

'I don't think she actually knows yet, boss,' Timon said. 'She hasn't seen you with me. It's the other one you need to worry about. I saw him when we were in the taverna talking, like I told you. He's the one who's seen us together. He's the one we need to get rid of.'

'No.' The first voice sharpened. 'I've already told you. I won't have it.'

'Just because he's a cop?' Timon sneered.

'Mind your own business. I make the decisions round here, remember.'

'Okay, boss, if you say so.'

Angel lay wondering what was going on. The other one must be Josh, she supposed. Why was this voice so familiar?

She knew she had heard it before – but it hadn't sounded nearly so harsh, had it? Could it be Gregor Doukas? Or even Jason Horowitz?

'How about this next bend, boss?' Timon asked presently. 'There's a good, sharp edge. If we put her over that she'll be finished. And it could so easily be an accident.'

'Yes, maybe. We should have brought the car with us, Timon. We need it to stage a proper accident. We'll have to go back and get it – you can drive it here, while I drive this car.'

'That's going to take ages,' Timon objected. 'We should have brought it at the time.'

'True. But it's not too late. Turn round and we'll go back.'

So. They were going to put her over the steep edge of the road. Angel shuddered in horror at the thought. No way was she going to lie still and allow that to happen. At the first opportunity, she would be out of the car and running. The darkness would help her. No matter what happened, it had to be better than passively letting them get away with it.

She lay still, listening. Timon was trying to turn the car. It wasn't easy, on the narrow, steep road. He grunted as he manoeuvred about, going backwards and forward. A seven point turn so far, Angel reckoned, laughing to herself. Serve him right!

Eventually, he had the Mercedes turned round and was starting to drive back along the way they had come.

Angel thought about it. It would be bad to let him get right back to the car. The accident would be so easy to stage then. She really needed to take action in some way long before he got there. She looked round her intently. Was there anything she could use? She suddenly realised that her shoulder bag was still hanging from one arm, resting on the floor so that she hadn't been aware of the weight. Was Josh's gun still there? If it was…!

Angel reached down carefully to draw up the bag silently, without attracting the attention of the two men in the front seat.

Got it.

Feeling inside it, she drew out the gun. Now what?

She sat up and leant forward, the gun in her hand. Poking it into Timon's neck, she said, 'Brake now, if you don't want me to shoot you, Timon!'

She felt the man's convulsive start, and went on talking. 'I mean what I say! I'm not going to wait. Brake, or I shoot, okay?'

Her hand was already on the door handle to her left.

'All right, all right! I'm braking! Don't shoot!'

The car jerked violently and a moment later it had stopped. Angel pulled on the handle, swung open the door, and a moment later was out and running.

She headed back the way they had just come, back away from where they had abandoned Josh's car. She had no intention of making things easier for them – she didn't want to go towards the car and help them to stage their accident. She had no idea where she was heading, but away was better than towards any direction that they wanted to go in.

At first she ran along the middle of the road, then it occurred to her that if they thought of turning the car again – and that would be the obvious thing to do, surely – they could very easily catch up with her no matter how fast she ran. The sensible thing to do would be to branch off the road up into the hill country.

Angel crossed to the other side of the road, climbed over the verge and headed upwards.

It was rough going, but at least she knew it was taking her away from Timon and his boss, whoever he was. She still didn't know, although vague suspicions were beginning to form in her mind. Doukas? Jason? Someone else? Someone whose voice was to some extent familiar. No time now to work it out. No time to do anything but climb and run.

The hill was covered in rough, spindly shrubs and grasses with a scattering of rocks, large and small. No doubt in daylight there would be wild flowers in all the colours of the rainbow as well, and the whole sight would be delightful to someone driving past. But to Angel, trying to make her way upwards as quickly as possible, it was far from delightful. Rather, it was nightmarish. Her feet continually slipped, and she dreaded that she would go over on one or other of her ankles and fall, helpless and incapacitated.

But so far, she was managing to keep going.

She kept her ears open for the sound of the approaching car, or the sound of someone crashing after her through the undergrowth.

So far, nothing.

Then, suddenly, the noise of an engine below her, going past and dying away.

Angel breathed a sigh of relief.

Then, just as she did so, she heard the sound she had been dreading. Someone coming up the hill behind her, crashing through the bushes. Coming ever nearer.

Chapter Forty Eight

If she went on running, her pursuer would hear her and be all the more easily able to track her down. Angel froze. It was important to make no noise.

But then, if she stayed still directly in the enemy's track, he would find her without any problem.

Angel decided on her course of action.

As quietly as possible, she wriggled off to one side, hoping that her movements would be drowned out by the sounds the pursuer himself – Timon? – was making. She kept going, her arms and feet working to move the bushes out of her way without noise. It wasn't easy, but she was prepared to put whatever effort was needed into it, so as to get out of the direct path of the enemy.

As she wriggled her way across the route she had been taking, suddenly the ground underneath her disappeared, and she found herself falling, falling, into a pit which had no rhyme nor reason to it, which simple let her down into the depths with nothing to support her. Down, down, down, she thought, like Alice in Wonderland. Then she landed unhurt on a soft bed of leaves, not too far down after all.

Angel breathed in and realised that she was safe, that now her pursuer probably couldn't catch her, since he wouldn't know where she was.

It was important that he shouldn't discover her. Angel lay still, breathless. She listened hard.

Timon, if that was who it was, crashed up close to her on the far side. He hadn't noticed the pit into which she had fallen. He was panting, out of breath.

'Boss?'

He had taken out his mobile phone, Angel realised.

'Boss? It's me. I can't find any sign of her. Come back. If you haven't seen her on the road yet, she must be somewhere up the hill. But it needs two of us, at least, to find her. I'm not getting anywhere on my own.'

There was a muttering which Angel couldn't make out.

'Okay, boss. I'll go down to the road and wait for you – then we'll try to find her up here, between us, okay?'

Then the crashing sound of Timon heading back down the hill.

Time to make some decisions, Angel realised.

There was no sense in keeping on heading up into the hills. She had no idea where she would come out, and at any moment she might trip on the rough, rocky hillside and damage an ankle or worse. Then she would really be in trouble.

She needed to get back to the road and if possible make her way to Josh's car – which wasn't too far away – and drive off in it – going in whichever direction took her further from the two men. She ought to hear the other car approaching in a few minutes. She'd let them get together and then begin to search for her. Then she'd have to bypass them very carefully and run back along the road.

If she had time to disable the other car, that would be even better.

Presently she heard the engine noises she was waiting for. The boss was back.

Then she heard voices, carrying clearly in the open air of the Corfu hillside. The men were agreeing to make their way up the hill together, and only to split up when it seemed necessary. It might be too dark, even with the use of torches, for them to see her tracks with any ease, they thought. Two of them looking would be better than one.

Angel hoped they were right. She knew that to begin with she had crashed wildly through the shrubs and growth. She must have left some obvious tracks. She moved quietly away to the left, trying to avoid the direction in which the searchers were approaching.

At first she moved in as straight a line as she could manage along the side of the hill. Then, presently, as she heard sounds of the men over to one side, near to where she had been a short time before, she took up a diagonal direction, moving away from them but at the same time downhill.

The main problem was to keep quiet enough to remain unheard.

Angel picked her way fairly silently down towards the road. There was one moment when she felt sure she was stumbling and tripping, but she gathered herself up safely and moved on as quickly as she could. She felt extremely thankful that she was wearing her trainers.

Just below her she could see Timon's car drawn in to the side of the road for safety, the lights flashing a warning for other cars.

For a moment Angel was tempted to steal this car instead of going back to Josh's Audi. Then she thought better of it. Instead, she lifted the bonnet and disconnected the distributor cap, making the car impossible to drive.

Then, head down to watch the road in the feeble moonlight, she ran hard, back along the road. She could feel the gravel under her feet. It wasn't the easiest of going. But it was a great improvement on the steep rough hillside with its rocks and harsh undergrowth. And it was much easier to stay reasonably silent.

The car couldn't be too far away. Angel began to raise her head to look out for it.

Suddenly she noticed a beam of light along the round ahead of her. Was it a light from the car, or from another car? Anyone willing to help her would be good.

But a moment later she realised that the light came from a strong torch shining along the road from behind her. Horror stricken, Angel knew what the light shining over her shoulders was. It was her two pursuers coming along behind her at top speed. The car was out of action, but they could run as well as she could do.

Angel tried to put on speed, and wrenched at her pocket to pull out Josh's gun.

Spinning round to face the men, she shouted, ' Stop! Or I'll fire!'

The answer was the crack of a bullet whizzing past her left ear.

Angel fired back, then dived off the edge of the road on the uphill side, to take shelter behind a huge rock she had spotted. There was nothing for it but to keep firing.

Chapter Forty Nine

It took Doukas some time to get the car back on the road, and to be sure that there was no serious damage. The front left wheel needed to be changed. With Josh and Doukas working together, that didn't take as long as it might have done.

'Okay,' said Josh eventually. 'Let's get moving.'

Doukas said nothing. He got back into the driving seat and started up the car, hardly waiting for Josh to scramble in to the passenger seat, then he backed carefully into position and turned off into the side road where about five minutes previously they had seen Josh's car, driven by Angel, heading after, they supposed, the Mercedes driven by Timon and containing his boss – the one man above all others that Captain Doukas wanted to see.

'I've told you about stuff we've found out,' Josh said presently. 'Suppose you tell me a bit about your own discoveries? For instance, we've seen you chatting with this guy Jason Horowitz. Angel thinks he's on the level – he told her he was working undercover – but I have my strong suspicions of him. Is he working undercover, like he claims. Or is he just one of the crooks?'

'Horowitz is working with me,' Doukas said. 'He's been going undercover with the gang. He's done a lot of good work so far. I can't think why you should have distrusted him, when it seems he told your friend Angel what he was up to – not that he should have done.'

'Okay. I've got a suspicious nature. Comes of being a cop.'

'Horowitz got in well with one of the gang members in particular, a woman, and got a lot of info from her. It helped us to track down some of the lesser members. We arrested three of them recently. Quite a coup. But there are a few more senior members. So far we haven't identified them. This woman, Rena, either didn't know who they were or hasn't been willing to give them away to Jason.'

'Okay.'

The car continued to roar on along the road. Josh wondered if Doukas would be able to keep going at his present speed on such a dangerous road without an accident. Then he saw something out of the front window.

'Stop!' he shouted.

But Doukas has seen it too, and was pulling to a halt.

The Audi was just in front of them, pulled in to one side of the road. Josh had leapt out almost before Doukas had stopped his car.

Josh wasn't sure what to expect. Angel lying, bleeding or unconscious, half in and half out of the car? But there was no sign of her, or of blood on the road, nothing to show that anything had happened to her.

Josh took a deep breath. He looked around him. Where had Angel gone? Had she been kidnapped? Or had the car broken down on her, forcing her to leave it and escape on foot?

'Let's drive on,' Doukas said. 'If she's somewhere on the road we'll catch up with her.'

'Okay,' said Josh. He was finding it hard to speak. He had sent Angel off on her own after people he knew were villains. He regretted it bitterly now. But he knew, at the same time, that it had been what Angel would have wanted and expected from him – trust that she could deal with the situation, and the enemy, herself.

Doukas pulled out round the Audi and stepped on the accelerator. He was driving at a dangerous speed for this mountain road. Especially now that they were coming to some sheer edges where the road twisted and turned with steep hills on one side and a drop on the other which Josh didn't like to contemplate.

They were winding up into the higher hills of Corfu. Not Pantocrator, but the hills to the west of it which spanned the island. Josh, who knew Corfu like the back of his hand, realised that if they kept on driving they would come down to the other side of the island with its beautiful beaches and the much visited monastery of Paleokastritsa. He had planned to take Angel there if the holiday had developed normally.

'I think you should tell me anything else you know, Doukas,' he said abruptly. 'It might help us to track these guys down. And if they have Angel –' He left the sentence unfinished.

Doukas was silent for a few minutes. Then he said. 'I understand. I, too, as I think you know, care about this Angel Murphy. If anything happens to her – well, if would be an extreme motivation for me to destroy this villain I've been chasing.'

Josh swallowed hard. He believed Doukas. But he knew, at the same time, that the concern Doukas had for Angel was nothing like his own.

'So, tell me anything you can,' he said harshly.

'Okay. I've answered your questions about Horowitz. I've told you that his undercover activities haven't produced much except small fry. But you must remember that Horowitz is not the only string to my bow. Don't you admire my expertise in English idiom, by the way?'

Josh ground his teeth and said nothing.

Doukas went on. 'I, myself, have been investigating the robberies since last March when they began. Various clues have led me to a number of possible men who might be 'the boss', as they seem to call him. I've been looking for a man who knows the well off people on the island, those who have jewels and who keep them in their homes. I had a list of half a dozen or so possibles.

'Some of those I've ruled out – one has been in America since April. This 'boss' seems to operate on the spot. There have been phone calls and meetings which we've heard of, but too late to be there. Another died two months ago, but the robberies have gone on, and the boss's presence has still been evident. And so on. I've whittled it down to three possibilities. I've a feeling, Smith, that some of what you know would allow me to arrive finally at his identity.' Doukas took his eyes off the road for a split second to look sharply at Josh, but immediately looked away again.

Josh's emotions pulled him two ways. It was true that he had had his suspicions. And that now, since Timon's meeting in the taverna with his boss, he was sure.

'Yeah,' he said in the end. 'I've been reluctant to say this –'

He broke off.

'Listen!' cried Captain Doukas. 'Wasn't that a shot?'

Even as he spoke more shots rang out.

It seemed as if they were coming from just round the next twist in the road.

Chapter Fifty

'Okay,' Josh jerked out. 'Let's get on.'

The car moved forward. Doukas stopped it just short of the bend in the road. He and Josh jumped out and made their way towards the corner. Josh had his gun in one hand. He saw out of the corner of his eye that Doukas had also drawn his.

They stopped and peered round the rocks and bushes at the verge of the road. Angel was crouching behind a huge boulder on the side of the road away from the steep edge. As they watched, more shots came from not far up the road.

'Okay,' said Josh. 'I'll go up the hill and come out behind these guys who are firing, if you'll keep an eye on what's happening here. Shoot as much as you like, as long as you don't hit me!'

He vanished up the hillside, bending low to keep out of sight.

Doukas made his way quietly and carefully over to Angel. As she heard him coming, she glanced round, gun in hand, but relaxed when she recognised him.

'I heard the car come up and then stop,' she whispered. 'I hoped it was Josh – but you'll certainly do, Captain.'

'Do you know who's shooting at you, Angel?'

'One of them is called Timon – he's part of the gang who've been doing these jewel robberies. Don't know who the other one is.'

'The boss,' Doukas said grimly. 'I've a pretty good idea who it is, but no proof. If I could just catch him now!'

'You could at least arrest him for abducting me and shooting at me,' Angel said helpfully. 'That wouldn't be a bad start, would it?'

As they exchanged thoughts, the bullets continued to whiz around them, and Doukas joined Angel in firing back. Presently he said, 'I should warn you that your friend Josh Smith was with me. He's currently trying to take these guys from the rear – so maybe you'd like to be a bit careful where you aim your shots.'

'Well, thanks for telling me!' Angel said indignantly. 'It's good to know that I might have been shooting at him!'

'I credit him with enough sense not to get in the line of fire,' Doukas said drily. 'Maybe you don't?'

Angel laughed reluctantly. 'Well, if you put it like that.'

'How are you off for ammunition, Angel?'

'That's a good question, Gregor. I'm afraid the answer is not too well. And since this isn't my gun, I don't have any back up. I've been trying to go easy with it – the occasional shot just to keep them uneasy. But I can't have many bullets left by now.'

As she spoke, she aimed the gun and fired again. Or tried to. Instead, there was a click. No bullets left.

'Okay, Doukas, there's your answer. You don't have any to spare, yourself, I suppose?' Angel asked coolly.

'Smith may have some back in the car, if you like to go and see. I'll keep them occupied here, okay?'

'Worth a try. Sure, he might have taken them all himself, but who knows?' Shrugging lightly, Angel backed away from the shelter of the rock on her hands and knees. Presently, when she was far enough away, she stood up and ran towards the car.

The night was still dark. Angel had a good sense of direction, but almost at once she realised that she needed to slow down and take it easy. She was looming dangerously close to the edge of the road with its fearsome drop. She slowed to a fast walk, and presently was able to identify the car, parked by the roadside, very near the edge. Its black silhouette reared up against the infinitesimally lighter night sky.

Moving carefully, avoiding the many stones which were scattered along the road and the ruts at the edges, she approached the car, wondering if she was wasting her time.

She wasn't particularly hopeful of finding ammunition that fitted the gun, a 9 mm calibre, which she remembered Josh usually carried. But it was worth trying. Better than throwing stones instead.

She opened the car door, leaned inside, and began to rummage in the glove compartment where she had found the spare gun. No spare bullets of any type. Josh, sensibly, must have taken all he had with him.

Half inside the car, leaning forward, she thought she heard a faint sound behind her. Someone coming up? Josh? She really hoped so.

'Josh?' she asked, beginning to squirm back out of the car.

'Alas, no, little lady,' said a familiar voice. 'I'm afraid your friend Josh is elsewhere. Will I do instead?'

Angel froze. She knew that voice. It belonged to the man Timon. Timon, who should have been crouched, with his unknown boss, behind the rocks further back, where she had been firing.

It seemed that, like Josh, he had had the idea of creeping round to take her by surprise from the back, while his boss kept up the firing.

Now what? With only her wits and an empty gun, Angel thought fast. What should she do?

Timon's gun was in his hand, pointing at her, and Angel was sure that it would be far from empty.

'What do you expect to achieve by this, Timon?' she asked coolly.

'That's for the boss to say,' Timon answered. 'We're going back to him now. You can ask him whatever questions you like. Come on, start moving.'

He pulled Angel round in front of him, and began to march her back along the road. Then suddenly he froze as he heard the snap of Doukas's gun, still some distance away from them, firing carefully spaced bullets from the boulder behind which Angel had been until very recently.

Timon halted and made an angry, frustrated sound.

Hearing him, Angel realised that he hadn't known she had company until now.

Was this something she could work to her advantage?

Chapter Fifty One

When he left Doukas, Josh climbed as far as he could up the hillside before beginning to circle round behind the enemy. He needed to go quickly and quietly. Easier said than done.

The hillside was rocky, covered in grass and wild flowers which looked grey in the darkness. There were some small bushes and shrubs which tended to trip Josh up however carefully he placed his feet. The rocks were a major problem. Josh found himself banging into them time after time.

Presently he was aware of tall shapes around him and realised that he was in the middle of a clump of olive trees. The low branches brushed his face and he had to put up one hand to shield his eyes. Moving from tree to tree, leaning against their trunks, he made his way to the other side and out onto the bare hillside again.

A stream trickled down in front of him, heading for the road, and Josh found that he had stepped into it before he realised it was there. Grunting, he scrambled on across it and paused to take off his shoes and the wet socks, and to wring out as much as possible of the water. Putting the socks back on wasn't the most pleasant experience, but he grinned wryly to himself. It had to be better than walking barefoot among the rocks and thistles. He moved quietly on. He must be past the man with the gun by now. Time he was going downhill.

Uphill hadn't been easy in the darkness. Going across had been better. But going down proved to be a lot harder still.

Every few steps Josh felt his feet starting to slide from under him. The damp on his shoes didn't help. Instead, it made the grass seem slippery underfoot, and added to the difficulty of making progress except at a snail's pace.

Josh paused for a few seconds to listen. He had been aware for some time that the sound of shooting had become far less frequent. Both sides were saving their bullets, he realised.

Timon thrust Angel in front of him as they moved a little closer to the boulder where Captain Doukas was crouching.

'Speak to him,' he hissed in her ear. 'But if you warn him, I'll simply shoot you both.'

Angel thought quickly. 'I don't know him,' she protested in a low voice. 'He doesn't know I'm here. He won't recognise my voice. You seem to think we're together. We're not.'

Timon halted, still holding Angel's arm and with his pistol thrust against her back. It was clear that he was momentarily at a loss. 'Perhaps I'd better just shoot him now, in that case,' he said after a few seconds.

'No!' Angel snapped. 'Can't you see that he's a cop? You'll be in serious trouble!'

'Ah, but if there are no witnesses to say it was me?'

'So, you mean to shoot me too?'

Timon paused again. 'I'm supposed not to, if I can help it. The plan is to make it look like a car accident, with no bullets involved. But maybe I'll have to.'

'Why shoot him at all? He'll be running out of ammo any minute now. Hear how slowly he's pacing his shots? If he had plenty of ammo, he'd just fire away. I see your boss man is doing the same, by the way. He must be running short,

268

too.' As she spoke, Angel was moving her feet, placing them carefully to give herself a better balance.

'This is nonsense!' Timon snapped out suddenly. 'You're trying to distract me. I'm going to shoot him now – and then either we'll shoot you or maybe you can be persuaded not to tell, who knows?'

He moved his gun from Angel's back and aimed at Doukas instead. This was what Angel had been waiting for.

Moving at the speed of light she twisted one foot round Timon's ankle and tripped him backwards. Recovering her balance instantly, she seized the gun with her right hand as he fell, and hit the wrist of the hand which still held it with the edge of her other hand. Timon let go as his hands went backwards in a vain attempt to break his fall. Angel covered him with his own gun, at the same time shouting for Doukas.

Doukas sprang up and came over to them. 'What's this?' he asked.

'His name's Timon, and I think he's the right hand man of the boss of the jewel thieves' gang,' Angel explained coolly.

'Not much of a right hand at the moment,' Doukas commented. Timon, flat on his back, was nursing his painful right wrist with his left hand, trying to rub some feeling back into it and only succeeding in giving himself more pain.

'So, he was planning to take me to his boss. I suppose he'd have called out to let him know not to shoot. But when he saw you, that complicated matters. He reckoned he had to shoot you first.'

'Perhaps we could persuade him to stick to his original plan?' Doukas suggested softly. 'But we could both go with him, instead of just you. He can walk in front, in case the boss doesn't hear him at first and there are still a few spare bullets flying. Do you hear me, Timon?'

'We have both the guns now, Timon,' Angel reminded the man sweetly. 'You haven't a hope, boyo!'

Timon staggered to his feet, muttering something in Greek which Angel couldn't understand – she thought probably it was just as well.

It wasn't clear yet if he would call out to his boss to stop him shooting. But in any case, they were on their way. It was as they began to come nearer to the rock where Timon's boss was hiding that the shooting stopped.

'Any ideas why your boss isn't firing, Timon?' Doukas asked, prodding the man with the barrel of his gun.

'He may have no more ammunition,' Timon offered sulkily. 'Or maybe he feels like a rest. He knows I went round behind you and he can hear that you've stopped firing. He's probably waiting to hear from me.'

'Any of those reasons will do,' Doukas said cheerfully. 'Okay, get moving!'

He prodded Timon again, and they continued to make their way along the edge of the road.

Josh came on down the hill as rapidly as he could. As he approached, he realised that the shooting had stopped. Not knowing why, he could only guess. Lack of ammunition or some other reason.

He could see a dark figure now, crouching behind a huge rock at the edge of the road, the twin of the one where Angel had hidden. Dark as it was, he knew he recognised the back. He knew who it was. He hadn't had any real doubt for some time. And the meeting in the taverna with Timon had confirmed his guesses.

Josh drew his breath in and stood still. 'Hi,' he said.

The figure whirled round and stood up.

'Well, Hamish,' Josh said. 'Quite a surprise. Maybe you'd like to explain to me what you're doing here?'

Hamish McPherson stared at him. For a moment he was unable to say anything.

Chapter Fifty Two

'Of course, I've had a good idea for some time that it was you who were masterminding the jewel robberies, Hamish,' Josh said. 'But I'm afraid I kept hoping I was wrong. Tell me, I'd really like to know, is Marge in on this?'

'Marge? Certainly not!' Hamish's voice flared out in indignation. 'I thought you knew her better than to think such a thing of her for a moment, young Josh!'

'I did think that. I thought I knew her well enough to be sure she wasn't in on it,' Josh said. 'But then, I thought I knew that you couldn't possibly be involved either. I was wrong there, wasn't I?'

Hamish said nothing.

'Why, Hamish?' Josh had remained silent, too, but then he felt compelled to speak again. 'Why did you get into some-thing like this? I should have thought that you were the last person.'

'Why, laddie? I'll tell you why. Money, that's why, money. I'd have thought you could have guessed that too. I worked hard all my life, Josh laddie, but when it came near to retiring time, what had I got to offer Marge? Nothing. The business had been going down the drain for long enough, and it wasn't picking up. What were we going to do for our last twenty or so years, except scrape and save and go short? Marge deserves more than that.'

'She deserves an honest husband, Hamish, and I know well that that was all she wanted.'

'You know nothing about it, laddie. What would your Angel girl think of you, if all you had to offer her after a lifetime of work was nothing? If all your efforts had gone for nothing at all, and you were as near to being a beggar on the streets as you could be?'

'She's not my Angel yet, Hamish – I thought I explained that to you. I hope she will be, before too long. And if she ever is, she won't mind if I have nothing to offer her in the end, except my honesty. That's what she thinks matters, and it's what I think matters, too.'

'Easy to say when you're not broke, like me a few years ago. I started up the gang during my last years in the States – it happened that I ran into an old friend who knew he could trust me. And after we'd had a few drinks together, he told me he was fencing stolen jewellery. If ever I needed his services, he said, he'd be very happy to give me a special deal.

'I laughed it off at the time. But then I got to thinking, why not? Marge and I'd been moving in the sort of circles where women wear jewels by the cartload at evening dos. I knew who to go for. I brought my assistant, Joey, in on it. I don't think you ever met him. He knew a couple of hard men who did the actual robberies for a reasonable cut. After we'd been going for a while I was able to plan the move out to Corfu, buying the villa, giving Marge the life she deserved.

'But when we got here I realised I needed to keep the money coming in – so I brought in Timon. Joey'd stayed in America, and I needed a second-in-command I could rely on. I've known Timon since we first came here on holiday, a long time ago. Timon picked up some local guys for me. Got to be quite a big operation in the end.'

'I knew the name was familiar to me,' Josh said. 'I must have heard you mention Timon some time or other. But for a while I couldn't place it.'

'Timon and me's about all there's left right now of the gang,' Hamish said ruefully.

'They've been dropping like flies this last day or two, haven't they? There was some sort of infighting going on, I'm told?'

'Yes, some of these people began to think they weren't getting a big enough cut. They took a shot at Marge and you – nothing to do with your Angel, although I know you both thought it was. They wanted you to think that, I suppose – sidetrack you from the truth. They didn't intend to kill either you or Marge, just to hurt me and make me give in to their demands. It was that nurse, Rena, who set up the shooting, but Bakis fired the actual gun – that's why I had Christos shoot him, while Dido distracted his attention. I'm not sure if Jason was in it too, but if I find he was, he'll be in trouble, just like Bakis.'

Josh debated whether to say that Jason was actually an undercover cop, but decided not to. 'Dido stayed on your side? And the two guys who grabbed me? One of the things that made me suspect you, was the telephone call from their 'boss' – you, Hamish – telling them to let me go, not to kill or hurt me. There had to be a reason for that.'

'I couldn't have let them hurt you, laddie. I never wanted that.'

'But you didn't care so much about Angel?'

'Och, that's a different thing, Josh, I know you like her, but there are plenty of other girls. She was getting too close to the truth – that's why I told Dido to deal with her. But then

Dido had that accident, and now the other two, Marios and Christos, are no more good, not now they've been identified. You might not give them away, but Angel would for sure. You and Angel between you have just about wrecked it all.'

'Happy to oblige,' Josh said dryly.

'Oblige? Och, you're joking, I see. Well, Timon can easily pick up a few others, presently. I've no intention of stopping now.'

Josh said nothing. He knew that Doukas was about to put a stop to Hamish's plans, but it didn't seem a good idea to warn him.

'Well, that's the story, laddie. Listen, I'd be happy to bring you in on it. What do you say? You've been like a son to me and Marge, y'know, Josh. Ever since our own boy was shot, and you came to tell us about it and were so kind. I'd like to do you a favour. I'd have made you the offer sooner, but I wasn't just sure how you'd take it. How about it, then? There's big money, enough for you as well.'

'Hamish, you know that you've been like a father to me since we met,' Josh said painfully. 'But you were right. No way could I come in on this.'

'Och, well. I was afraid of that,' Hamish said. 'But you won't give me away, will you, Josh laddie? You couldn't do that!'

'I don't think I'll have to, Hamish,' Josh said. 'Listen!'

They could hear the footsteps coming, more than one person. Hamish froze.

Round the edge of the huge rock came Captain Doukas, gun aimed straight at Hamish, pushing Timon before him. They were followed by Angel. She was carrying the gun she'd taken from Timon, and it, also, was pointed straight at Hamish McPherson.

Chapter Fifty Three

Hamish laughed.

'Two empty guns,' he said. 'You have Timon's gun, haven't you, Angel? I recognise it. Don't you realise that he left me to get some more ammo from the car?'

Angel clicked the trigger, and knew at once that Hamish was speaking the truth.

'And you, Captain Doukas. Why did you stop firing if you still had some bullets?'

Doukas said nothing.

'And you, Josh.' Hamish's voice grew softer. 'I can't quite bring myself to believe that you, you who might as well be my son, would shoot me?'

Josh, like Angel and Doukas, remained silent.

'So I'm not worried that I'll be shot. I'm going, now. See – I'm walking away. I'm heading back to my car.'

Hamish McPherson moved across the road towards Angel, Timon and Doukas. It seemed as if he was going, as he had said, towards the place where his car had been parked.

Then, as he passed Angel, he swung suddenly round and grabbed her.

'Get behind me, Timon!' he snapped.

Timon moved equally quickly, and McPherson backed towards the edge of the road to where it plunged down steeply far below, in a cliff edge. He had Angel by the arm, twisting it behind her back as Timon had done not long before. His gun was pointed against her temple.

'Now, just listen to me!' he said. 'I didn't stop firing because I was out of bullets. I stopped because I heard Josh coming up behind me. You know that's true, don't you, Josh? I've got plenty of ammo left. And if any of you move, I'll shoot and Angel will go plunging over the cliff here with a bullet in her head. I don't somehow think she'll survive that, okay?'

'You wouldn't do that, Hamish?' It was Josh who spoke.

'Wouldn't I? I wouldn't shoot you, Josh. But this lassie's a different matter. I know you like her, but, hey, there are plenty more fish in the sea. You'll find one just as good in no time, laddie.'

'If you hurt Angel, I'll never have anything to do with you again, Hamish.'

Hamish's face twisted in a sudden pain. 'I don't believe that, laddie,' he said eventually.

'You'd better believe it, Hamish.'

Captain Doukas spoke.

'McPherson. Forget about this guy. Maybe he wouldn't want to kill you. But I'd have no hesitation. I'm a professional – I don't run out of bullets. I reloaded a while ago. I stopped firing for the same reason you claim you did – because some-one came up behind me. Two people, Timon, and Angel. Now, I wouldn't like to shoot Angel. But from what I've seen of her, I might not need to. What do you think, Angel?'

Angel took the hint. She had escaped from a very similar position with Timon a short while ago. Doukas was suggesting that she should repeat her tactics of then.

'I don't think you will have to, Gregor,' Angel said cheerfully. 'This guy's no professional. Up until now he's had his tough guys to do the dirty work. This must be the first time he's been out at the cutting edge. Right, Hamish?'

'I think I can aim to hit you, McPherson,' Doukas said, 'without damaging Angel.' He aimed carefully at Hamish McPherson.

'No!' Hamish yelled. 'If I go over the cliff, she goes with me!'

He stopped pointing his gun at Angel's head and tried to aim at Doukas instead. The gun wavered between the two.

It was Angel's opportunity. Driving her elbow into his stomach and stamping on his toe with one foot, she twisted her other foot round his ankle and sent him staggering. As she did so, she sprang away out of range of his gun.

And Doukas levelled his pistol, aiming straight at Hamish McPherson, and fired.

Hamish groaned and fell forwards on his face. His legs hung over the cliff edge, and he clung desperately to a bush which seemed about to give way at any moment. 'Josh,' he said feebly. 'Josh. Look after Marge for me, won't you?'

Josh sprang forward. But it was too late. The bush slipped. With a final groan, Hamish McPherson toppled over the edge of the road and disappeared.

Angel slept deeply that night at her room in the Villa Callidora. Marge had been told nothing, except that Hamish had died by accident. Both Angel and Josh knew that she would have to learn the whole truth, but neither of them felt that now was the time to tell her about Hamish's role in the jewel robberies, let alone the deaths involved. The replacement nurse had arrived, and had given Marge something to help her sleep.

The next morning, both Angel and Josh felt strangely shy. They ate breakfast, then Josh suggested a walk. They headed out to the road which ran beside the Villa's grounds.

'Angel,' Josh began. He stopped, unsure of what to say.

'Yes, Josh?'

'Angel.'

'Come on, darlin', say what you want to, why don't you?'

'I'm finding this hard, sweetie.'

'Sure, I'd noticed that, boyo.'

'Okay, Angel. Here goes. I risked your life last night rather than shoot Hamish McPherson. Gregor Doukas shot him without hesitation. I could understand it if you thought Gregor was a better man than me. I know he cares about you. If you – if you think you'd be better off with him than with me, I'd have no kick coming. I'd deserve it. But tell me, won't you? Don't keep me wondering.'

Angel's eyes were soft. 'Agh, Josh, you're a right eedjit!' she said. 'Listen, darlin', you did the right thing. How do you think I'd have felt about you if you'd shot a man who was like a father to you? Doukas was doing his job. It was okay for him. But it wasn't like that for you. You were torn two ways, I know. You did what was best.'

'Angel!' Josh started forward and put his arms round her.

'Besides,' Angel said mischievously, 'you did me the honour of trusting that I could get myself out of trouble, and that Hamish wouldn't have a chance against me when it came to the bit – and neither he had!'

'You rascal!' Josh said. 'And I did trust that you could! No one can win over you, sweetie, when you get going!'

Chapter 53

He swung round to face her and held out his arms. ' I love you, Angeline Murphy. Come here till I kiss you.'

And Angel did.

About the author

Gerry McCullough has been writing poems and stories since childhood. Brought up in north Belfast, she graduated in English and Philosophy from Queen's University, Belfast, then went on to gain an MA in English.

She lives just outside Belfast, in Northern Ireland, has four grown up children and is married to author, media producer and broadcaster, Raymond McCullough, with whom she co-edited the Irish magazine, *Bread*, (published by *Kingdom Come Trust*), from 1990-96. In 1995 they published a non-fiction book called, *Ireland – now the good news!*

Over the past few years Gerry has had around seventy short stories published in UK, Irish and American magazines, anthologies and annuals – as well as broadcast on *BBC Radio Ulster* – plus poems and articles published in several Northern Ireland and UK magazines. She has read from her novels, poems and short stories at several Irish literary events.

Gerry won the *Cúirt International Literary Award* for 2005 (Galway); was shortlisted for the 2008 *Brian Moore Award* (Belfast); shortlisted for the 2009 *Cúirt Award*; and commended in the 2009 *Seán O'Faolain Short Story Competition*, (Cork).

Belfast Girls, her first full-length Irish novel, was first published (by *Night Publishing*, UK) in November 2010 (re-issued July 2012 by *Precious Oil*). *Danger Danger* was published by *Precious Oil Publications* in October 2011; followed by *The Seanachie: Tales of Old Seamus* in January 2012 (a first collection of humorous Irish short stories, previously published in a weekly Irish magazine); *Angel in Flight* (the first Angel Murphy thriller) in June 2012; *Lady Molly and the Snapper* – a young adult time travel adventure set in Dublin (August 2012); *Johnny McClintock's War* (August 2014) – a historical novel set during WWI and early 20th century Ulster and *The Seanachie 2: Norah on the Beach ... and other stories* (September 2014).

Hel's Heroes – *a romantic comedy* – was published in June 2015 and *Dreams, Visions, Nightmares* – a collection of literary and award-winning Irish short stories, including the *Cúirt Award*-winning story, *Primroses*, and the *Seán O'Faolain* commended story, *Giving Up* – in January 2016. *Not the End of the World* – a humorous, futuristic, adult fantasy novel – was published in February 2016 and *The Seanachie 3: Seamus and the Shell and other stories* in August 2016.

Belfast Girls

The story of three girls – Sheila, Phil and Mary – growing up into the new emerging post-conflict Belfast of money, drugs, high fashion and crime; and of their lives and loves.

Sheila, a supermodel, is kidnapped.

Phil is sent to prison.

Mary, surviving a drug overdose, has a spiritual awakening.

It is also the story of the men who matter to them:–

John Branagh, former candidate for the priesthood, a modern Darcy, someone to love or hate. Will he and Sheila ever get together?

Davy Hagan, drug dealer, *'mad, bad and dangerous to know'*. Is Phil also mad to have anything to do with him?

Although from different religious backgrounds, starting off as childhood friends, the girls manage to hold on to that friendship in spite of everything.

A book about contemporary Ireland and modern life. A book which both men and women can enjoy – thriller, romance, comedy, drama – and much more ...

"fascinating ... original ... multilayered ... expertly travels from one genre to the next"

Kellie Chambers, Ulster Tatler (*Book of the Month*)

"romance at the core ... enriched with breathtaking action, mystery, suspense and some tear-jerking moments of tragedy.

Sheila M. Belshaw, author

"What starts out as a crime thriller quickly evolves into a literary festival beyond the boundary of genres"

PD Allen, author

"a masterclass, and a vivid dissection of the human condition in all of its inglorious foibles"
WeeScottishLassie

From the author of Belfast Girls

Gerry McCullough

Danger Danger

Two lives in parallel – twin sisters separated at birth, but their lives take strangely similar and dangerous roads until the final collision which hurls each of them to the edge of disaster.

Katie and her gambling boyfriend Dec find themselves threatened with peril from the people Dec has cheated.

Jo-Anne (Annie) through her boyfriend Steven finds herself in the hands of much more dangerous crooks.

Can they survive and achieve safety and happiness?

"starts with a bang and never quite lets up on the tension ... it will hook you from the beginning and keep you spell bound until the very last sentence."

Ellen Fritz, Books 4 Tomorrow

"The emotional intensity of the characters is beautifully drawn ...   You care for these people."

Stacey Danson, author

an amazing, page turning, stunning novel ... equal to Belfast Girls in every respect. I can't wait for her next novel to be published.

Teresa Geering, author

an attention-grabbing plot, strong writing, and vivid characterization, ... fast-paced and highly addictive

L. Anne Carrington, author

Angel in Flight:

the first Angel Murphy thriller

Is it a bird? Is it a plane? No, it's a low-flying Angel!

You've heard of Lara Croft. You've heard of Modesty Blaise. Well, here comes Angel Murphy!

Angel, a *'feisty wee Belfast girl'* on holiday in Greece, sorts out a villain who wants to make millions for his pharmaceutical company by preventing the use of a newly discovered malaria vaccine.

Angel has a broken marriage behind her and is wary of men, but perhaps her meeting with Josh Smith, who tells her he's with Interpol, may change her mind?

Fun, action, thrills, romance in a beautiful setting – so much to enjoy!

"it's a fast-paced read, ... exciting, and you can not put this book down"
Thomas Baker, Santiago, Chile

"I could not stop reading! ... a gripping thriller from beginning to the end"
SanMarie Lamprecht

"a fast-paced, exciting read. From the moment I read the first line, I was hooked"
Cheryl Bradshaw, author, Wyoming, USA

"a sassy bigger then life heroine in an action packed adventure thriller in Greece"
Book Review Buzz

Johnny McClintock's War:
One man's struggle against the hammer blows of life

The story of one man's struggle to maintain his faith in spite of everything life throws at him.

As the outbreak of the First World War looms closer, John Henry McClintock, a Northern Irish Protestant by upbringing, meets Rose Flanagan, a Catholic, at a gospel tent mission – and falls in love with her.

When Johnny enlists and sets off to fight in the War he finds himself surrounded by death and tragedy, which pushes his trust in God to the limit.

After more than five years absence he returns home to a bitter, war torn Ireland, where both he and Rose are seen as traitors to their own sides.

John Henry and Rose overcome all opposition and, finally, marry. But a few years later comes the hardest blow of all. Can John Henry still hang on to his faith in God?

"brilliant .. this book had me captured from the start ..
moves at a fair pace throughout"
Tom Elder, *Amazon.com*

"characters you will truly care about ..

a gut-wrenching emotional ride .. a must read"

Tom Winton, author, USA

"Gerry McCullough's best book yet ..
a powerful tribute to those who died for their countries and what they believed"
Juliet B Madison, author, UK

"an emotional roller coaster ride .. an epiphany .. highly recommended
.. a book that will make you think about how wonderful life truly is"
Thomas Baker, Amazon.com, Santiago, Chile

"will hold you spellbound until the very last sentence
.. I love this book"
Sheila Mary Belshaw, author, UK, Menorca, Cape Town

Johnny McClintock's War

*One man's struggle against
the hammer blows of life*

Gerry McCullough

Published by

www.preciousoil.com/publications

Chapter One

John Henry McClintock met Rose Flanagan when she was sixteen, and he a year or so older.

They met at a tent mission, which is a gospel meeting in a large tent. It was in a field miles from anywhere, in County Down, in the depths of Ireland.

It was a soft, warm summer night. Music poured from the lighted tent as John Henry drew nearer to it. He was one of a large crowd of people, stepping cautiously through the long grass at the field's edge – soon to be trampled flat by the hordes of visitors – and trying, not always successfully, to avoid the still wet sticky cow pats laid down that day, and the big purple thistles which grew everywhere.

The huge dirty beige tent, which looked dull by daylight but now, in the gathering darkness, shone out as a bright focus of warmth and good fellowship, had no ribbons or other decorations. There was only a cardboard placard set up at the entrance giving the times and the dates of other meetings, in bright red against a whitey-yellow background, with the name of the speaker in a bold dark green. There was a similar placard attached to the gate at the entrance to the field, where a blossoming hawthorn hedge spread its white, sweet-smelling flowers close enough almost, but not quite, to obliterate the writing.

John Henry hadn't seen Rose yet. He had gone along to the tent with friends of his own age, just as she had done a few minutes earlier. A tent mission was one of the free entertainments on offer in Ireland, in these days just before the First World War. You could be sure of meeting a large crowd of young people, who would seldom be gathered together in one place otherwise.

They pushed into the tent, nudging each other and whispering.

'There's Annie Kilpatrick! She's a whizzer!'

'Get off my toe, you great lump!'

'Aw – sorry, Tommy! Hey, there's Sadie Wilson with Geordie Milligan! Didn't know they were walking out!'

'Pity – she's a lovely girl!'

1

John Henry listened in amusement, but didn't contribute much. He liked his friends, Tommy, Willie and wee Artie, but he sometimes wondered how much he had in common with them. They had all left school early and had shown no reluctance to do so. John Henry himself had done the same, but not by his own choice.

When John Henry had left school at the age of fourteen, a few years before, it had been at his father's insistence, in spite of his evident ability. And in spite of the desire of his teacher that he should stay on, even try for teacher training eventually (the idea of university an impossible dream in the minds of most).

The master of the local Church of Ireland school in the village, Michael Patrick Fyfe, was a descendent of the French Huguenots who had come to those parts a couple of centuries ago, driven out from their homeland by persecution, and had brought their linen making skills with them. Fyfe was a clever man who deserved to be doing more than teaching in a village school. He felt this particularly when a pupil who should have achieved much more was forced to leave by his family's desire that he should go out and earn his living.

In John Henry's case he had felt it so strongly that he'd called round with the boy's father to make his protest.

Fyfe rehearsed in his mind what he would say as he knocked on the door of the three storied house beside the church grounds. He could see that the house had once been an impressive building. Tall, built in grey stone, it was covered nearly up to its second story in sweet smelling rambling roses. And the garden spread around it on all sides, neglected and overgrown with nettles and thistles now, had clearly at one time been a pleasure to see. The owners had obviously gone downhill, and the house with them. He knew that Douglas McClintock, John Henry's father, was a widower, and had heard that he drank. Maybe that was where the money for house repairs went to.

Fyfe, who was a small, thin man, still young and unsure of himself, wondered again if he was doing the right thing. Would his intervention make any difference? He took in the scent of the pink roses growing beside the door as he waited apprehensively, listening for the sound of approaching footsteps inside.

The door opened at last in response to his repeated knocks, and a tall dark haired man with a craggy face peered out at him.

'Mr McClintock?' Fyfe said nervously. 'I'm Michael Fyfe, the village school-master. I'd like a word with you about your son John Henry.'

'What's the wee skitter been up to now?' roared McClintock. He made no effort to open the door wider or to invite Michael in.

'No, no, it's not that he's in any trouble,' the schoolmaster said hastily. 'Far from it. He's a first rate scholar. That's why I'd like to suggest that you allow him to stay on for another year or two and eventually take his teaching certificate. I know you've said you want him to leave at the end of the school year, next month, but I really think it'd be a crying shame. A waste of the boy's ability. He could do so much more with his life.'

McClintock's face, which had been growing red with anger as he listened to his visitor, began to swell up alarmingly. Fyfe noticed in apprehension that he carried a strong blackthorn stick in his right hand. As he stopped leaning on this stick and raised it threateningly, Fyfe took a hasty step back. McClintock advanced on him.

'I'll be the one who says what my son should do with his life!' McClintock roared. He pushed his red swollen face so close to Fyfe that the schoolmaster could smell his rotten breath, an unpleasant reek of onions and alcohol. 'Don't come round here again telling me what to do with my own! I say it's time the lad got out and earned his living, and that's the end of it!'

The young schoolmaster jumped back out of reach of the blackthorn stick, just managing not to trip over the crumbling front doorstep, and the heavy wooden door slammed in his face. He tottered away down the village street, thankful to have escaped unmolested. He was very sorry for John Henry. But he was quite clear that there was nothing more he could do for him.

So John Henry had taken a low-skilled, and low paid, job in a linen factory, and was now contributing to the family income, like his older brother and sister, and helping to support his younger sister. To his father's great satisfaction.

John Henry was philosophical about it, but he wanted quite fiercely to get out of the linen factory, to do something that mattered with his life. He knew his abilities – his quickness to learn and to understand. He had been top of his class by a mile every year since he first started in the small local school. He wanted to make use of the intelligence he had been given.

Rose Flanagan was also working, as nearly everybody of their age and social class was; helping, mainly in the kitchen, at a nearby farm, fortunate in that she had been able to find work near her home and could return to her father's cottage most nights.

She'd got the job through the good offices of her parish priest, Father Donnelly, who knew her father well and who still thought of Rose as a sweet, innocent child, one he was glad to help. Her new employers, the Reillys, owned a small farm and were currently looking for more assistance, since their former kitchen girl had moved away to the other side of County Down when she married recently. By recommending Rose, Father Donnelly knew he was helping the Reillys, also parishioners of his, as well as helping Rose's father who could do with the extra income Rose would bring in. And, of course, he was earning the gratitude of the pretty wee girl herself. All good, Father Donnelly told himself.

'You'll work hard for these good people, won't you, my dear?' he said to Rose, giving her a toothy smile.

'Oh, certainly, Father,' Rose answered. She wished Father Donnelly would stop stroking her arm. However, her father was there, so it was safe enough. Rose wouldn't have liked to be on her own with Father Donnelly. She'd heard stories.

Annie Reilly was a kind, motherly woman, and although the work was hard, Rose enjoyed it well enough. She was used to working hard. Her mother had been a bit of an invalid in the years before she died, and since her death Rose had carried the burden of the household work at home. The work at the Reillys' farm wasn't much worse.

It was her friend Mary McCartney who'd suggested going to the tent meeting.

'There'll be lots of talent, Rose. I heard Frankie Murphy and his pals are going. They think it'll be a laugh, see? I really fancy Frankie, Rose! And you know rightly that his pal Peter O'Rouke fancies you, girl! Peter was asking me if you and me might be going. Let's tell them we'll join in and go with them!'

'I don't think we should go just for a laugh, Mary. And what if we get into trouble? They might not like people from our church going.'

'Not at all! The poster says, "All Welcome!" So they want us, see?'

'I think it might be interesting, Rose,' put in Maggie Kilmore. 'I've never been to a Protestant meeting. I'd like to know what they say that's so different. And I heard the preacher was a Jesuit before he left it. I was wondering if he'd tell us why he left. That would be interesting, too.'

And Peggy McCracken, a schoolmate of Rose's since early childhood, had also been eager to go, and said, shaking back her red hair, 'Ach, come on, Rose! It won't be any fun without you!'

'Oh, all right, then,' Rose agreed at last. But not without a lingering worry.

The girls met up with Frankie Murphy and a few other boys by arrangement at the field gate, and made their way across the rough grass, avoiding the cow pats and the stinging nettles until they reached the tent door.

Chapter 1

They and the boys went in together, greeted at the flapping doorway of the tent by a beaming, friendly man, with a red, wrinkled face, who had lost most of his hair. This man was holding out sheets with the words of the choruses, and the huge crowd had already begun to sing, as a warm-up to the meeting proper.

A group of boys whom Rose had never seen before were entering at the same time as Rose and her friends. As the two groups stood near to each other at the door of the tent, taking the sheets in turn from the friendly man, John Henry and Rose each noticed the other. Rose saw a tall, well built boy with dark hair falling over his pale face, and a sweet smile which switched on, as if instinctively, as he caught her eye.

John Henry saw a small, slim, and very pretty girl, with light brown hair, blue grey eyes, and a perfect complexion. Roses and cream, he thought, thinking of one of his favourite songs, *The Mountains of Mourne*. There was a bright intelligence in her eye as she glanced in his direction which attracted him even more than her looks. They were strangers, but through the mind of each went the fleeting thought, *Perhaps – not for long?*

Chapter Two

They went on in, and found places with their own friends, in different parts of the tent.

'This is daft, Johnny!' hissed John Henry's closest friend Tommy Maguire. Tommy was tall for his age with an attractive boyish face, smooth sandy hair and very bright blue eyes. He never had any problem getting off with girls. 'What the heck are we doing here?'

'Well, it wasn't my idea!' said Willie Morgan on Tommy's other side. His freckled face was one large grin at the idea, as he wriggled his fat, overweight body in the hard seat, trying to get more comfortable.

'Or mine!' retorted John Henry.

'It must have been yours, then, Artie!' said Tommy, nudging the small, dark haired boy beside him. Artie, the usual butt of the group, flushed bright red.

'I just thought it might be fun, Tommy!' he protested. ' See, just look round you. What about that for talent?'

Tommy looked round. Yeah, there were lots of girls, some of them quite pretty.

'Got a point there, Artie,' he admitted grudgingly, sweeping his hand back over his smooth, sandy coloured hair, as always held down by hair pomade. 'Not a bad idea, old man.'

Artie flushed again, but this time in delight at being praised by Tommy and addressed as 'old man'. The youngest of the group, he was constantly running to catch up with the others, and trying hard to seem as sophisticated as his idol Tommy.

Gradually the singing drew to a close, and the meeting opened.

The speaker was a gifted orator.

'Friends,' he began, in a soft, gentle voice, 'you all know that there's someone out there. Someone who made you. Someone who loves you.'

A collective sigh went round the tent. John Henry stirred uncomfortably. He didn't much want to be moved by this man, to respond. He was only here for a bit of fun, for company.

The speaker went on, 'Yes, friends, it was St Patrick who first opened our eyes, as Irishmen and women, to the presence of God in all nature. But St Paul said it before him, and David said it in his psalms, the songs he wrote from his shepherd's heart, "The Heavens declare the glory of God!" '

The speaker's voice grew louder, more emphatic. John Henry's attention wandered.

For a few moments he was back in his very early teens, experiencing again the wonder of the beauty of the earth in springtime. The freshness of early morning. The pink and white of the apple blossom all around. The still nights. The feeling of something – something. A presence that was trying to speak to him – which he longed, but was afraid, to listen to.

When he came back to the here and now, the speaker was quoting the Irish poet Joseph Plunkett, the young Christian Brother who had recently joined the republican movement.

> *'I see his blood upon the rose*
> *And in the stars the glory of his eyes.*
> *His body gleams amid eternal snows,*
> *His tears fall from the skies.*
>
> *I see his face in every flower;*
> *The thunder and the singing of the birds*
> *Are but his voice – and carven by his power*
> *Rocks are his written words.'*

The speaker dropped his voice, which had been soaring to the skies a moment before, and went on, speaking quietly.

> *'All pathways by his feet are worn,*
> *His strong heart stirs the ever-beating sea.*
> *His crown of thorns is twined with every thorn.*
> *His cross is every tree.'*

Something caught at John Henry's heart, stirring and exalting him. He no longer wanted to resist; to fight whatever it was that was drawing him, reaching out to take him captive.

The speaker went on. He was quoting from the Bible now, referring with all his eloquence to the death of Christ, to the need for surrender to him. All at once, John Henry knew what he was going to do.

In another part of the tent, tears streamed down Rose's face as she listened with her whole heart to the speaker's emotional words. She was miles away from that place, wandering in a bright garden, hand in hand with someone who loved her so much. The pain and the joy were intermixed to an unbearable extent. The need for action, for response, overwhelmed her.

The speaker, dropping his voice to its initial softness, drew to the end of his message.

For a moment there was silence.

Then came the final prayer, and the appeal.

At its close, when the speaker called for people to come forward, as a sign that they wanted to give their lives to the Lord, Rose Flanagan stood up and walked to the front.

While she was waiting afterwards for her turn to pray with one of the counsellors, she noticed someone standing next to her, also waiting. It was the young man she remembered seeing as she came into the tent before the meeting started. It was John Henry McClintock, although as yet she didn't know his name.

Coming out of the tent, John Henry spoke to her. 'Marvellous evening, isn't it?'

'Yes, it's lovely,' Rose agreed. The clear starry night of early May, with its dark navy blue sky studded with distant silver stones, was very beautiful.

'Come from round these parts?'

'Dromore,' she said. This was a village some five or six miles away.

'A fair distance,' said John Henry. 'If you'd like some company for the walk home, I'd be glad to go along with you.'

Rose had plenty of friends who had come with her and would have kept her company on the way back.

But for all that, she accepted the offer.

Over the next months, they saw each other regularly. John Henry made a point on the first Sunday of going to the church that had organised the tent mission where they had met. But he found that Rose, like himself, didn't belong there, and had come only for the mission. The following week, having found out which was Rose's own church, he went there.

It was then that he realised that Rose was a Catholic by upbringing.

The Seanachie:
Tales of Old Seamus

Gerry McCullough

A humorous series of Irish stories, set in the fictional Donegal village of Ardnakil and featuring that lovable rogue, *'Old Seamus'* – the Séanachie.

All of these stories have previously been published in the popular Irish weekly magazine, *Ireland's Own*, based in Wexford, Ireland.

"heart warming tales ... beautifully told with subtle Irish humour"

Babs Morton (author)

"an irresistible old rogue, but he's the kind people love to sit and listen to for hours on end whenever the opportunity presents itself"

G. Polley (author and blogger – Sapporo, Japan)

"This magnificent storyteller has done it again. Each individual story has it's own Gaelic charm"

Teresa Geering (author – UK)

"evocative characterisation brings these stories to life in a delightful, absorbing way"

Elinor Carlisle (author – Reading, UK)

The Seanachie 2:
Norah on the Beach and other stories

Gerry McCullough

Another series of twelve humorous Irish stories, set in the fictional Donegal village of Ardnakil and once again featuring that lovable rogue, *'Old Seamus'* – the Séanachie.

All of these stories have previously been published in the popular Irish weekly magazine, *Ireland's Own*, based in Wexford, Ireland.

"gentle stories laced with Irish humour ...

Like the first collection ... very well written and an effortless read"

Bookworm

"so well written that you find yourself flying through the stories"

Tom Elder

Lady Molly & The Snapper

A young adult time travel adventure, set in Ireland and on the high seas

Gerry McCullough

Brother and sister Jik and Nora are bored and angry. Why does their Dad spend so much time since their mother's death drinking and ignoring them? Why must he come home at all hours and fall downstairs like a fool?

Nora goes to church and lights a candle. The cross-looking sailor saint she particularly likes seems to grow enormous and come to life. Nora is too frightened to stay.

Nora and Jik go down secretly to their father's boat, the *Lady Molly*, at Howth Marina. There they meet The Snapper, the same cross-looking saint in a sailor's cap, who takes them back in time on the yacht, *Lady Molly,* to meet Cuchulain, the legendary Irish warrior, and others.

Jik and Nora plan to use their travels to find some way of stopping their father from drinking – but it's fun, too! Or is it? When they meet the Druid priest who follows them into modern times, teams up with school bully Marty Flanagan, and threatens them, things start getting out of hand.

Meanwhile, Nora is more than interested in Sean, the boy they keep bumping into in the past ...

"the story ... flows in authentic Irish lilt and dialogue, captures the imagination"
Book Review Buzz, USA

"excellent prose to suit the intended audience and has enough antics to keep any young mind turning the page"
J.D., USA

The Whore and her Mother:

9/11, Babylon and the Return of the King

Raymond McCullough

Could the writings of the ancient Hebrew prophets be relevant to events taking place in the world today?

These Hebrew prophets – Isaiah, Jeremiah, Habbakuk and the apostle John, in *The Revelation* – wrote extensively about a latter day city and empire which would dominate, exploit and corrupt all the nations of the world. They referred to it as Babylon the Great, or Mega-Babylon, and they foretold that its fall – 'in one day' – would devastate the economies of the whole world. Have these prophecies been fulfilled already?

Is Mega-Babylon the Roman Catholic Church?
A world super-church?
Rebuilt ancient Babylon?
Brussels, Jerusalem, or somewhere entirely different?
Should this city/nation have a large Jewish population?
Why all the talk about merchants, cargoes, commodities, trade?

Can we rely on the words of these ancient prophets?
If so, what else did they foretell that is still to be fulfilled?
Do they refer to other major nations – USA, Russia, China, Europe?
What about militant Islam?

"AMAZED when I read this book ... in awe of your extensive knowledge on so many levels: Christian, Jewish, and Muslim culture; the Jewish diaspora ... Greek & Hebrew; ... thought-provoking and troublesome ... many will be offended, but you consistently build your case instead of being sensationalistic."
James Revoir, author of *Priceless Stones*

Oh What Rapture!

Is a *'Secret Rapture'* going to spare believers from the tribulation to come?

Raymond McCullough

Many are convinced that very soon an event known as *'The Rapture'* will take place, where bible believers all over the world will suddenly disappear, leaving society at a loss to explain the disappearance of so many. Many non-fiction books, fiction thrillers and movies have capitalised on this theme, earning a fat revenue for their authors/ producers.

But is this really what the bible teaches?
Is *'The Rapture'* genuine, or a false hope?
Are those who trust in it being duped, so that they do not get ready for what is coming?
And are they being disobedient to the clear command of the Lord?

Written by the author of Amazon best-selling book, *The Whore and her Mother*, also on the topic of bible prophecy, this volume focusses on the false teaching of a *'secret and separate Rapture'* – an event which is NOT supported by scripture!

This book investigates the scriptures used to back up the *'secret Rapture'* theory and clearly compares them to the other scriptures concerning the return of the Messiah, Jesus (Yeshua). The evident truth is revealed and the origins of the false *'secret Rapture'* doctrine are exposed.

Believers around the world are taught to expect persecution, sometimes even death, for their faith. More have been killed in the past century than in previous centuries combined – in China, Cambodia, Nigeria, Iran, Egypt, Indonesia, Vietnam, etc. Yet many believers in the west confidently expect to avoid any persecution and be *'beamed up'* out of any coming tribulation!

If you thought believers were soon going to be lifted out of a worsening world situation, be prepared to meet the exciting challenge of scripture head on!

More info from: *preciousoil.com/publications*

www.ingramcontent.com/pod-product-compliance
Lightning Source LLC
Chambersburg PA
CBHW051410170626
46809CB00006B/2098